COURT OF THE GRANDCHILDREN

MICHAEL MUNTISOV

GREG FINLAYSON

Published by Odyssey Books in 2021

www.odysseybooks.com.au

A Cataloguing-in-Publication entry is available from the National Library of Australia

ISBN: 978-1922311146 (pbk)

ISBN: 978-1922311153 (ebook)

"When you see a walnut it is almost invariably an old tree. If you plant a walnut you are planting it for your grandchildren, and who cares a damn for his grandchildren?"

George Orwell

PROLOGUE

The United States Court of Appeals has ruled that Concord's controversial interstate border control practices are unconstitutional. The governor is speaking right now, let's watch.

" ... we call on the Federal Government to stop its program of harassment of our hard-working men and women at the borders. We must protect our State's sovereign rights and our citizens. Therefore, we will be launching an appeal to the Supreme Court against this decision. In the meantime, we will continue to enforce the State Law."

*Well, fighting words there. Let's go back to today's ruling. There it is on the screen ... to watch Judge Groden deliver the judgment, just say *Link2* while synced.*

United States Court of Appeals for the Fourth Circuit

Robinson et al v. State of Concord

[July 9th, 2059]

In 2057, the State of Concord enacted a statute limiting the entry of out-of-state residents into Concord. The scheme was justified on the basis that the State of Concord was unable to cope with the "unrelenting flood of climate refugees" from other coastal states, which "overloaded the financial, cultural, and social capacity of the State."

The question presented by this case is whether the 2057 statute was constitutional when it was enacted.

The Court concludes that citizens of the United States, whether rich or poor, have the right to choose to be citizens "of the State wherein they reside." U.S. Const., Amdt. 14, § 1. The States do not have any right to select their citizens.

The Fourteenth Amendment, like the Constitution itself, was "framed upon the theory that the peoples of the several states must sink or swim together, and that in the long run, prosperity and salvation are in union and not division." Baldwin v. G. A. F. Seelig, Inc., 294 U.S. 511, 523 (1935).

The judgment of the District Court is affirmed.

And now to our commentators Suzy Ashdod, chair of the Constitutional League, and Randolph Vann, head of the Concord City Blue Caps Movement. Welcome to both of you. Suzy, let's start with you. Are you surprised by this ruling and what does it mean?

Suzy: It means we are all Americans, like the Constitution says. Look, a million people have already left Florida. There are millions more whose homes are unlivable along the coast. We should all—

Randolph (interjecting): You got one part right. There's millions of refugees and no room in our state—

Suzy: Let me finish.

Randolph (shouting): No, it's too easy for you. I don't see you giving up your fancy house for the coasties. Who's gonna pay? You expect us young people to pay, don't you? Well, we didn't create this problem.

1

LILY

THE INTERRUPTION MADE HIM PAUSE. HE CLOSED HIS EYES. I remained still and waited. When his eyes reopened, they were distant, focused on the turning of his mind.

"I invited you here … I don't know that there's an easy way …" He hesitated, then drew breath. "I'll get straight to the point. I want to die."

"What the …" The words popped out with my gasp. I stared with astonishment at my great-uncle.

"I want to have my life ended rather than continue," he said.

I leaned away from him and waited for an explanation. But apparently, it was my turn to speak. I cleared the lump in my throat.

"Why would you want to die?" I scanned his face and hands, searching for some tell-tale sign of medical horror.

"It's my right," he said without emotion.

My feet shuffled nervously under the table. "Is there anything I can do for you?"

"Yes, there is," he replied. "I would like your permission."

"My permission?"

"Yes," he said, as though anyone would understand his request.

A pall of silence descended on us. My nails dug into my palm as my mind swept over the last few days looking for answers.

* * *

It started when his carer called me a few days ago. Out of nowhere, I had a great-grand-uncle. His name was David Moreland. He was my grandmother's uncle and he wanted to see me.

When I told Ava about the call, she said I shouldn't go. For Ava, this was black and white: all people of his age were burners. They put us in this mess, and we should have nothing to do with them. But I wasn't Ava, and the invitation reminded me of Grandma, so of course, I accepted.

As a kid, I would have lived with Grandma if I had the choice. She always had far fewer opinions and more patience than my mom. But after Mom's divorce, we moved to Concord City and I only got to see Grandma at Thanksgiving. I couldn't wait for those visits. The long slow afternoons sitting in her kitchen, talking about the 'old' movies she saw when they first came out and learning how to make tea her way. But what I most looked forward to was hearing about Mom's boyfriends when she was a teenager. Grandma had a knack for making Mom's life sound like a crazed soap opera, one where each episode was more outlandish than the last.

Thinking about Grandma reminded me of her insistence on good manners. I needed to take a gift to my great-uncle's. What would Grandma have been happy with? A cake, a bottle of wine, flowers? I chose flowers.

He lived in an apartment building on the other side of a bad neighborhood, near one of the big tent cities, so I ordered a car instead of riding my bike. I avoided cars whenever I could. They always smelled funny and the greasy marks and litter reminded me of the countless others who had come before. The trip was thankfully uneventful, and the car dropped me at the curbside outside his building. I brushed myself down and entered the building.

In the elevator, my reflection gazed back at me from the mirrored sidewall. I fixed my hair and straightened my creases. The bright yellow flowers glowed against my crimson top and gray pants. They were a good choice.

"Level Eight." A stark white corridor greeted me as the elevator doors opened. I gathered myself and followed the sign to my great-uncle's apartment.

The corridor had doors along one side and windows on the other—just like any apartment building. But, after a few steps, a familiar anxiety stirred in me. My gait slowed. Why this sudden apprehension? After a couple more steps, my feet slid to a complete stop. What the hell? My eyes darted up and down the corridor, looking for the source of my unease. They landed on the flowers in my hands. The flowers? I swallowed hard but it caught in my throat. Now my heartbeat was thumping in my ears. I turned back to the elevators and reached for the pad.

"Lily ... Lily," a voice called. "This way."

I turned. A middle-aged woman was scurrying toward me.

"Hello, I'm Sarah." She pointed behind her. "David's apartment is down there." Her voice was familiar. She was the carer who had called me.

I stood frozen. Shivers pulsed down my arms. My hands twitched. Sarah didn't seem to notice, so either I looked normal, or she was being polite.

"I'm so glad you came," she said as the elevator tone signaled its arrival behind us.

Sarah guided me toward the apartment. My head was light, my breathing fast. Oh god. Don't faint! Focus on the white roofs through the windows. Breathe. Deep. Breathe. The harsh tiles of the corridor floor echoed in my head on every step. My hands squeezed tight, strangling the flowers, as though they held the secret to my strange reaction.

We arrived at the open door of the apartment. Sarah gestured to me and I stepped inside. The foyer was a different world. Subdued lighting, ochre-colored walls, and a textured beige rug. And it was warm, much warmer than the corridor.

Thud! Sarah closed the door behind us. The vibration shook me back to normality.

Stepping into the lounge room, I was met by an elderly man in a wheelchair. My great-uncle. He stared at me blankly, saying nothing.

Sarah stood to one side, watching but not speaking.

"Hello. I'm Lily," I said, recovering enough to speak. "Umm, do I call you Uncle or something? I don't even know ... "

"Just David will do," he said in a gravelly voice.

He had the typical hunch seen in elderly people. Despite his thinning silver hair and age spots dotting his wrinkled face, I could tell he was handsome when younger.

I bent to kiss him. My eyes glimpsed a close-up of the back of his hand. Tendons bulged and prominent veins criss-crossed under his pale translucent skin. As I straightened back up, a whiff of urine rankled my nostrils.

He wore a dark blue jacket over a collared shirt and a red, old-fashioned tie. The collar was too large for his neck, leaving a gap and highlighting the billows of skin hanging from his chin. It was like he was dressed for a wedding. Grandma wouldn't have dressed up for a visit from me.

With a wince, he beckoned me to sit at the dining table.

"I brought some flowers, Uncle David." I held out the flowers. "Do you have a vase?"

A silence followed for longer than was comfortable. Had he heard?

"They look gorgeous," Sarah replied eventually. "Just what the apartment needs. We don't have a vase—perhaps one of the tall glasses would do? They're in the cupboard above the sink."

I headed to the kitchen, grateful for a few moments to collect my thoughts while Sarah navigated Uncle David's wheelchair to the table.

The apartment was one of those designed for the elderly. The kitchen, lounge, and dining areas were part of one large space, and all appointed with high-end fixtures. The entries to the adjoining bedroom, and from there to the bathroom, were wider than normal and had no doors. This allowed the wheelchair to move around. Fortunately, I didn't need to use the bathroom, because I couldn't see how things could be private.

Through a sliding glass door off the lounge area was a balcony with a solitary white polymer chair. The balcony balusters were conspicuously high, with the railing set around shoulder height. The cage-like enclosure made the chair look like it was on display in a zoo.

Inside the kitchen, I found the tall glasses. They were no good for holding flowers.

"Yes, these should be fine," I said diplomatically.

On the bench, the wooden handle of a knife poked out from a pile of plates and bowls. I carefully extracted it without disturbing the stack. The knife's serrated blade, covered with an oily film, was not ideal but good enough to roughly crop the flower stems. I divided the bunch between three glasses.

"How about we put the flowers here?" I balanced them on the oak coffee table. "They look good against the white of the sofa, don't they? They're tulips."

"Thank you," Uncle David said. "Please sit so we can talk."

I took my place next to David at the table and Sarah joined

us. The glass over the tabletop was cool to touch, a stark contrast to the room that was a lot warmer than I liked.

"Thank you for coming to see me," David said. "It's a pleasant surprise to find that I have some family connections after all."

"Now that I know you're here, maybe I can visit occasionally." The words came out but I wondered if they were true. Right now, it wasn't like a visit to Grandma's.

"Visits would be nice," Sarah said after David was quiet for longer than seemed reasonable.

Sarah's words prompted David to continue. "I remember your grandmother. When I last saw her, she was probably ten years old."

"Do you remember any stories about her? I'd love to hear them."

"My memories of her are a little vague."

"Did you talk much with her?"

"Not really." The conversation fell to a dead end.

Why was I having to make the discussion? Still, I needed to say something or the visit would never end. I stuck with the simple things.

"Your apartment is nice. Is it government-sponsored?"

"Absolutely not," he scoffed. "There's already too much government meddling in our lives."

"Definitely, its—"

"We've become a welfare state." His voice rose. "The government knows everything. Artificial intelligence controls everything. Humans are becoming redundant."

Sarah interjected. "David, it might be best if you avoided this topic." She smiled at me. "You can see David feels strongly about it."

I ignored Sarah. "There's a growing movement of people who want less technology and AI in our lives," I explained.

David's eyes widened.

"It's called 'Humans First'. You should join." Oh shit! Why did I suggest that? The image of Vince in his blue cap at our last Humans First meeting flashed through my mind. He and his friends wouldn't much like having some old person as a member.

"There's too much AI," David agreed. "During my career, we didn't have to rely on artificial intelligence ..."

We continued our discussion, David talking about his concerns on humans being shut out of decisions, and I told him more about my group.

When David talked, his eyes darted between me and Sarah, his head remaining still. It was creepy, like one of those statues whose eyes follow you around the room. As the discussion went on, he became more animated, but with each movement came a wince.

After a particularly loud moan, Sarah interrupted. "David, I don't think talking about this is in your best interest."

He closed his eyes for a moment. When they opened, they were focused into the distance.

"I invited you here ... I don't know that there's an easy way ..." He drew breath. "I'll get straight to the point. I want to die."

This was not a dream, or a nightmare. Those you could wake up from.

Sarah broke the silence. "David wants to exercise his rights under the State Euthanasia Law. He needs his next-of-kin to give permission."

"Am I the next-of-kin?"

"You're David's closest surviving relative."

I turned to David. "Do you have a medical sign-off?"

"I don't need one. I'm ninety-six now," David said.

"There's nothing seriously wrong with you, is there?"

"It might look that way." His eyes turned to Sarah. "I have a terminal illness."

"Terminal?"

"I don't want to go into details." His eyes shifted back to me. "It's a complicated medical situation, which young people like you wouldn't be familiar with."

He paused, then continued deliberately, as if scripted.

"I have so many ailments and take so many medications. I'm in constant pain. I'm losing my senses. I don't have opportunities to interact with people. Everything is dominated by artificial intelligence. Life has become a constant, painful chore. I would like to go while I still have my dignity."

This was a long way from my fantasy of chatting about Grandma.

"I'm sorry." My eyes turned down to my lap. "This is a big question from someone I hardly know."

"I hope the fact that you don't know me makes it easier for you," he said coolly.

Images flashed through my head. A woman lying in a hospital bed, shrunken and fragile, and covered in wires and tubes.

"I saw my mother die. She suffered a lot." My shoulders shivered as a bead of sweat ran down my back. "I don't want to be part of another death." My mind instructed me to leave, but my feet were anchored to the floor.

"I know it's a shock." David's voice was steady and considered. "But this is what I want."

What *you* want? What about me? How dare he sit there serenely while my emotions were tossing me around? Stand up and leave. But my motor functions still refused to cooperate.

My eyes locked onto the caged chair on the balcony, trapped just as much I was. "So, the only thing you need to die is my permission?"

"There is one other requirement," Sarah announced.

"No there isn't!" David glared at her.

"David has a social obligation he may have to fulfill."

"No, I don't!" David countered. "I'm getting a medical waiver."

"He's been called to appear before the Climate Court," Sarah said.

My ears pricked up.

"That's enough!" He threw up his arms. "Ooff!" he winced. Color faded from his face. His shoulders drooped.

The discussion froze.

Eventually, Sarah spoke. "Lily, I know this is a lot to take in. Is it all right if we end the visit and get back in touch after a few days?"

"Sure."

But I was not sure at all. I had come expecting some sort of chat about my family from years ago. You know, sharing stories and looking at photos. Instead, I was caught in the middle of an argument about choosing to die. A part of me had an impulse to help, but mostly I didn't want anything more to do with this man and his unreasonable request.

As I walked out of the building, I was met by a display of framed photos of old cars—people driving on the way to somewhere. This little celebration of excesses from the past reminded me that Ava had told me not to come. She was right.

2

DAVID

My planned welcoming words and offer of refreshments evaporated the moment Lily walked through the door. I was surprised, unsettled. I hadn't anticipated it; how could I? My whole plan was disrupted and, under pressure, I had defaulted to my old business mode.

"Why didn't you tell me about her face?" I chided Sarah after Lily left.

"Here's your *Zepraxonyl*." She placed the tablet into my cupped palm. A white ellipse with an etched band.

I threw it into my mouth and washed it down.

"Why didn't you?" I persisted.

"I didn't think it was relevant."

"But it is."

"Why?"

I didn't bother to answer. Sarah wouldn't understand. How could she? She isn't family.

"And those tattoos," I scoffed.

"They're 'kumadori,'" Sarah said. "It's the Japanese word for face painting."

"Why would you change your face like that?"

"They're not permanent," she explained. "Some people change them every week. They're very popular with the young."

I shook my head at the folly of this latest fad. It won't last.

Despite being flustered by her appearance, it was refreshing to meet someone who could see past the artificial intelligence hype and know the dangers to society at large. It gave me hope that this generation might avoid the disaster we're heading into. I was surprised that young people had groups like hers who understood these dangers. All I ever heard about the younger generation was that they wanted nothing to do with us older people. And those bizarre face tattoos, those kumadori, won't make them any more approachable for us.

Still, it wasn't Lily I was mad at, it was Sarah. She had sabotaged my whole plan and confused the issue by bringing up the court.

She finished her cleaning chores and sat at the table with me. "Is everything all right, David?"

"Don't ever contradict me again."

"I didn't contradict you," she replied calmly.

"You brought up the Climate Court."

"I was saying what was true."

"You know I'm getting a waiver."

"That's not certain. And I didn't say anything when you lied about a terminal illness."

"For god's sake, Sarah. Stop resisting for once." I could tell she was trying to manipulate me, which of course would fail.

"How are we going to get her permission?" I asked, turning to the more important point.

"It might be best to avoid a face-to-face meeting next time," she replied. "We should do a Holo call. There'll be less emotion."

I grunted in agreement. The kind of emotion that Lily brought was not a familiar event in my apartment. Usually I had nothing to be emotional about other than mundane annoyances from Sarah.

"Do you think she'll give permission?" I asked.

Sarah paused. "She will. When the time's right."

Lily must have noticed that I was of sound mind and able to make my own decisions. So, Sarah was right, it was only a matter of time before Lily would approve my wish.

With that more positive outlook, I could enjoy beating the crap out of Fred. I called my joint pain Fred. It seemed childish to name the pain at first, and I ignored the suggestion to do so from the specialist when she first made it. But now I saw the merit in personalizing the pain. The *Zepraxonyl* pushed back against Fred and his army. It was my fleeting moment of winning and I cherished every second of it.

I visualized a battle, and I made up different scenarios. One of my favorites was imagining force fields around my knees being re-energized by the Zep. Fred's henchmen were pushed off their footholds into the abyss below—to the bottom of my feet. And for the rest of the day, when I remembered, I paced around the apartment and felt tiny prickles all over the soles of my feet as their bodies exploded under my weight. I got a lot of satisfaction from these fantasies. I dared not tell Sarah about them, although she would notice me walking, almost dancing, and ask if everything was all right.

This time I imagined the gremlins being pushed off the tops of my shoulders and falling right down into my fingertips. I hung my arms straight down by my sides and shook them to make sure the gremlins didn't get hung up along their fall.

During one of these pleasant winning moments, I came up with a theory that the name *Zepraxonyl* derived from its shape. The tablet looked like a miniature Zeppelin and it had a shiny surface, like the membrane on the airships themselves. I recounted this observation to Dr. Bartok. He didn't know what a Zeppelin was. It startled me how quickly the past had faded and was lost to the present.

Alas, the pleasant moments didn't last long. The pain receded as the Zep-powered force fields hit peak strength and then they started their slow decline ... and Fred's fog rolled in.

3

DAVID

TO GET BACK AT SARAH, TO SHOW HER WHO WAS BOSS, TO ANNOY her, I did something different when it was time for my coffee. With my walking stick in hand, and the Zep kicked in, I ignored Sarah's protests and made it down to the lobby café on my own.

"Welcome to the Courtyard Café, Mr. Moreland. A server will be with you momentarily," said the automated greeting in my hearing piece.

A carefully rotund woman wearing a dark blue uniform approached.

"Hello Mr. Moreland. It's lovely to see you again." I'd never seen her before.

"Now, last time … you sat at that table by the window." She gestured to my right. "You were with Sarah. Will she be joining us today?"

"No." Sarah was hard to escape.

"Would you like that table again, Mr. Moreland?"

As I surveyed the rest of the largely empty room, she continued without waiting for my answer: "Wonderful, let me help you." She led me to the table and pulled a chair for me. The cushion was soft but too low. Sarah was not there to help me. Somehow this made the discomfort more annoying and I fidgeted in the chair to get more upright.

"Make yourself comfortable. You can see the menu there." She pointed at the screen projected onto the corner of the table. "I'll be back in a moment."

The café décor had not changed since my last visit. It was largely browns and oranges, a color scheme that reminded me of my childhood. The floor was timber—real or fake, I couldn't tell. The fireplace and chimney were made of mortared iron-stone blocks and, on either side, large Aztec design rugs adorned the walls.

My server was back. "Now that you've settled in, Mr. Moreland, let me introduce myself. My name is Gabriela and I'll be serving you today. I hope you've had a chance to look at the menu. Last time you were here ... you had ... a black coffee and chocolate cake. Wait ... oh, that was nearly a year ago. You need to visit us more often! We still have chocolate cake on the menu. Would you like that again?"

"Yes."

"Okay, one black coffee and one piece of chocolate cake," she said deliberately. "Done. I'll bring it out to you shortly."

"Wait. How do you know so much about my last visit?"

"My 'Sherpa' is synced to the café AI." She pointed out the device that looked like an earring: circular, black with a silver perimeter. "It briefs us in real-time."

She saw the look on my face. "Have you not seen a Sherpa?"

"What's it called ... a Sherpa?"

"Yes, like the guides to Mt. Everest."

"I have an earpiece." I pointed.

"Oh no, that's a much older device. It needs a separate Guide." She looked down at my belt where my Guide was attached. "A lot of our customers still use them. How do you find it?"

"It helps my hearing. I don't use the other functions. I don't know what they are." It was a lie. I knew there were many options but didn't want to use them. I also didn't want to explain myself to some server. That's how things worked when you got older. It was easier to pretend ignorance than explain your uneasiness with some elements of a new world.

As she left, music faded into my ear. It was a classical piece. Stravinsky. I squirmed in my chair. I knew the music well, and it pulled me into a past I tried not to visit. These days, the past was more vivid than the present.

Alone in my study, I stared at the emails on my laptop without reading the words. Without those subtle noises from the presence of others, the house echoed and moaned. And with no need to have lights on in other rooms, the dark seemed to dominate. Since the cleaners had been, even the air smelled thinner. I didn't think it would feel like this. An empty house. Jenny and Stephanie weren't about to walk in from the supermarket any time soon. One thing I knew better than most: once Jenny decided on something, it was decided. I put some music on. Classical would be best. Stravinsky.

The music in my ear faded out. Gabriela was coming with my order.

"Here's your coffee, Mr. Moreland." She placed the cup and saucer in front of me.

The coffee cup was small. "Is this size right?"

"It's the new standard size," Gabriela answered. "Would you like a larger serve?"

I was content with that serve for the moment.

"And here's your chocolate cake." She placed a dark, lumpy mass beside the coffee. "It's been a pleasure to serve you, Mr. Moreland. My shift is ending now, so Helen over there will be looking after you." She pointed to a younger woman near the servery. "Make yourself comfortable and enjoy the rest of your day." And just like that, Gabriela was gone.

The aroma of the coffee settled me after the whirlwind of the service.

Coffee was one of the few foods that I could still smell and taste; perhaps it was the bitterness. Sarah made a good coffee, but Dr. Bartok limited me to only one a day as it interfered with my medications.

Sarah made a chocolate cake for me every day too. I liked the texture and sensation of eating it even though I had lost the ability to taste.

I took a bite of the chocolate cake. It stuck straight to the roof of my mouth. Damn! With a sigh of resignation, my tongue went to work to dislodge the stuck cake. A big chunk came off easily, but the rest was harder. I tried a couple of techniques. Pressing around the edges worked best. I got most of it off, but it took another couple of mouthfuls of coffee to swirl away the stickiest remnants. I leaned back into the chair. What a chore. I went to take another sip of coffee. It was empty.

The new server appeared on cue. "Are you done, Mr. Moreland?"

"I'd like another coffee."

"Another coffee? I am sorry, Mr. Moreland, but your Guide is not permitting a second cup of coffee."

"But this was only a half serve."

"I am sorry, sir, but your Guide is not permitting it." There was no compromise in her voice. "As I'm sure you're aware, this café is bound to respect instructions from your Guide, and it tells us that more coffee is not good for you."

I contemplated whether to argue, but couldn't find the energy. Even coffee was restricted by the system.

"Mr. Moreland, is there something wrong with the chocolate cake?"

"I didn't like it."

"I'm very sorry to hear that, Mr. Moreland. We will deduct that from your bill and make a note in your record. Rest assured, Mr. Moreland, that we will not disappoint you again."

This new server was more efficient and matter-of-fact than Gabriela. I studied her ears. "You don't have a Sherpa?" I asked.

"No, sir, I am a full AI-driven android."

It was getting harder for me to tell. They needed to make it more obvious who was AI and who was not. It was the androids that should have face tattoos, not humans. I'd been making these points for a long time, but no one was listening. The time when people did listen to me had passed.

The cake and coffee had been a disappointment but the view out the window provided a more optimistic outlook. The public courtyard was bathed in sun. The lightly leaved trees cast dappled shade over the wooden benches underneath, creating an inviting, peaceful setting. Some sun would help.

I made my way to the door. Neither pushing nor pulling would open it. A different server came up to me. "Your Guide is not authorized to use that door, Mr. Moreland. I am sorry, you will need to get your Guide reprogrammed."

"Can't you open it for me?" I said.

"I am sorry, Mr. Moreland, we are not permitted to do that. As you know, we segregate areas for your safety." She left me to attend to another customer.

I stood there alone, leaning on my walking stick, for how long? Ten seconds? Five minutes? My brain was in a fog.

The door opened as a couple entered the café. Their sudden entry cleared the fog enough for me to instinctively gesture to them and they propped the door open for me.

The tinted windows had disguised the ferocity of the light outside, forcing me to squint, almost close my eyes. A puff of wind blew against my face and hair. The same pleasant sensation as when I sat on my balcony.

"Mr. Moreland, please return to the café," ordered the voice in my earpiece. I ignored it.

One of the benches in direct sun was free and I made my way toward it. The Guide started to vibrate. People in the courtyard stared at me. I ignored them.

I sat gently on the bench. The burning heat of the wooden slats seared through my pants but quickly subsided to a tolerable and increasingly pleasant sensation. The warmth radiated through the rest of my body. I imagined the harsh edges of the slats leaving a branding mark on my thighs, which Sarah would no doubt ask me about that evening.

"Mr. Moreland, for your safety please return to the café. Please return ..." I turned off my earpiece, closed my eyes, leaned back, and let the sun bathe over my face. It was the nicest thing of the day, or even week, perhaps a month?

Penetrating the quiet peace, just discernible but distinctive, was a sparrow's cheep. The bird's song threw me back into the past as quickly as Stravinsky had earlier. My thoughts ventured back to the first years with Jenny.

Jenny loved the beach, even the long drives there and back. I wasn't an outdoor sort of person, but I was swept away by Jenny's passions. She made everything fun.

My favorite was Marathon Shores, one of the magnificent beaches near Beachport. We stayed at a little shack on the first street back from the dunes, surrounded by woods. Every morning we woke at sunrise to a chorus of birdsong and closest of all to our window was a sparrow nesting.

The beach was expansive. At low tide, it took a good five minutes to meander from the top of the dunes to the water's edge.

One day, at the end of a relentless winter, we were the only ones there. We played at being the last survivors on earth. The chilling ocean breeze contrasted with the warmth of the direct sun—the back of my head was burning, while my face was frozen solid.

The contrasts made me feel alive.

"David … David." It was Sarah. She sat next to me and took my hand. "David, you know that you can't go out here alone. Your Guide is warning you."

"Let me sit in the sun. You know it's one of my few remaining pleasures."

Sarah obliged me, but a few moments later we were interrupted by two young couples.

"We have this bench reserved," demanded one of the group, a thin young man with a tone of superiority. "And even if we didn't, your kind should stay behind closed doors. Where you belong."

"Can I see your confirmation?" Sarah requested politely.

The movements were too fast and the light too bright for me to see what happened next, but Sarah turned to me. "They have the bench reserved, we need to go."

"Why?" I said. "There are empty benches all around us."

The man's companion, who had prominent black marks on his cheeks, thrust a pointed finger at me.

"You should be in jail, old man!"

"Don't, Aaron," one of the girls urged, coming from behind him and pulling his raised arm down. This seemed to further infuriate him.

"You're a criminal. You're a fucking criminal!" He moved closer. Visible patches of skin reddened on his face.

"Leave him alone," the girl pleaded. She stepped between me and the man.

"Burners should pay. Burners should pay!"

The man's friend echoed his shout, and they started to chant.

"Burners should pay—"

"This man is in my care." Sarah stood and faced the aggressive men. They were stunned into a momentary silence. "He is leaving the area now."

Sarah helped me stand and we shuffled back toward the door.

"You're a murderer." The ranting started up again, emboldened by our move to leave. "You shouldn't be allowed in public. You fucking piece of shit!"

"Burners should die! Die!" I heard as the door closed behind us.

My pee started to flow. I willed it to stop but it kept coming until my bladder was empty. The warm, unpleasant sensation spread and surrounded my crotch.

"Don't worry, David," Sarah assured. "You're safe with me." She sat me down at a vacant table. I squelched onto the seat. The wetness was suddenly cold. My whole body trembled.

'Die!' The chant repeated over and over in my head.

I wanted to die.

But not because some young thug thought I should.

4

LILY

Could I say yes to death? Should I say yes? Did I even need to answer the question? Sarah mentioned the Euthanasia Law. I knew it existed, but I didn't really understand what it was for, or where it came from.

I asked Michael, my Sherpa's AI, for a brief history.

It turns out that early this century euthanasia was uncommon. It was opposed on mostly religious and ethical grounds, but a group of people argued that staying alive with a terminal illness and unrelenting misery was cruel and withheld a basic human right.

With the advances in medical technology since then, more people could live past one hundred years, and a lot of them didn't want to keep going. The world they grew up in was gone forever. Many of their cities were unrecognizable and borders changed or meaningless. Hardly anyone they knew was left, having been swept away or forced to move in the wake of the GISC disaster.

Death and loss were so common in the aftermath of the

GISC that life itself seemed to be less sacred. Michael explained that it was out of this trauma that the Euthanasia Law was born. When it was finally enacted, it was supported by all sides of politics and barely got any opposition. That part was surprising to me. My experience of my mother's death had seemed the opposite of 'right' and, as far as I could tell, life was precious and not to be put aside so easily.

The history of opposition to euthanasia made the requirement to get some form of a statement from a close relative easier to understand. Making sure that everyone understood and agreed made sense ... at least in the abstract. But now that I was the one facing the rules, the choice seemed impossible.

In moments like these, my first reaction was to turn to Goldie.

It was Grandma who gave me Goldie. Goldie was the right name; it matched her pink saddle with its gold trim, and I fell for her straight away. We became inseparable. Early on, some of my friends made fun of me; a plush horse was such an old-fashioned toy. But somehow, Goldie became a fixture in my various houses over the years.

My good friends greeted her when they visited. "Hi Goldie," they said, making a fuss and stroking her mane. Rituals were like that, they started small and then they stuck.

But what drew me most to Goldie were her amber eyes. They changed with my mood. When I was happy, her eyes joined in with a celebratory glint. And when I was upset and I turned to her, her eyes were comforting and invited a hug. Goldie never let me down. That's why she was still there, standing in the corner of my bedroom next to the laundry basket, ready to give me whatever look I needed.

Right now, Goldie gave me her sympathetic look.

"Time to make some calls," I announced. I lifted her by the

saddle and put her under one arm, and with the other grabbed the Holo platter and lobbed it onto the foot of the bed.

With Goldie on my lap, I leaned back against the pillows. "Call Ava," I instructed.

I could have called Ben or Lucy. But Ava was that friend you called first when there was real trouble. I've known her since high school. She was a member of the student senate and always the activist, pushing various causes. In class, she was the leader of any discussion. Ava was one of those people you looked up to, and who made you feel good when they agreed with you.

"He just wants to die? Is that it?" Ava seemed disinterested, as if I had just asked her what color shirt to wear.

"Yeah."

"Then just say yes. What's it to you? You don't know the guy. This is what the Euthanasia Law is for."

"I'm not sure ..." I wanted empathy and help, not to be told to choose the red shirt and stop messing around. "It brought back horrible memories of Mom dying."

"Well, say no, and have no more to do with him."

"But what if he keeps hounding me?"

"Block his calls," she suggested coolly. "He's one of the burner generation anyway. Why should you be concerned about him?"

"I'm related to the guy." I glanced at Goldie. "I mean, he knew my grandmother."

"So?"

"I don't know, it sort of means something."

"But you said he was weird."

"He was. He was." I groaned. "Maybe he's just too old ... Oh, I don't know ... I wish this never happened." As my words spilled out, the reason for Ava's attitude became clear. I had not followed her advice to not visit David in the first place, and so it was me who had created this mess.

"Lily, you're going to have to say yes or no."

I waved my hand in the general direction of the Concord City courthouse. "His carer said he'd have to appear in the Climate Court first."

Her head lifted as if this information had changed the equation. "What's his background?"

"He was some sort of department head here in Concord," I explained. "I looked him up to check it was all legit."

"What's his name again?"

"Moreland. David Moreland."

"Yeah, I think I've heard of him."

"And he was so anti-AI. He hadn't heard of Humans First, but he liked the idea. Maybe we should do something with him?"

"Most old people are anti-AI," she said. "It's the younger group we need to get involved."

"Yeah."

"Well, what are you going to do?" Ava wasn't disguising her impatience.

I paused to think, but my mind remained blank. I had no choice but to ask: "What would you do?"

Ava's projection switched to her avatar and the audio went blank. She had overlaid a transmission shield while she took a moment to reply. Was she getting more information about David?

Her face came back to life, her eyes gleaming. "You have to say no. Let him face the court, not slip away untested. If he was one of the good guys, then the court will say so, and you can make your decision." She spoke with an air of finality. "Sorry, Lily, I have to go. I'm still at work. There's stuff I have to finish."

Her pixels shrank down into the projector pinholes.

The sudden silence in the room highlighted my sense of

abandonment. Sure, I hadn't followed Ava's original advice and now she was telling me in her own way that she wasn't pleased.

But still, I had called Ava for empathy and advice, and instead, I had been given orders. I wondered whether I would follow them.

5

DAVID

SARAH CAME IN AND STOOD AT THE FOOT OF MY BED. "GOOD morning, David. How are you feeling today?"

She moved to my bedside and activated the controller. The bed jolted as it started to move and Fred took the opportunity to give me a spike.

And so began our daily dance. No music played, but we were like an old couple on the floor, so familiar with each other's motions that no toes were crushed even though the steps were stilted. We took our cue from each other's actions: set the bed to recliner mode, take the medications, wait ten minutes, lie flat, change diaper, recline again, up for toilet and shaving, clothes on, then to the table for breakfast.

Breakfast was always warm porridge, a small banana, half a piece of buttered toast, and half a cup of tea. I couldn't taste any of these but I liked their textures and the astringency of the tea. We tried other things; eggs felt too slimy, bacon too hard to chew, pancakes too dry. So, we stuck with the proven. Except this morning there was a large slice of preserved peach instead of the banana. Sarah said the shops were out of bananas.

After my toast, I picked at a crumb stuck between my teeth. It wouldn't budge. Instead, it packed in tighter. I worked to dislodge it with my tongue and made a whistling sound as I sucked air through the gap in the offending teeth, hoping to coax the crumb out. I paused for a moment and saw myself from outside, a man whose last days on earth were consumed with an undignified fight against a crumb. With a sigh, I gave up and cleared my mind enough to see the day to come.

"When's my call with Lily?" I asked.

"In about twenty minutes." Sarah took away the plates.

Getting up carefully from the table, I turned to face the sofa. I walked on the spot for a few moments, provoking Fred's prickles in the soles of my feet. Mapping out a meandering path between me and the sofa, I set out with short calculated steps, pushing down hard on each landing as if squashing an imaginary spider.

"Do you need a hand, David?" Sarah came up to me. I waved her away.

After a productive journey, I eased onto the sofa, put my walking stick to one side, and brought a soft velour cushion to my lap.

"Can we make the call from here?" I asked.

"Sure, I'll set it up." She brought the Holo platter over from the charger and placed it gently on the coffee table in front of me.

I was keen to get the Holo call going. But time became slow just when you wanted it to go fast. Time was like that. You couldn't get it back and it moved at a pace that you wished it wouldn't.

Outside, summer storm clouds rippled with the wind. Spots of rain drifted onto the window, surviving only a few minutes before evaporating away. This rain would surely be a source of discussion on the news streams today, as summer had gone by unblemished last year.

"David ... David." It was Sarah. Lily was on the Holo.

Lily sat serenely with a light-filled birch forest as her surround. Her kumadori did not shock me this time. The elaborate artwork of the green vine twisted symmetrically, climbing up her cheeks and around her eyes, coming together at the bridge of her nose. Pale yellow flowers bloomed on her forehead.

She was holding a toy horse. I had a sudden fantasy of the horse running away through the forest. I pressed against my cushion to refocus.

"Lily, I know my motivation for meeting you last week was not what you expected and I'm sorry. I hope you understand."

"That's okay," Lily's Holoprojection said, her face beaming. "To think that a member of my family was a department secretary. I told my friends about you, and they were impressed too."

This unanticipated compliment triggered a smile that broke my planned earnest expression. It's been a long time since someone had said anything like that to me.

"This is Goldie." She raised the stuffed horse. "Grandma gave her to me. Isn't she beautiful?"

"She is."

"She's family." Lily's infectious charm and the soft forest light drew me closer.

Suddenly the lights flickered. The Holo transmission cut out. I jerked away in surprise. "Ooff!" Even the Zep couldn't fully suppress Fred.

After a second or two, the transmission returned but with reduced fidelity. Lily was transformed into a brown cloud of jumbled pixels.

A few seconds later the lights stabilized.

"The back-up has kicked in," Sarah said.

"You okay? You still there?" Lily's audio wasn't affected, even if her projection was.

"Still here," I replied.

"These dropouts are so annoying," Lily complained.

I took a moment to regain my composure and got straight to the point. "Have you thought about what I asked?"

"I have given it a lot of thought," she said. "I'd like to see you appear before the Climate Court first. I'm sorry, David, I just can't agree to your request right now."

"I'm getting a medical waiver." I willed myself to stay calm. "I won't be appearing at this so-called court."

"But you seem okay. Why couldn't you appear?"

"You don't understand. My medications are masking my true condition."

"Doesn't that mean your medications are working?"

"It's more complicated than that." My thoughts weren't coming fast enough. I shouldn't have taken my Zep this morning.

The Holo transmission popped back to normal definition. Lily's face had lost its smile. The forest was gloomier behind her.

"The Climate Court is serious about having people like you appear." Lily's voice had a force of certainty behind it.

Sarah intervened. "David will be seeing his doctor next week, so we should get his advice first. In the meantime, David, it might help to plan for the possibility of appearing in court."

"We don't have to plan for anything," I protested.

"If you appear before the court, you will need a lawyer," Sarah explained. "You don't like AI lawyers, so finding a suitable human lawyer might take some time."

"I'll use my personal lawyer." Damn! I'd been tricked into a discussion I didn't need to have.

"I've already spoken to your lawyer," Sarah said. "He runs a family practice. He's not qualified for the Climate Court."

"I know a good lawyer." The light in Lily's forest glowed as her face regained its original sparkle.

"Who would that be?" Sarah asked.

"It's irrelevant," I growled.

Lily ignored me. "I'll get in touch with him."

6

LILY

THE VEIL OF WORRY THAT SURROUNDED ME WAS SHIFTING.

Sarah was edging David in the same direction as me—to attend the court. Sure, David argued about legal representation and finding a human lawyer. But finding a human lawyer was going to be easier for me than having to make a life or death decision. I wasn't going to let David off the hook. I knew where to go. Matteo Bernal.

I met Matteo when he gave a talk at a Humans First evening seminar. He was standing with Ava in front of the wall screen before the session started, so I went up and introduced myself.

"It looks like you've drawn a crowd," I said, waving at the people congregating at the back of the meeting room.

"Amazing," Matteo said. "Who would have thought that the law would be that interesting?"

His presentation was about the challenges of being a human lawyer when you were competing against AI. This was ironic as Matteo had the olive complexion and shaved head that was currently such a popular choice for AI male androids. The androids were usually designed to be classically handsome, and Matteo could have passed for one at a glance.

In his talk he started with the obvious: in law, like so many other professions, not many clients sought out human lawyers. AI was more precise and not prone to procedural or factual errors. Clients liked AI because they provided quick and unbiased opinions.

Someone asked him what it was like financially to be a human lawyer. He said his hourly rates were low—the lowest in the professions.

He turned off the screen, stepped down from the elevated podium, and wandered through the disorderly array of seats in the audience.

"Why would you engage a human lawyer?" he asked of us.

"To support the needy," came the first response. We laughed.

He moved closer to me. "What about you, Lily?"

"For a case where I needed someone who could understand social contexts and emotions better," I answered.

"Perfect. Thanks for following my script," he joked. "Yes, many cases need that level of understanding. It's crucial in more cases than you imagine. I'll give you some examples in a moment. Anything else?"

There followed an interesting discussion that brought up many factors favoring human lawyers, on which Matteo elaborated and gave some case studies.

By the time Matteo wrapped up, he seemed like the embodiment of our Humans First vision: young, passionate, and articulate.

After the presentation, with the lights turned up and switched to a warm yellow, several of us stood around Matteo with drinks and discussed our experiences.

"Why don't you wear a kumadori?" asked Ben in our group. "We encourage wearing them. They show our uniqueness as humans—not to mention playing havoc with facial recognition systems."

"Doesn't work for me." He smiled. "They don't go well with older clients."

"Do you ever get mistaken for an android?" I asked.

"Oh, Lily," Ben gasped, taking a step back with embarrassment. The others stared at me as if I had just turned into a witch.

Matteo's face reddened.

"Sorry, Matteo, if I said something wrong." I tried to read the messages on everyone's faces. "Excuse me." I left the group and made a beeline for Ava.

"Didn't you see his bracelet?" she said. "He's a recovering Trainer addict. Too much sex with androids."

"Oh, shit!"

Ava grinned. "Plenty of sex addicts around. Very few openly admit it."

I was surprised because Matteo seemed more human-centered than most people. The important thing was he was a human lawyer and that's what David wanted. David didn't need to know about Matteo's seedy side.

7

LILY

MATTEO REMEMBERED ME WHEN I CALLED HIM ABOUT WORKING for David.

He agreed to meet in person at his office. Most people didn't want to meet. But if you wanted to understand someone properly, you needed to sense all their pheromones and micro-gestures. Unfortunately, the convenience and ubiquity of AI and Holo overrode this truth. Maybe that was something the old found different? It probably made things hard for someone like David.

I was lucky that my job at the Department of Resettlements involved face-to-face meetings. I could make better decisions. But there was always a reluctance from our clients to an initial meeting; they usually preferred Holo. However, we insisted on a meeting and, almost without exception, their views changed afterward. We had no problems with them returning. I found meetings more rewarding too. It had to be the same with lawyers. Or at least human ones.

Matteo greeted me in the small waiting room. "It's nice to see you again."

"You too." We shook hands.

He invited me into his office. The frosted glass walls on three sides made for plenty of light even though the office didn't have an external window. His screen was in the parked position looking down at us from the ceiling, and his polymer white desk was clear except for an AI portal.

I placed my bag beside one of the two visitor chairs at his desk. The other had a Holo platter on the seat.

"Over here, Lily." He beckoned me to sit on one of two worn chairs next to an occasional table in the corner.

"I thought you might have had a Holo chair?" I nodded at the platter.

"I rent the chairs in the conference room on this floor when I need to. It's not that often. The platter works fine for most clients, and it's cheaper," he said as I sat down. "Let me get you some water."

On the table was a trophy. I reached out to pick it up. It was heavier than I expected. The top was made of clear acrylic and looked like a mountain peak. The etching read:

2058
Jeffrey R. Hansen Award
MATTEO BERNAL
Concord City Bar Association

I cradled it in my lap to emphasize its weight. "This is impressive. What's it for?"

"For some volunteer work I did for the Association." He placed a glass of water next to me.

I put the award back, making a loud clunk. "Oops." I smiled meekly. "Thanks for taking the time to see me."

"Sure." He sat. "Tell me more about what you had in mind. I

understand you want some legal advice regarding one of your older relatives?"

I told him about David and the court, or at least as much as I understood.

Matteo summarized. "So, Mr. Moreland wants to die, and he has to fulfill his obligations at the Climate Court to qualify under the Euthanasia Law, and then you have to file a No Objection Deed. We call it a NOD."

"Yes, I have to give permission."

"Not exactly. How about we check the exact legal situation that applies here," he suggested. "Is Mr. Moreland over ninety-six? There are fewer conditions."

I nodded.

"Okay, Karrie, please summarize the qualifying tests for a person over ninety-six under the State Euthanasia Law."

Karrie answered from the portal: "A person over ninety-six years old has to meet three tests to qualify under the State Euthanasia Law. First, they must fulfill all outstanding social obligations. This means they must discharge any mortgages and debts, have a legally valid will, complete any outstanding civic duties, jury duty and the like, and not have any proceedings outstanding against them."

"Why did you choose a female name for your AI?" I asked.

Matteo frowned. I glanced at his bracelet and bit my lip.

"Just asking." That was all I had, and it sounded lame even to me.

"Karrie, continue," Matteo instructed, regaining his poise.

"The second test is that the person must complete a *ratio decidendi* statement, which receives the approval of the Euthanasia Review Board. It must be at least 250 words long and is normally recorded in the person's own voice."

This was new. Matteo clarified it for me. "That's a formality. They must explain the reason they want to die. It's a way of demonstrating that the person is, you know, of sound mind. Has he done that?"

"It hasn't been mentioned." How complicated can this get?

"Karrie, continue."

"The third test is that their next-of-kin must lodge a No Objection Deed. Next-of-kin is defined in the Euthanasia Law by a consanguinity not exceeding the fifth degree of relationship."

"The NOD is a pro-forma document you have to sign and get witnessed," he explained. "It's not strictly a permission. You're just not objecting to his assisted death."

"It's the same as giving permission."

"Legally not, but practically yes. One difference is that you would have to give some well-argued reason for objecting. Do you have a reason?"

I didn't want to go into my feelings, so I stuck to the facts. "I'm not ready to give permission, and that's what I've told David."

"Did you give him a reason?"

"No." I glared at Matteo. Why all this pressure about a so-called reason? It should be obvious that people don't want family members to die. "I want to know more about his condition, more about him," I continued. "I think his appearance at the Climate Court would be valuable. He influenced climate change policy. We should hear about it."

"Do you understand how grueling the Climate Court can be?" Matteo cautioned.

"Well, it couldn't be harder than normal courts."

"That's what most people think. I can tell you it's tough. Is he well enough?"

"I thought the court was designed to accommodate the elderly." The pulse in my temple started to throb.

"Well, yes, but it's still difficult and the court can't always control everything."

"He's getting checked by his doctor," I said, finding another line of argument.

"All right then … and Mr. Moreland wants a human lawyer to represent him at the Climate Court? That's not surprising, most old people prefer human lawyers."

"Would you do it?"

He grimaced. "My experience at the Climate Court hasn't been positive. I've represented two clients recently. The same experience with both. They got tripped up by the AIs and their own hubris. The outcome was not positive for them or the court, or for me." He paused for a moment. "All things considered, I must say no. If you like, I'll make some inquiries and send you a recommendation for someone else."

"Why don't you meet with David first?" I said. Meeting with David was a risk, but it was the only option that popped into my mind. "Please consider it."

Matteo studied me for a long moment. "Let me think it over."

I left with a deflated ego and a pounding pulse. I tried to think of a movie where the hero couldn't hire the lawyer. None came to mind.

8

RATIO DECIDENDI STATEMENT BY DAVID MORELAND

The pain in my joints makes life unbearable. I call my pain Fred. Naming Fred allows me to curse at him; to plead with him.

Because of Fred, medications and their side effects rule my life now. They have to. Could you sit in a dentist's chair being worked on 24/7 without anesthetic?

The main culprit is *Zepraxonyl*. It's the best drug for keeping Fred and his army at bay. It's the machine gun that kills most of the enemy. But it sprays bullets at my own side as well.

One side effect is my loss of taste and smell. Incontinence is no fun either. I don't look forward to lying down to have Sarah remove my diaper, wipe clean my shriveled genitals, leave them exposed for an interminable time to 'air dry', to then have barrier cream applied and a new diaper put on.

But the worst side effect is the mind fog. It makes it hard to read or focus, or even keep company. Sarah is okay, but her presence is a combination of annoyance and a reminder of my diminished state, so I mostly prefer silence. Occasionally I resort to visiting the communal room at the end of the hall, but it's just a bunch of old people, most of whom can't speak coherently or just mutter under their breath. In any case, I don't want to talk about trivia or play games when I can't focus.

To be honest, the main reason I don't join in with the residents is that most of them live through their children and grandchildren, sharing stories and photos. I can't tolerate the regret and unintended cruelty, even after all these years without family.

I can't control Fred. I can't control all the horrible consequences of him being in my body. Fred is happy to torture, but not to kill.

That is why I want to die.

This is my solemn and true desire, made in sound mind and good judgment.

I, David Moreland, wish to die. To leave and to never return.

Status of ratio decidendi statement: APPROVED

9

LILY

Two days after our meeting I got a call from Matteo. He had thought about it, and called David and arranged to meet him. And then asked me if I would like to come as some sort of after-thought. I know it's not all about me ... but really?

As a briefing, I gave him some vague background about David and his apartment. I warned him about the lack of doors. Now I wish I hadn't. With a serious discussion underway, I was worrying about toilets with missing doors. I blocked the thought from my mind and tuned back into the others. David was speaking as the three of us sat at his dining table.

"They tried to unsettle me by asking me the same question in different ways, but I knew more about natural gas than their expert witnesses did," David recounted.

"It's a common tactic," Matteo said.

"You lawyers like to pose a string of questions asking for yes or no answers." David smiled. They were like buddies reliving the good old days. "I learned never to answer any question with a yes or no because you can get trapped."

"Exactly right." Matteo was agreeing with David a lot more than he did with me.

"I got some warnings from the judge about my answers," David added, emulating the judge's finger-pointing, "but I was able to stick to the plan."

"That's impressive," Matteo acknowledged. "Most witnesses under cross-examination haven't got the discipline. For most people, it's their first time in a court. Many of my clients tell me afterward, 'I should have said this,' or 'I shouldn't have answered that way.'"

"That happens to me too," I said. "Not in court, but other situations."

David turned to me with a 'so what?' look, and then back to Matteo. I bit my tongue and resisted the temptation to speak my mind.

"Here are your drinks." Sarah's entrance stopped the conversation, and we all leaned back in our chairs.

On her tray were our drinks and a plate of chocolate cake slices, all neatly sized and arranged. David promptly reached for a piece of cake. He took a bite and, with an open mouth, started chewing loudly, oblivious to his surroundings. I expected Sarah or Matteo to speak, and maybe they expected me to, but in those few moments, we missed the chance to politely disrupt the routine. Now we were committed to drinking and watching in awkward silence as this scene played out.

Seeking a distraction, my eyes were drawn to a couple of old-fashioned picture frames on the mantle beside the wall screen. In the larger one closest to me, three people stood together. One of them looked like former President Kristen Wade. She had that same distinctive profile and smile. It was a little too distant to be sure. I made a mental note to have a closer look later.

My speculation was interrupted by the vibration of my

sleeve screen. The alert was for images of friends and news. Nothing new or interesting. So, my attention returned to David.

He had finished his cake. Now, with brows furrowed in concentration, he was pressing the tips of his fingers firmly into the tabletop. With a smirk, I turned to Matteo and shrugged. He shrugged right back. At least my experience of oddness here was being shared with someone else.

"What did you think of the cake?" Sarah broke the silence.

"Hmm?" David woke from his hypnotic state and took a moment to get his bearings. "You know, I've lost my ability to taste and smell most foods."

"What about chocolate cake?" I asked.

"I can't taste it."

"No taste?" He had given a good impression of someone who could taste.

"I like the texture."

"Matteo, what sort of people usually come to you as clients?" Sarah gently steered the discussion, now that David was back with us. "Who is it that wants a human lawyer rather than an AI lawyer?"

"It's interesting. I would put my clients into two groups," Matteo explained. "The first is an elderly cohort who grew up with human lawyers and feel uncomfortable about the real ability of AI lawyers."

"So, you must be familiar with people like me?" David said.

"I am. The second group is some of the younger generation, like me and Lily, who are suspicious of the reach of technology. This younger group is expanding and I hope it'll be part of a new long-term trend. I rarely get inquiries from the rest, who are set in their view that AI is the best, cheapest, and quickest."

"Human lawyers understand emotions better," I chimed in.

"That can be important," Matteo agreed.

"And how have you found working against AI lawyers?" Sarah asked.

"It's challenging, more so in some cases than others."

"What about in the Climate Court?" Sarah seemed intent on finding some flaw in Matteo.

"I think a human lawyer is best suited to that court." Matteo didn't appear bothered by her questioning.

"And you've had successful experiences at the Climate Court?" she prompted.

"Not as good as I would've liked. It depends very much on the client. And, as I'm sure you know, the Climate Court is not like other courts, so success is harder to judge."

"Yes, I see," Sarah replied, unconvinced. She collected the cups and plates from the table.

"It's irrelevant anyway," David scoffed. "I'm getting a medical waiver."

"That's possible," Matteo said. "A serious illness will qualify you for a waiver."

"You should appear," I insisted. "You'll be fine in court."

"It's difficult in this court," Matteo said. "There's pressure over a long period of time."

I lined up my shoe to kick Matteo under the table but didn't go through with it. Instead, I gave him a wicked frown. Why was he siding against me?

"We can't pretend it would be easy," he said.

"I'm not pretending anything," I shot back. Was I shouting? "I think David should appear." I was flushed, the excessive warmth in David's lounge room suddenly more apparent.

Matteo turned to David. "It's a big decision, Mr. Moreland. Do you have any questions?"

"No, I don't. Thank you anyway. I'm familiar with court situations, unlike your clients. In any case, I won't be attending court, so this is all academic."

Matteo glanced at me, uncertain what to say next.

"I've also appeared under oath before congressional hearings," David added, reverting to his reminiscent tone. "They can be very adversarial, but mainly they're a sideshow. I didn't have any problems handling them."

"The Climate Court is different," Matteo cautioned. "I'm more than happy to provide you with some background."

"Thank you, but that won't be necessary. I'm sorry you've wasted your time." David was polite but firm, and Sarah took the cue.

"Lily and Matteo, thank you so much for coming to visit David. We learned a lot and I'm sure it will help us work through the next steps."

Leaving David's apartment, I hummed a nonsense tune in my head as Matteo and I navigated the corridor of dread.

In the elevator, I pondered my dilemma. If David gets his waiver, I'm the only barrier to his death wish. If things continue like this, I'll have to reject signing a NOD. Then he'll be going to court just because of me. Will he cope? Matteo doesn't think so. As the elevator announced our arrival on the ground floor, I brushed the questions aside. I have to stay strong. The alternative doesn't bear thinking about. I can't be responsible for another death.

10

LILY

Outside, I stopped to rummage through my bag. "Just looking for my sunglasses." The glare off the white pavement drove needles into my eyes.

"It's bright, isn't it?" Matteo squinted, his contact lenses not correcting fast enough.

I put my glasses on. "That's better."

"He's a feisty old guy, isn't he?" Matteo said as we headed toward our cars.

"Actually, he was less intense than last time. He was calm and spoke more naturally. He moved around. He was just more normal."

"But what about that cake trance thing?" He laughed.

"Yeah, that was strange. We might have been stuck there for hours … the gateau gaze." I stuck my arms out like a sleepwalker.

"The tiramisu trance."

"The stare … of the strudel." I giggled, enjoying our game, and waited for Matteo's riposte. It didn't come. He turned more serious.

"It's a shame he has a terminal illness," he said. "What is it exactly?"

"Don't know. It's awkward to ask." I had a more pressing concern. "Why did you support David about the waiver?"

"Because it's true."

"The waiver isn't going to make any difference," I insisted, not appreciating the implication that he should have somehow misled David.

"The Climate Court's hard," he argued. "And he's exactly the kind of person who struggles with it."

"Too bad. I'm not giving him permission if he doesn't attend."

"That's tough talk. Forcing him to attend court against his wishes, despite a waiver, seems heavy-handed to me. And you're going to have to present a compelling reason in your NOD. Which is?"

"But he's asking me for permission to die."

"Just no objection, actually," he quipped.

"Don't be a smart ass." But I did have doubts. After all, only a few days ago I didn't even know who David was. Why should I object to him following through on his wishes if no one else was against it?

We arrived at our pick-up station and stood in the shade of the arched roof. Our cars were on their way.

"Do you want a drink?" I asked Matteo.

He shook his head.

Standing in front of the dispensing machine, I synced my Sherpa and ordered through Michael: "Small iced tea."

I needed a drink after David's sauna of an apartment. I had hardly touched my drink there to avoid the bathroom problem.

"So, will you represent him?"

"I don't think it's going to happen," he declared.

"I'm going to insist."

"Well, there are three problems," he said.

"Oh yeah?"

"Number one." He raised his thumb like he was making a closing argument to a jury. "David doesn't want to appear."

"Yep, we can solve that."

"Number two." His forefinger now. "Sarah doesn't want me to represent him."

"We can convince her."

"No, we won't. She was clear, and her reasons were good."

"Sarah's not in charge. David wants a human lawyer, so he'll get what he wants. And the third?"

He dropped his hand. "I don't want to take on the case."

"What?" I turned to face him. "You're trying to promote human lawyers, and you're refusing to take on a case where a client wants a human lawyer? What gives with that?"

"Are death threats a good enough reason?"

"What?" I gasped.

"Lots of climate fanatics out there." His tone was low and steady. He was completely serious. "You know the ones—they think the Climate Court is a cover-up, that everyone who appears is guilty and should be convicted. So, if you represent someone, you become a target too. Those groups see a young human lawyer as an absolute traitor."

"How can you be a traitor if you're seeking the truth?"

I knew about the protest groups. The more extreme ones were convinced there was a global conspiracy on climate change, that a whole generation knew what was coming and just window-dressed the problem. Then when the GISC disaster happened, the cover-up was exposed. They blamed that generation, and particularly the leaders, for all the problems since.

The actions of these groups varied from peaceful protests to media campaigns and, in some cases, to out-and-out terrorism.

The irony was that their extreme actions were in part responsible for the creation of the Climate Court that they now hated. Most groups were not satisfied with the structure of the court, even the more moderate ones like the Blue Caps. They felt there were not enough convictions. So, they persisted with their protests. But this was the first I'd heard about death threats. I made a note to ask Michael more about it later.

"That's not actually the reason that I won't take on Mr. Moreland," Matteo continued.

"What is it then?"

"I've dealt with too many of his type and I know what's coming, and it's not good."

"What does that mean?"

"He'll ignore my advice because he thinks he knows what he's doing. When things turn to shit, it'll be my fault."

"You're so negative." I preferred the death threat reason. I threw my empty drink in the bin.

"I've seen it before. And in the Climate Court especially."

"Maybe AI lawyers are better after all. Let's organize one for David, shall we?"

He laughed grimly. I started to laugh too. The idea of David with an AI lawyer was so unworkable.

"Please reconsider. I mean, I'll be there. I'll—"

"Hey. Hand it over!" a voice yelled.

I spun. A crouched man with a red kumadori and disheveled hair pointed a wide-bladed machete at us.

"Sync now. Hand over five thousand dollars. Now!" He crept closer, waving the dull blade in one hand and a Guide in the other.

Matteo stepped forward. "We can't do that."

Swish! The man leaped and slashed at Matteo's face. Matteo jumped back.

"Okay! Okay!" I shouted. "I'm doing it. I'm doing it."

"Quick!" the man barked.

"Michael." My voice quivered. "Sync with this man's Guide and transfer five thousand dollars to it."

"You don't have sufficient funds in your account," Michael warned in my ear.

"Confirm transaction," I pretended.

As I spoke, a police drone in stealth mode descended behind the man. "Drop your weapon!"

Without looking behind him, the man dashed toward the trees beside the shelter.

Two pneumatic pops emanated from the drone. The man's feet stopped in place as if suddenly glued down while his momentum toppled him over, face first. He hit the ground with a soft thud. The machete slid away, scraping along the pavement.

The drone hovered over the man for a few seconds, then one of its cameras turned to us. Matteo and I stood frozen.

"This is Police Drone 'Veatch6.' The offender is sedated and in a stable condition. You have no more to fear from him. He is an undocumented refugee from Florida, so I have notified the Department of Resettlements Security, who will arrive shortly. I assess the scene as 'safe.' I assess your conditions both as 'shaken but satisfactory.' I have your details and have transmitted the incident reference number to your Sherpas. You are now free to leave the area. Would you like any further assistance?"

Neither of us spoke.

"Would you like any further assistance?" the drone repeated.

"No ... no," I mumbled.

Matteo shook his head.

The drone descended on the machete, picked it up, and stowed it away. In an instant, it flew up and out of sight over the trees.

Matteo's face was white, his eyes blank.

"That was close." My voice trembled. I drew Matteo into a one-sided hug and pressed my head against his chest. My cheek slid against the smooth fabric of his shirt. His heart pounded against my face. He remained silent and unresponsive, arms to his side.

"Your car has arrived," Michael said in my ear.

11

DAVID

Dr. Bartok was patient and took his time with his examinations and explanations. He never hurried me, and we often chatted about things other than my illness. He planned to retire soon, but I would be gone before then.

My routine appointments involved the review of my vital signs and the doses of my various medications. It was an ongoing challenge to get the dose levels right. I once asked him why the medical system couldn't formulate simple and effective drugs to treat my conditions, especially with the dramatic advances in medicine that I'd witnessed in my lifetime.

He explained that the system I grew up with was funded by major pharmaceutical companies investing in drug research and development with a payback over long periods of patent protection, and with patients who lived a long time with problematic conditions taking expensive medications every day. The world was different now, and that system wasn't profitable or relevant anymore.

With safety approval granted, new techniques in genetic engineering were now used routinely on most infants. They led to the eradication of many 'old' diseases and aging mechanisms. For the young, most old diseases were controlled.

But for old people like me, already afflicted with legacy diseases, there was no cure. And no new medicines. And no profit in finding them. It was an odd case of discrimination against those still alive but too old to benefit from gene therapies.

Understanding the reasons behind the lack of effective drugs didn't reduce my pain or side effects, and just increased my frustration with being alive today. I had outstayed my welcome and it was time to go.

Sarah took me to Bartok's suites. This appointment was too important for a remote consultation. So, before I took my Zep this morning, I prepared a note of prompts. I didn't want to go off-script with Bartok or be distracted from the critical questions.

Bartok already knew that I wanted to die. I had raised it every time I saw him over the last year. And he had reviewed my *ratio decidendi* statement before I recorded it.

"The Climate Court is something you need to avoid," he warned. "It's tough, especially psychologically. I'll give you a waiver."

This was going to be more straightforward than I imagined.

"The Climate Court says its systems are designed to accommodate people of your generation but I don't think they're sufficient," he continued. "I don't want to alarm you, but people have died at the Climate Court."

"The way things are going, it might be the quickest way for me to go."

He chuckled. "I can grant you a waiver on psychological grounds." He studied his screen. "Your results aren't definitive on their own. I'll have to do another brain scan to get up-to-date data."

The scan involved sitting on a chair that rotated into a skeletal pod where various sensors were mounted. He lowered something like a crown to within an inch of my head. I remained still while various images and videos were projected in front of me, all in silence.

My heart skipped when the image of my daughter Stephanie appeared for a brief moment, and I recognized the video extract of the aftermath of the Beachport Disaster. The other images were more random like flowers, war scenes, the sea, a fireplace, an eagle, the GISC. The screen suddenly went blank and music played in my earpiece. It was the same Stravinsky piece that played at the café. Then more images.

Just as I had acclimatized to the rhythm of the test, everything stopped. The contraption opened and Sarah helped me back into the large recliner facing Bartok's desk.

"Psychological suitability?' Bartok asked of no one in particular.

"Age-adjusted score of 65. Repeat 65," came the AI voice after a few seconds.

"Whoa, David. You like close calls." He smiled at me. "You should be proud. There are few people your age who would score that high."

"What does it mean?"

"It means I'm preparing a waiver for you right now." He winked.

Bartok dictated his conclusions.

"Given these factors, Mr. Moreland's condition prevents him from contributing to the Climate Court. His attendance would pose a serious risk to his psychological health, a not insignificant risk of death, and the potential to damage the reputation of the court. On these grounds, I grant him a medical waiver from appearing before the court. End Recommendation."

"Recommendation captured."

"Please submit."

"Submitting now," the voice said. Suddenly: "Error, submission not accepted."

Bartok's eyes widened. "What's the error?"

"Recommendation is not consistent with the data."

"What's happening?" I asked.

"I'll sort it." Bartok pulled his chair closer to the desk. "Please clarify. Brain scan data result is at the automatic waiver limit."

"Brain scan result needs to be outside the test device sensitivity band at the limit," came the reply.

Bartok leaned back into his chair, brought his hands to his face, and gently rubbed his eyes, his previous confidence a distant memory.

"Is there anything else that David could do?" Sarah asked.

"I don't think so. The data says he doesn't qualify for a medical waiver, no matter what my gut and better judgment tell me."

I looked for my prepared note. It was crushed in my clenched hand. I unraveled it and brought the crumpled paper up to my face. "Do you know someone else who might be more familiar with the waiver system?" I asked bluntly.

"I'm sorry, David, but I have even worse news. I am obliged by law to provide an assessment to the court whenever I receive a request for a waiver. I'll have to submit a Certificate of Fitness for you because that is the data-based assessment. It won't accept my judgment."

I took a few moments to process Bartok's answer. Stripped clean, it was clear. I was being judged by an AI, not a human.

"Intervention has gone mad. Where's it going to stop?" I felt more resigned than angry. "It wasn't like this when I worked in government."

"Believe me, I don't like it either," he said. "This was brought in to stop people from cherry-picking doctors."

I looked at my note again. There were no other options. Perhaps I would have thought of some, had I not taken my Zep this morning.

"Hold on. Let me check something else ..." Bartok said, turning back to his screen. He scrolled through some pages. "Okay, let's try this. Edit recommendation."

"Mr. Moreland suffers from severe psychological disturbances that are not detected by his scans. He believes that there are beings living in his body, whom he communicates with on a regular basis. He is also vulnerable to incoherence when he is in stressful situations and his medication balances are not optimum. He therefore fails the court's 'known future stress factor test.' End Insertion. Please submit."

I held my breath.

"Submission accepted."

"Wait," Bartok cautioned.

"Submission approved. Waiver granted," the voice said.

Bartok thumped his fist against his chest. "Common sense prevails." He turned to me with a grin. "You can fulfill your wish."

Bartok had outsmarted the system and was now celebrating my wish to die. I should have celebrated too. But somehow Bartok's reaction pushed me in the opposite direction. The stark reality of what was to come made me slump, even though I had faced the exact same reality with anticipation, even excitement, only a few days earlier.

With my mind in turmoil, Sarah guided me out of the building. Out the front, a man sat on the ground facing people as they left, staring at each of them as they walked past, ignoring him. His face was covered with speckles of blue and white, as if his kumadori had been incompletely removed or had worn out. He held a sign:

I AM NOT FROM FLORIDA. I AM FROM BEACHPORT.
CAMPS TOO DANGEROUS. PLEASE HELP.

As we approached, his eyes locked onto me. "Spare some cash?"

We went right past.

"Keep your money! You fucking burner!" He grabbed some stones and threw them, but his aim was off and they pinged off a sign next to us. The building security guards immediately pounced on the man and dragged him away as he pleaded with them. "He's the problem, arrest him. Arrest him!"

12

DAVID

When I woke the next morning, the doubts and confusion I felt at Bartok's suites were gone. The rare rain from yesterday had stopped, but I knew the air pressure remained low because the demons went into action early. Thanks Fred, for bringing me back to reality.

"Sarah!" I called out. "Let's Holo Lily. Hold back my Zep until after the call."

"Of course." She activated the controller.

Our morning dance went at a slower tempo this morning to avoid over-stimulating Fred. Sarah selected loose-fitting clothes on these more difficult days. A different costume for a different dance.

When I finally leaned back into the wheelchair, the worst was over. In the bathroom, Sarah wiped the perspiration from my forehead, spread cold shaving cream on my face, and we continued our routine.

At breakfast, she spoon-fed me like a child—a demeaning but necessary survival mechanism without the Zep. It freed up my brain to rehearse the call with Lily.

When the time arrived, Sarah placed the black disc on the dining table chair opposite me. "Hello Lily," I greeted her projection, which hovered over the platter.

"I've got good news," she announced.

"What's that?"

"Matteo has agreed to represent you in court."

"That ... that won't be necessary," I stammered, her news upending my planned talking points. "I won't be going to court."

"You have to, David. The court is important, you need to appear."

"No, I don't. I have a medical waiver." The words didn't come out right. I sounded like a child with a certificate.

Lily's smile vanished. "I'm not going to grant permission unless you appear."

I changed tack. "People have died appearing at the court."

"Isn't that what you want?" Her words carried a hint of hostility, which set me back in my chair. I kept my face and voice calm and responded.

"I want to die on my own terms. Not in pain while answering pointless questions."

"I'm not giving you permission." Now she was the one sounding like a child. "I'm not going to be the one who causes your death."

"That's cruel," I moaned. "You're torturing me."

"No, you're torturing me!" She was on her feet now. "Out of the blue, I find I have family, and you want nothing to do with me except this horrible request."

"I just want to die," I pleaded. "You don't have to do anything other than sign a piece of paper."

"Is that how you did climate policy? Just ticking boxes."

"I achieved more than you imagine."

"Well, show me," she said. "Go to the Climate Court and show me and everyone else."

"Young people haven't got the attention span to notice. I've kept it simple—a simple permission to die."

"I can't live with that," she declared.

"It would be the same as if I never contacted you again."

"I didn't ask for this. The court matters, and I think your doctor is wrong. Listen to yourself. You're perfectly able to argue with me. Court would be easier."

"I just want to die. Forget you ever met me."

"Is that what you want?!" And suddenly her projection disappeared.

I sat in silence. My mind threw me back in time.

Jenny's eyes seethed with anger. 'Is that what you want?' she screamed and stormed out of the room. When Jenny had threatened to take Stephanie and leave me, I didn't take her seriously. Somehow my inner self felt challenged. So, I didn't just ignore her, I taunted her ... I dared her ...

Sarah broke into my flashback. "It might be best to ask for the signed permission through Mr. Bernal."

Before I could think through Sarah's suggestion, Fred launched an attack.

Sarah gave me a Zep and the counterattack began.

As the fog rolled in, the tension in my body began to ease. To clear my mind, I made my way toward the balcony. The sun was breaking free of the wispy clouds but an unseasonal chill in the wind made me hesitate at the door. I stepped out. The direct sun on my skin made a difference. I sat in the chair, hoping for some protection from the breeze. The memories of the Beachport shoreline came flooding back—the warmth of the sun mixed with the chill of the breeze. It didn't last long. My thoughts swung back to my call with Lily. How was this so difficult? She was an adult. She hardly knew me and I was dying anyway. Was I missing something?

My thoughts circled in the Zep fog, like ships waiting for the lighthouse to turn on.

I came back inside.

"Sarah, I'd like my coffee now."

"It's early," she said. "I can make it if you want."

The coffee was tasteless. Nothing but hot liquid. I couldn't finish it.

The call with Lily kept replaying in my mind. The sincerity in her voice bothered me. The hints from the past didn't bode well.

I stopped circling the lighthouse for a moment. "What do you think I should do?" I asked Sarah.

"You know what Lily would like you to do."

"Should I?"

"She's family," she replied.

That was hardly an answer. I changed tack.

"The court's very demanding apparently."

"How does that compare with your life now?" she asked. "You always complain about the boredom and the routine. At least the court would be different."

That was one way of looking at it.

After a pause, she continued: "Could you be convicted?"

"I never did anything wrong," I said. "How could you even ask such a question?"

"What are you afraid of then?"

Was I afraid? Sarah had a good response to each of my questions. Perhaps I was overthinking it. After all, I've been through much tougher courts than anything these young people could put me through.

"I'm going to the common room," I said. A new environment might help.

"Let me prepare your Guide." She attached the Guide to my belt.

The door to the common room was open. I entered and was met by the watch-dog eyes of an old woman. She sat at one of the tables, prune-faced, scowling, eyes fixed on the doorway.

I slinked past, not saying anything. By the windows at the far end was a loose circle of upholstered chairs, recently used for a discussion group, or a game, or god forbid, a sing-along.

With some effort, I turned one of the chairs to face the wall-to-ceiling window. I liked this view. You could see downtown in the distance. The shards of bluish-green skyscrapers poked just above the dirty haze caused by the summer wildfires. Closer, the tent encampment just across the expressway had expanded yet again. But mainly my view was of the nearby suburban expanse of grainy white and green. I was an advocate of the white roof and road policy. It made sense. Increase the albedo of urban surfaces and you have a measurable impact on temperatures. You didn't need AI to understand that.

"She's late!" The woman's screech nearly bumped me off my chair. "My daughter, she's late."

I squirmed in my seat.

"They don't care. They just want your money. They just want you to die," she ranted. "To make you feel miserable so that you die. That's all they want. Do you know what she said? To my face. 'I want you to die.' That's what she said. Can you believe it?"

Nowhere was safe. I pressed the button on my Guide.

"Everything is about money. No one cares. If I didn't have any money, she'd be gone. Even now, she doesn't show up. I didn't treat my mother like that. She has no respect."

Chairs and feet shuffled behind me. My muscles tensed as I fought my inclination to look around.

The touch on my shoulder jolted me. Then came the sting from a blow against my ear.

"Where's my daughter?"

The woman struck harder on my shoulder. I jerked forward to move out of her reach.

"Mrs. Wheeler!" It was Sarah. "Put your walking stick down."

"Are you all right, David?" Sarah came around to face me.

"I'd like to go back to the apartment."

Mrs. Wheeler was lost in the swirl of her own thoughts and words. And they were undignified words. It didn't matter whether they were hers or her daughter's. Words meant something. They created imaginary worlds in the mind of the listener. And those worlds counted.

Rather than distract, this clash with Mrs. Wheeler and her screeching about her daughter merely brought back the harshness of Lily's words this morning.

It was early afternoon by the time I called Sarah over to the sofa. I had circled the lighthouse in the fog for long enough. There was only one way to act and retain any sense of dignity.

13

DAVID

It was best if Sarah told Lily of my decision. That way I could avoid any unexpected emotion and confusion. And I could skip the need for an explanation. It was more dignified when you took the emotions out, when you made a firm decision and moved on.

"Sarah, she's family."

"Lily?"

"Yes, she's family. Tell her I will appear at the Climate Court."

I heard the call. Lily sounded pleased. My tension melted into nothing. By the time Sarah reported back, my mind was drained. "I need a nap."

"There are some matters we'll need to deal with to get ready for court," Sarah said with an enthusiasm that didn't match my mood.

"Just organize it so that it happens as soon as possible."

"You need to appoint a lawyer," she added. "The court can appoint one for you. That'll be the quickest way."

"I don't need a lawyer," I insisted. "Especially not an AI one. You know that."

"The Climate Court requires you to have a lawyer."

"Lily's man. He's young but he'll do."

"Mr. Bernal's court record is not good."

"I won't discuss this any further."

Sarah hesitated, giving the appearance of backing off, then stiffened.

"His background holds some risks. It could work against you."

My concentration was too weak to understand her words. "Stop talking in riddles."

"He was a sex addict," she said. "The court will know."

Sex? I fought through the mind fog to find relevance in her accusation. "I don't care."

"There's another thing—"

"For god's sake ..." This whole dying and court and waiver experience was like a set of Russian dolls. Every time you finished with one, there was another lurking inside.

"There are pre-briefing sessions for people new to the court," she said. "It's recommended that you attend. Even Mr. Bernal recommended it."

"Come on, Sarah," I moaned. "I know how courts run. I just want this over and done with."

14

LILY

"THAT'S DIFFICULT," SIGHED MY BOSS, CRYSTAL FERGUSON, AFTER I explained the David story and my desire to attend the hearings. "I totally understand why you want to attend, and we will, of course, support you." She took a breath. "But why didn't you tell me earlier? We need to let clients know as soon as there's a change in their appointments. We can't leave it till the last minute."

She was right. The Department of Resettlements prided itself on its person-to-person counseling and support, so we needed to prioritize our clients. It was that focus on real human interactions that had attracted me to the department in the first place.

The Department of Resettlements was created soon after the GISC, to support climate change refugees from damaged coastal areas like Florida, so my work meant I met lots of people. Those that had the courage to move early tended to be people without much money but with lots of drive. It was rewarding watching them rebuild their lives with just a little help from me.

Despite encouragement to relocate early, most people held

out. No matter how much the ocean rise was known, it was hard to imagine that your hometown was doomed until the time came. Then the constant trickle of refugees became a flood. Our health systems couldn't cope. Our infrastructure was busting. Everything was out of control. It was a crazy time, working twelve-hour days and most weekends.

I breathed a guilty sigh of relief when the out-of-state restrictions were put in place and we got back to some reasonable workload. The decision was not popular in D.C. or the other coastal states. They said it was unconstitutional. The State has appealed to the Supreme Court to keep the restrictions. Now everyone was saying we were going to lose. What then?

Crystal suggested I take the next two days off, reschedule my client meetings, and let my work colleagues know what was happening. The support Crystal and the department were giving me justified my stance with David. Yes, some doubts had started to creep in, especially after David received his waiver. But waiting in the courthouse foyer, my conviction was stronger than ever that I had taken the right path.

A burst of activity near the building entrance caught my attention. David and Sarah had entered the foyer. They stood on the black and yellow circular State seal that was embedded in the marble floor. Courthouse officials came up to meet them.

David's hunch and frailty appeared exaggerated. Maybe it was him being in the wheelchair, or perhaps it was the scale of the foyer with its wide expanse and grand staircase. He looked small and out of place. Had I done the right thing making him come here?

As he reached me, I took one of his pale hands in both of mine and flinched. His hand was like a sheet of ice. "Are you ready for your big day?" I asked, sticking with my lines.

An eternity seemed to pass.

"Yes," he finally replied.

I glanced at Sarah, concerned.

"We had to battle through some protestors," she explained, anticipating my question.

"Well, I'm sure you're going to be great," I reassured David. "I'll be rooting for you from the gallery."

He made no acknowledgment. His stiffness and darting eyes brought back the uneasiness of my first visit. He even wore the same oversized shirt collar and necktie.

"Would you like some water, David?" Sarah asked.

"Mr. Moreland!" The voice came from behind me. It was Matteo. I smiled in anticipation and turned. "Hello Lily." He spoke matter-of-factly and strode past me. "I've booked a briefing room," he announced. His stern and flat demeanor was new. He leaned down to speak to David.

"There are a few things we need to go through," he said. "It's important you start the hearing in the best possible way."

Without waiting for an answer, Matteo stepped behind David and wheeled him away.

"Wait, I'll come with you." I ran after them.

Matteo glanced back. "That won't be necessary." They disappeared behind one of the many doors adjoining the foyer.

I stood, abandoned in the vast expanse of the building, wondering why I was there.

15

DAVID

SARAH WARNED ME ABOUT ATTENDING COURT IN PERSON. THE court had sent me a loan Holo chair for use during the hearings. But remote meetings never came close to replicating in-person meetings, no matter how cutting-edge the technology. Sarah tried to convince me that the Holo technology used at the Climate Court simulated the feeling of being there. I wasn't prepared to take the chance just on Sarah's word, especially for my first appearance. The difference in interactions recently with Lily in person versus Holo showed how things can get confused. So, I stood my ground and insisted that I attend in person.

The court was supportive and seemed to understand the needs of older people. They sent a suitable vehicle, so getting me set up in the car proved to be uneventful. Sarah sat in the front, and I was in the back in my wheelchair, snugly held in the specially designed compartment. Six stainless-steel anchor points secured my wheelchair, with two sashes crisscrossing against my chest. The vehicle appeared sturdy, with thick glass and a purposeful style, perhaps reflecting the security needs of a court.

The courthouse was located in the historic part of Concord City, about thirty minutes away. The ride was smooth thanks to the epoxy surfacing on the roads. Sitting in the back, facing rearward, I watched as the white pavement and black markings flashed past.

We came off the expressway at the Commerce Street downtown exit. My old department offices were right on Commerce Street. I hadn't passed there in a long time. The department building was a classic example of 1960s Brutalist architecture, the forerunner of the current white concrete neo-Brutalist style. It was a horrible building to work in. Low ceilings, poor ventilation, and limited natural light. But it was heritage protected, so it remained there, an imposing monolith.

We turned into Jackson, the beginning of the historic district. The car started to judder off the uneven cobblestone pavement. My eyes clenched shut. My hands gripped the armrests. I held my breath. The vibrations turned into rusty razors slashing at my joints. Hang on! The courthouse was only around the next corner.

As the car turned, the centrifugal force forced me to sway one way and then the other. The bumping rhythm accelerated.

"Ahh! Ahh! Ahh!"

The car slowed down and stopped. "Are you all right, David?" Sarah asked as she reached back and touched my hand.

"It's the bumps," I whimpered, glued to the wheelchair.

Sarah joined me in the enlarged compartment of the car. She carefully studied my face and hands. She wiped the film of perspiration from my forehead. "Is the pain still there?"

"The shadow aches."

"The courthouse is only a hundred yards down the road," she said. "Can you handle that?"

"No!" I dreaded the thought of Fred's razors starting up again.

"How about you take your *Zepraxonyl* now?" She placed my bag of medications beside my wheelchair. "Or we could get out here, and wheel you down the sidewalk."

"Let's do that."

Out of the car, the dust in the gusty hot wind stung my face. Sarah placed a blanket over my lap and hands. From nowhere, a dozen helmeted security people appeared in their green fluorescent uniforms. One of them talked to Sarah.

"Sure, we'll hurry," she replied.

Sarah immediately came around behind me and started pushing me down the sidewalk with the security men surrounding us like a moving guard of honor.

Looking ahead to the courthouse plaza, a small crowd had gathered. They were wearing blue hats and caps. Some had blue painted faces. They stood on either side of makeshift metal railings, manned by more security guards.

Sarah bent to my ear. "Ignore them, it'll be done in a moment."

The crowd spotted our convoy. A man's voice rang out. People began waving placards. One of them read: 'Punish the Burners.' Chanting started as if responding to a conductor's baton. Three or four people at first, building to the whole crowd.

For a moment I thought nothing of it, then my pelvic muscles tightened. The chanting was directed at me.

"Turn back!" I cried, almost to myself. Instead, Sarah sped up, making the bumps over the sidewalk more prominent, but the pain was not the threat now.

Contorted faces scowled at me. The ferocity of their screams caused a fine spray of spit to rain out of their mouths like venom. I raised the blanket over my head.

Losing sight of the mob made time slow down. Our convoy moved into the eye of the storm. The intensity of the chants rose to a crescendo. My flimsy, soft blanket somehow deflected them, muffling the calls into an indeterminate angry rumble accompanying the rhythmic chant.

As soon as we were past, the chant intensity died down, like the change in tone when an ambulance siren roars past. I lowered my blanket. The guard of honor stopped and we were in the courthouse foyer. My heart was racing.

Three uniformed officials were waiting near the entrance. They came up smiling and were unreasonably calm.

"Welcome to the Climate Court, Mr. Moreland. Please ignore the protestors out front. As explained in our briefing materials, they are not singling you out. They're here every day."

"They're terrorists," I gasped, out of breath like I had run a marathon. "Keep them away."

"We try to manage them. They do, of course, have a democratic right to voice their views. We apologize if they upset you," the lead official said. "Please be our guest and move to the more private part of the foyer." He gestured to a roped-off area guarded by a couple of security guards. "Please take your time and have some refreshments before your hearing."

"Lily's waiting there," Sarah said.

Lily greeted me enthusiastically, making a fuss.

Sarah intervened. "How about some water?"

Now Matteo was dragging me into a room on the side and explaining something at speed.

"Matteo." I stopped him mid-sentence. "How long before the hearing starts?"

"About ten minutes before we move into the courtroom."

"Let me gather my thoughts."

He hesitated. "Sure, I'll stay until we're ready to go in."

I took some deep breaths and closed my eyes. Fred was quiet

for the moment. I concentrated. What am I here for? The court. Stay focused. Don't get distracted. It's a court, you know what to do. Fred, you need to back off. What else? Don't answer yes or no. Don't get distracted. Stay focused.

I listened for the rhythm of my breath and heartbeat. They were normal.

"We'll have to go now," Matteo announced after what seemed like only a minute. He wheeled me in—he was jerkier than Sarah, giving Fred an opportunity to play. I started to doubt my strategy of deferring my Zep.

The courtroom was small, much smaller than I had imagined. After the grandness of the courthouse foyer, this room was bland and informal. I expected an elaborate setting, something more like the rich wood-paneled congressional hearing rooms.

Matteo parked me at a table to one side of the courtroom, partly facing the public gallery. Lily sat in front with Sarah. She waved at me. I smiled back.

With everything in place and time approaching, nerves jangled in the pit of my stomach. Although an unpleasant sensation, this was a good omen; it would help me perform better when the moment arrived. Some people thought that nerves were a problem, but they gave me more energy.

A door behind me gently clicked open and then closed, followed by rapid footsteps. The judge appeared in my peripheral vision. She sat at the wide desk in the center of the room, beside a Holo chair.

She made some opening remarks and turned to me. "Welcome, Mr. Moreland, are you ready to proceed?"

"Yes."

An official wheeled me toward the central desk and positioned me next to the judge, directly facing the gallery. I stared out at the young faces. The looks I got back were grim … and hostile. Most of them wore kumadori and, for a brief second, I imagined I was in a Hieronymus Bosch painting.

16

TRANSCRIPT

JUDGE MBEKI: Can the witness please state their full name?

DAVID MORELAND: My name is David Xavier Moreland.

JUDGE MBEKI: Thank you, Mr. Moreland. I hand over to you, Attorney Bernal.

ATTORNEY BERNAL: Thank you, Your Honor. Mr. Moreland, let's start with some background. Can you please give the court a brief summary of your academic qualifications?

DAVID MORELAND: I have a Bachelor of Arts degree from the University of Michigan majoring in Marketing. And I received a Masters of Public Policy degree from Stanford University.

ATTORNEY BERNAL: Thank you. And can you give us some of the key milestones in your professional career? Perhaps starting with your first job after college.

DAVID MORELAND: My first job was with NG Star Energy, initially in Marketing and Public Relations. I moved on to be Vice President of Business Development in the company's subsidiary, Energy Solutions West. After I was promoted to president, I built the business to over twenty billion dollars in revenues.

ATTORNEY BERNAL: How long were you at NG Star Energy and its subsidiaries?

DAVID MORELAND: I was with NG Star for seventeen years.

ATTORNEY BERNAL: What made you leave?

DAVID MORELAND: I wanted a greater influence on policy. When Secretary Papakouris offered me the opportunity to lead the policy and regulation team at Concord's Department of Energy and Climate Change, I couldn't turn it down.

ATTORNEY BERNAL: What were some of your achievements at the department, initially and later on?

DAVID MORELAND: Initially, I was responsible for developing strategies for the energy mix, and developing climate change targets. One of my first initiatives was to introduce strict energy efficiency rules. That allowed us to shut down our oldest coal power plants. Then I moved onto transition strategies into renewables. Most people would have heard of the 'Gas or Mass' program that I instigated. It was very successful. It won many environmental awards. After Governor Brown's election, I was appointed department secretary. During my time in charge of the department, I installed the largest fleet of fourth-generation nuclear reactors ever developed in America.

ATTORNEY BERNAL: They are all outstanding achievements, Mr. Moreland. But there's more, isn't there? You also played an important national role, didn't you—at the Helsinki Climate Accord?

DAVID MORELAND: Yes, I led the U.S. negotiating team at the Helsinki Accord. It was the biggest breakthrough ever in climate policy history.

ATTORNEY BERNAL: Yes, it's well known and still recognized today. Now, you were with the department for a total of twenty-nine years. Is that right?

DAVID MORELAND: Yes, that's right.

ATTORNEY BERNAL: That's a long and distinguished career, Mr. Moreland. Congratulations and thank you for your service to our state and nation.

DAVID MORELAND: Thank you.

ATTORNEY BERNAL: At this point, I would like to explore the methods used in developing policies and regulations when you first joined the department. To start, could you please describe to the court the type of information you sought out or commissioned in formulating climate change policies in the department?

DAVID MORELAND: When I first came to the department, State policy was prioritized around encouraging the transition toward renewable energy. So, we did a lot of work on the impact of renewable supplies on the energy mix, on the network, and of course their climate change impacts.

ATTORNEY BERNAL: What consultation processes did you follow?

DAVID MORELAND: We consulted with utilities, industry, and the Federal Government. Consultation with the community was mostly done by the utilities.

ATTORNEY BERNAL: How widely did you consult with utilities and industry?

DAVID MORELAND: Very widely, particularly with the energy industries in both the renewable and the fossil fuel sectors.

ATTORNEY BERNAL: What happened when Governor Brown was elected and changed direction on energy policy?

DAVID MORELAND: Secretary Papakouris was let go, as often happens, and I was approached to be the new Secretary.

ATTORNEY BERNAL: Did your department's consultation approach change when you became the new Secretary?

DAVID MORELAND: Well, given that the government policy changed to a carbon price, we also had to change.

ATTORNEY BERNAL: How would you characterize those changes?

DAVID MORELAND: We had to go broader because a much greater cross-section of industry was affected by the carbon price. From memory, we sought several rounds of submissions from the affected industries. It helped us adopt some very practical measures, such as the stepwise introduction of carbon prices over—

[Interruption from the gallery. A member of the gallery is sanctioned.]

JUDGE MBEKI: Apologies for the interruption, Mr. Moreland. Please proceed, Attorney Bernal.

ATTORNEY BERNAL: Mr. Moreland, let's move to the negotiations at the Helsinki Accord. You were the leader of the American negotiating team?

DAVID MORELAND: That's right. I was there under the instructions of Secretary of State van Berkel.

ATTORNEY BERNAL: How did that opportunity arise?

DAVID MORELAND: I knew many people in the Department of State including Secretary van Berkel. I kept them in the loop on our whole program here in Concord because it had national significance. They were impressed with what we were doing and how we went about it. One day, I got a call asking me to lead the negotiating team.

ATTORNEY BERNAL: Very good. On to the Accord itself, could you please elaborate on what your team's objectives were and what information you had to rely on?

DAVID MORELAND: Our objective, stated in simple terms, was to get agreement to the temperature target. That meant accelerated and binding emissions reductions from the top ten emitting countries. It included stopping deforestation and peat destruction in countries like Indonesia and Brazil.

ATTORNEY BERNAL: And what information and modeling did you have access to in order to form and justify this position?

DAVID MORELAND: We had the official IPCC modeling and we had our own modeling work.

ATTORNEY BERNAL: Mr. Moreland, how would you describe the outcome achieved by the negotiating team at the Accord?

DAVID MORELAND: The Helsinki Accord was an outstanding success and it's been recognized by everyone as a key milestone event. We achieved the first-ever binding commitment to meet a target.

ATTORNEY BERNAL: Thank you, Mr. Moreland. Your Honor, that is all for our introductory session.

JUDGE MBEKI: Attorney Marsaud, do you have any questions?

ATTORNEY MARSAUD: Yes, Your Honor. Mr. Moreland, going back to your time in policy and regulation at the department, can you please elaborate on the energy companies you consulted with and what form that consultation took?

DAVID MORELAND: It would have taken many different forms. I can't remember the specifics.

ATTORNEY MARSAUD: Can you give us some examples?

DAVID MORELAND: Well, we would have sought formal responses from industry to specific questions or potential scenarios. It was a range of approaches. I can't remember the details.

ATTORNEY MARSAUD: And the companies you consulted with?

DAVID MORELAND: I think we would have talked to all the major and mid-tier energy companies over my time.

ATTORNEY MARSAUD: And which company did you consult most with?

DAVID MORELAND: I can't remember. We talked to all of them.

ATTORNEY MARSAUD: Do you think you met with NG Star more than the others?

DAVID MORELAND: No, I don't.

ATTORNEY MARSAUD: Well, let me refer you to the—

JUDGE MBEKI: Attorney Marsaud, Mr. Moreland has responded to your question. This is just the opening statement. You will have time for cross-examination and presentation of your evidence later. Please move on.

ATTORNEY MARSAUD: Certainly. Mr. Moreland, if we look at the Helsinki Accord, is it not true that your negotiating team was given an objective target of 2-degree temperature rise?

DAVID MORELAND: We were given an objective, but we had to take into account the position of other countries. It was a negotiation.

ATTORNEY MARSAUD: You didn't achieve the 2-degree objective, did you?

DAVID MORELAND: We got fully binding agreements, which was a world first.

ATTORNEY MARSAUD: But not the 2-degree target trajectory.

DAVID MORELAND: We got agreement to 2.5 degrees plus all binding commitments. Most of those key countries delivered on the Helsinki commitments. It was the most successful climate change accord ever.

ATTORNEY MARSAUD: Mr. Moreland, you have seen the havoc wreaked by climate change events, not only in the United States but on the whole world. Do you accept any responsibility at all, even the tiniest amount, for the creation of the conditions that caused the chaos we now face?

DAVID MORELAND: No.

ATTORNEY MARSAUD: We will return to this issue, Mr. Moreland. But for now, that is all from me.

JUDGE MBEKI: Thank you, Mr. Moreland. We will adjourn for the day.

17

DAVID

MATTEO WHISPERED SOMETHING TO ME WHEN THE HEARING WAS adjourned, but I was looking for Sarah. Fred was unbearable. Even the movement of my chest from breathing was an invitation for Fred.

I pleaded to Sarah as she came up to me. "Give me the Zep!"

"It's in the car," she replied.

"Go. Now!"

"Do you need to talk to Mr. Bernal?"

"Just go!"

Sarah understood the urgency and quickly maneuvered me out of the courtroom and started across the expansive courthouse foyer.

An elderly man suddenly stepped up and stood in our way.

"David, do you remember me from NG Star days?" He paused. "I'm Jake Pauley."

His face was unfamiliar. He was unkempt, his disheveled gray hair far too long and his fly was undone.

He leaned closer. "We worked together way back. Remember the Gas campaign in Oregon? I still laugh when—"

"Out of the way!" I moaned.

Pauley didn't let up; his skunk breath distracted me from putting any meaning to his words. "The judges and attorneys look disinterested, don't they?"

"Sarah!" I called.

"That's good," he whispered. "Pretend you don't know me."

"I am sorry, Mr. Pauley, but Mr. Moreland has to go." Sarah wheeled around him and toward the exit.

He followed. "Don't be fooled. They'll trap you. But it's all right; I still have the files." He fell behind Sarah's pace. "Don't worry!" His voice faded as we left the building. "I'll stick with you!"

A group of the green-clad guards surrounded us. I willed Sarah to go faster across the plaza, but we were already traveling at speed. I shrank down into the chair to absorb the bounces. At each bump, I grunted—trying to expel Fred from my body. On reaching the car, the jolts stopped and my moaning turned to a pathetic sigh. Sarah got the Zep.

With my mouth open like a baby, she placed the tablet on my tongue. I sucked on the water bottle she put to my lips. That relaxed me even though it had no immediate effect on my pain.

Sarah got me into the car and put the blanket on my lap. The weight of the blanket and the quiet of the interior, muffling the growl of the crowd, calmed me. The precise clicking of the brackets into the stainless-steel restraining anchors added to my sense of security. Sarah switched the car windows to opaque mode, shutting out the view of the outside world. The Zep worked with the stillness, the force fields gradually spinning into action.

Suddenly the car started to rock from side to side. I grabbed the armrests. My head swayed, pain stabbed through my neck.

Shouts rang out. "Hey! Hey! Stand away from the car! Now!"

The rocking stopped after a few seconds; the angry shouting continued.

The car windows went transparent as a security officer came up. "You better go now, ma'am."

The car took off. Bang! Bang! Bright blue fluid covered and dripped down the side windows. The car stopped.

"Keep going," Sarah commanded. The car started up again and accelerated.

The cobblestones, the vibrations … "Ahh! Ahh! Ahh!" Every nerve slipped under the force field. The car stopped. "Screw you, Fred!"

"Do you want me to sedate you?" Sarah asked, beside me in a flash.

"Yes!"

The needle pushed deep into my vein and the *vrr … vrr … vrr* of the impulses delivered the yellow liquid payload.

As the sedative took me away, the shouts from outside the car started to fade.

"Jail for the murderer! Jail for the murderer! Burners must pay!"

And then nothing.

18

LILY

THE STATE OF CONCORD COAT OF ARMS DOMINATED THE BACK wall of the courtroom. The American and State flags were posted on either side. The bulkiness of a Holo chair stood out among the low profile of the rest of the courtroom furniture. Without these features, it could well have been one of the rooms we use for our Humans First meetings.

Sarah and I sat in the gallery front row.

Matteo brought David in and took up the table to the right of the judge's desk. We shifted across to be closer. I waved at David. He didn't react. He sat expressionless, waiting.

The judge strode into the room with an air of purpose. She sat and activated her screen and the court AI. She looked around to check everything was in order, checked with Matteo and then the other attorney, and got nods of acknowledgment from both.

The judges for the various Climate Courts and hearings were drawn from a pool of contributing countries. I had bet with Ava that the judge would be from Europe; she said America. We both lost. The judge's opening remarks were delivered in impeccable English but her intonation and accent gave away that she was from an African country.

David spoke with assurance, but he sat rigid in his wheelchair, a permanent frown on his face. I was fascinated to hear of David's career and some of his achievements. When he described his role at the Helsinki Accord, a sense of pride sprang up in me and some of my concerns washed away.

As David's testimony went on, his and Matteo's language turned to corporate-speak and seemed less relevant. Observing Matteo more closely, he was stroking his top lip. He had done the same in the foyer.

I whispered to Michael, "Message to Matteo. Watch your lip, you look nervous."

Matteo dropped his hand from his face.

Suddenly, a male voice emanated from the room speakers. "Miss Lily Miyashiro, please deactivate your Sherpa. Final warning."

All eyes turned to me as I slunk down in my chair. My face was on fire.

"Turn off your Sherpa," Sarah whispered.

"Michael off."

"Please proceed," the judge instructed.

The next several minutes of testimony were a blur as I settled down from the public humiliation. It could've been worse; at least the gallery was not full. Some questions from the other attorney probed at David, but my sense of shame from the stupid Sherpa incident was stopping me from following the details. The judge stepped in to bring the other attorney into line.

My attention was now drawn to the judge, who had no more attention for me, thank god. She had a nicely proportioned face with prominent cheekbones. But more than her physical appearance, my eyes were drawn to the scarf she wore. It was a beautiful piece in vibrant red and yellow on white, contrasting dramatically with her black suit, just like the Clyfford Still painting I had seen on my recent visit to the Concord City Museum of Art. The painting was on semi-permanent loan from MOMA, which had loaned out its most valuable works to museums in safe cities around the country.

In the midst of these musings, the judge spoke up and closed the proceedings for the day.

Sarah was already up and tending to David. She wheeled him out of the courtroom, looking like she wouldn't stop for anyone. I started to follow, changed my mind and stopped, and started again. In the end, I stayed and watched as Matteo conferred with the judge and other court officials, hoping to catch his eye. The discussions went on much longer than I anticipated, and, being the last person in the gallery, I left to find David.

The foyer was empty, so I moved out onto the courthouse plaza, where a blast of hot air whistled through my hair. David was not in the plaza either, only some stragglers milling around —and the homeless refugees camped around the perimeter of the building. The refugees had set up tents along the building wall, which offered additional shelter from the elements. The authorities tolerated these makeshift camps as long as they did not grow too large, at which point they would sweep through in an after-midnight raid and move them on.

In front of the tents, a solitary dog, tied to a bike rack, watched me with sad eyes. My hand reached out to pat the dog, but it backed off, cowering.

"C'mon, fella." I moved closer and rubbed the soft bristles on his head and then the back of his ears. His eyes sparked up and his tail sprang to life.

If only people were this easy. If only I could make eye contact with the homeless, smile, and get the same result. But it was worse than that. If I recognized any of them, my heart would sink—I had failed them. Could I have done more? Did I miss something? Thoughts like these were not good for my conscience. So, I avoided looking in their direction.

"Go home, you old burner! Get out of here!" The raised voices drew my attention to a handful of blue-capped protestors at the road curb. Their target was an elderly man. He had been one of the observers in the court.

Without warning, a Blue Cap burst out of the pack and shoved the old man, who toppled to the ground. He lined up a kick. I averted my eyes. The sound of a heavy thud carried on the breeze. After a second, with teeth clenched, I glanced back at the scene.

The Blue Cap towered over the motionless man. "You should be in jail! Nah, that's too good for you!"

A couple of cops ambled toward the fracas as the taunting continued. They managed to disperse the protestors, who couldn't resist cursing at the prone man even as they left. Bullies sure can be bold when they're not under any threat themselves.

The police leaned down and spoke to the old man, checking his condition. To my relief, they were able to help him onto his feet and dust him down. After a few wobbly moments, the man found his balance. Then, abruptly, the cops turned and left him standing alone as if nothing had happened. Part of me wanted to help the man, so it was with a tinge of guilt that I headed back toward the courthouse to get out of the wind. Matteo was striding toward me.

"Where's Mr. Moreland?" he called out as he approached.

"He's gone." I pointed. "The only thing out here is a bunch of Blue Caps beating up an old man."

"Shit!"

"What's wrong? Do you know him?"

"No ... no, it's Mr. Moreland. I told him to wait for me," he explained. "We need to debrief and plan."

"I thought he spoke well." I hesitated. "Didn't he?"

"Today was easy. It's going to get tougher." His eyes scanned the plaza as if David might still be hidden in some corner. "He needs to be prepared. The hard questions have already started and his answers weren't perfect. He doesn't listen to me."

"How do you think an AI lawyer would've gone?"

His lips betrayed a hint of a smile.

"Let's grab something to eat," I suggested.

19

LILY

MATTEO RECOMMENDED A LITTLE VIETNAMESE STREET HAWKER A couple of blocks away, but as we started to walk, the squally hot wind and our stinging eyes made the decision for us and we ended up choosing the closest option, a Food Ink outlet. Pricier than I would have liked, but at least it was bright and cheery. Bright and cheery, just like Matteo's words weren't.

"I don't want to discuss this any further," he said, "but it's important you don't contact me again in the courtroom. It makes me look unprofessional and could harm David's case."

I had nothing useful to say, so I nodded, and we walked in silence.

Ahead on the sidewalk, a man and woman were panhandling passers-by, showing those who stopped a hologram. Matteo noticed and he gently pushed against my forearm, directing me away from them. Instead, I sped up and headed straight toward the couple.

"Lily!" Matteo called out.

"It's fine."

They were former clients of mine. Jonah and Poppy. Originally from Louisiana. Data Scientists. I set them up at the White Hills camp and got them short-term casual jobs. They could never convert them to permanent. They used to come back to me as the casual jobs expired. It was hard for the out-of-staters ... even for good people, and you didn't need much time without a paycheck to run into trouble.

They didn't recognize me and started their spiel.

I stopped them. "It's me ... Lily Miyashiro."

They gave me a blank look and restarted the spiel. I sensed a harder edge to them. Their faces were gaunt beneath the do-it-yourself kumadori on their cheeks.

Matteo pulled me away but I shrugged him off.

"Your daughter," I said to them. "How is she?"

"Oh, Lily!" It was Poppy who clicked first. "Here, look." They turned on the hologram. It showed a girl, sullen-faced, lying in a hospital bed. Surgical steel pins jutted out of her leg.

"She was attacked at the camp," Jonah said.

"That's her? Poor thing," I sympathized. What more could go wrong for these two? I felt overwhelmed for a moment. But then a nagging doubt crept in. The hologram had that tell-tale cloudiness around the edges. Was it a fake?

"We need help," Poppy begged. "To cover her care. We can't afford—"

"The department can help." I discarded my doubts. "Make an appointment to see me."

I synced my details and turned to leave, but Jonah grabbed my wrist. "We need help right now." His eyes were suddenly menacing. His grip on me tightened. Poppy stepped up and tugged at my shirt. I gave a fake smile, knowing Matteo's eyes were on me. Jonah twisted my wrist, and my smile felt more like a grimace.

"No problem." I transferred two hundred dollars to Poppy's account. Jonah released his grip.

They thanked me profusely as if this exchange was perfectly normal, and moved on down the sidewalk. I returned to Matteo, unnerved, and with a wrist I feared would bruise up.

"You need to be careful," he warned. "Coasties can be dangerous—"

"Don't call them coasties," I hissed, ignoring my own hypocrisy.

"The city isn't happy when people encourage them," he added.

I knew the city's position on refugees better than anyone, but I didn't bother to reply.

What do you do about people like Jonah and Poppy? I knew deep down they were good people. And when you saw enough people in trouble as I did, you realized there was not much distance between them and you. Maybe that was the real reason I tried not to look at those worse off than me. To avoid that thought. To avoid that fear.

20

LILY

THIS WAS ONE OF THE OLDER FOOD INK OUTLETS. IT STILL HAD the full-height glass wall that divided diners from the food preparation area. You could see the robot food printers spring to life as each order arrived. They even had the colorful decorations and animated faces that so appealed to me as a kid. My favorite robot was 'Betty,' who made the pizza dough and then shot it out at the precise force to make a perfect round base on the conveyor. And Food Ink was the first food chain that went fully to android staff, a novelty at the time.

The dining area had modern brightly painted walls but retained the old-fashioned brushed metal table tops with embedded screens.

We ordered from our screen.

"I still find it strange," Matteo mused. "You know, that Mr. Moreland … he'd never met you, or even knew you, then he makes this request to die."

"Yeah, our very first meeting," I said. "I'm so glad the Climate Court thing was there. Otherwise, I would have freaked out."

"More than you did."

I laughed nervously. "Was it that obvious?"

He nodded. "People like us in Concord City haven't had much experience with death, so that makes it even harder."

"Actually, in my case, it's the other way around," I said.

His eyebrows raised, but he said nothing and motioned for me to continue.

"My mother died when I was seventeen."

"Oh. I'm sorry."

"I'm okay talking about it." I took a sip of water. "I think this David thing is more traumatic for me because of my past. If I didn't know what death of a close relative was like, I might've been able to give David his approval."

"I see what you mean," he said.

"I don't mind talking about my mom's death," I admitted. "I actually find it therapeutic."

Matteo didn't seem inclined to stop me, so I continued with my therapy.

"She fell ill suddenly. Just collapsed on the floor mid-sentence right in front of our neighbor," I said. "Some sort of brain bleed."

"What a shock."

"She was going to recover too, but the AI made a mistake in the hospital."

"A mistake? How can they make a mistake?"

"Yeah, I couldn't believe it either."

I explained that an error by an AI nurse, a software glitch, was a rare occurrence. Something like ten thousand times less likely than a human nurse. But that statistic didn't make me feel any better. I guess you could think of it as human error in a different way: an error in programming. But there was no shaking the fact that it felt like an AI killed my mother.

The worst part was that my hopes had built as I watched her initial recovery. She started to talk again. Then they gave her the wrong drug, and she shriveled up. They found their mistake straight away, but there was nothing they could do to reverse the process. I went from hope to despair in a single day.

Matteo said nothing.

"I regret that Mom never had the opportunity to tell me how much she loved me, to say goodbye. It was in her eyes; she wanted to tell me but she couldn't get it out. So, I told her instead. I told her everything. All my feelings spilled out over those last two days. But she couldn't speak at all."

Matteo didn't interrupt. If anything, I detected in his body language an invitation to continue. A lot of my friends hadn't let me get this far through the story.

"You know what was worse? The frustration in her eyes. She knew she was dying. She just wanted to get her emotions out. They were locked in her body. She was in pain, putting all her remaining energy and strength into trying to speak, or communicate with her hands, or any way she could. It was like she was trying to get a flame to light, to start a fire that wouldn't take. And then there was nothing."

Matteo stroked his top lip. Otherwise, his expression gave nothing away.

"Here's your pizza, ma'am." The mood broke. "Vegetarian with an extra layer of cheese," continued the server, placing the perfectly patterned and sliced pizza in front of me.

One thing you could say for AI servers: they didn't judge the emotional weather before they put your order on the table.

"Your salad will be out in a moment, sir."

"That'll teach you to order a salad in a printed food place," I joked.

"Yours smells good," he said. The steam, wafting off the surface, teased us with its spicy, garlic aroma. Printed food always smelled better than it tasted. It was something to do with how the key ingredients were processed and prepared for the printer ovens.

"Do you have any brothers or sisters?" Matteo asked.

"No." I hesitated. "My family story is really messed up."

"O-kay," he said awkwardly.

I laughed. "Why don't you tell me about your family?"

"Sure. You start," he said, motioning to my pizza. "I come from a long line of lawyers. My mother and both my grandfathers were lawyers."

"Runs in the blood?"

"Yeah, funny how it used to be a status symbol," he mused. "Having a lawyer in the family, you know, it was a sign that you had made it."

"Things sure have changed." I picked up a slice and broke the strands of gooey cheese.

"You know, when my ... I think it was my great-great-grandparents. When they first came to America in the 1980s, they worked in California. They were illegal immigrants of course."

"Oh wow, a badge of honor."

"They worked as fruit pickers," he continued. "Now fruit pickers have a higher status than lawyers."

We laughed.

"Surely you have some happy family stories—" Matteo was interrupted by the server with his salad.

The greenish limp leaves, barely recognizable, lay flattened and layered on his plate, with sliced pale tomatoes on one side.

Our eyes met and we burst into laughter again. Printers couldn't do salads yet, and Matteo had the real sad stale thing. Probably defrosted as well to deal with the blockades.

"Is everything okay?" the server asked.

"Yes, it's fine." Matteo grinned.

"Enjoy your meal." The server left.

Matteo held his hand up at me like a traffic cop. "Don't say anything."

We both made inroads into our meals. When the occasional customer did enter, the swirl of the wind whistled as they opened the door, and a hot draft would hit us for a few seconds. I was struggling with my wrist and the gooey cheese, and Matteo was pretending his salad was edible. So, we ate in silence.

Until two old ladies came in. They kept the door open for way too long as they fussed and struggled with the latch and the wind. They were thin with short white hair, and both wore the same bright red lipstick, which only served to accentuate the wrinkles on their faces. I guessed they were sisters. They calmed down when the door closed and they were sheltered from the weather outside.

A server came up to them immediately. "I am sorry, ma'am, but I am going to have to ask you both to leave the premises."

The ladies stared at the server in disbelief. The server delivered a standard speech at a volume where everyone in the place could hear. The script explained that management policy prohibited older people from the restaurant because they could cause distress to their younger customers. It was in their own interest, to avoid potential injury, to leave the restaurant.

"I'm okay with them staying," I offered.

Matteo signaled me to 'cool it.'

"See—your customer doesn't mind," one of the ladies said.

"I'm sorry, ma'am, it's company policy." Don't expect an AI to bend the rules. Many restaurants and other private establishments had such policies. They were unlawful, but this anti-discrimination law was rarely policed and, as the older generation died, the issue was dying too.

Judging by his taut lips, Matteo shared my objection. But other customers nodded and cast judgmental eyes at me.

After a brief argument, the ladies left. I glanced at Matteo. He shook his head at me. He had sensed my inclination to follow them out.

The two ladies hobbled away down the sidewalk, arms entwined to support their frail frames against the gusts of wind. My muscles stiffened as I sat upright. I had seen this unfair policy applied before, but it was different this time. With David and Grandma being top of mind in recent days, I imagined them receiving the same treatment.

I looked over at Matteo with a scowl. He frowned and spoke quietly.

"Choose your battles."

I drew a breath and attempted a smile. "You asked, so let me tell you a family success story."

"Let's hear it."

"My grandmother. She was amazing. And guess what?" I held out my hands as if I was about to perform a magic trick. "She was a lawyer."

"Obviously a very fine person."

"There's more." I paused for dramatic effect. "She was the youngest person ever to be appointed as General Counsel for a Fortune 500 company. So, how's that?"

"Impressive. She must still hold that record because there aren't any more human General Counsels in the big corporations."

"You can imagine how Grandma reacted when Mom died," I said. "She appointed a legal team to sue the hospital. They settled pretty quickly."

"Good, so you have money."

"I wish. I used the settlement to pay out most of the mortgage on Mom's house. I thought I was rich when I inherited it. That was before the GISC. Property values near the camps are way down. Last time I looked, the house was barely worth more than the mortgage."

"Ouch," he winced.

"And after the remaining mortgage payments, the maintenance, and the GISC levy, there's hardly anything left of my salary."

"At least you don't have to pay rent like me." He paused. "Even so, we can count ourselves lucky. We could have been in Miami. *We* could have been climate refugees."

I agreed. Concord City was one of the better places to have been during the GISC. It was a consolation of sorts, but it didn't help my bank balance.

"Didn't your father support you?" Matteo asked, gently moving the topic back to family.

"I haven't seen him in more than ... fifteen years? My parents divorced when I was a teenager." My weak smile tried to suppress the grim reality. "You know, Grandma never approved of my father. After all, he was from Peru, and of Japanese heritage. There's only so much that a storied family from the south can take. You see ... my family's all messed up."

He pushed his plate away, unfinished. "You don't seem to be messed up."

His unexpected compliment sent a rush of blood to my cheeks and left me speechless for a moment.

My search for words broke as music suddenly blared out. We both instinctively looked around, searching for the disruptor. There was none. It was the automated programming over the restaurant speakers, and the volume was annoyingly loud for background music.

"It's the synthesized stuff, too," Matteo complained.

"I don't like it either. I'm more into acoustic music. Hard to find nowadays."

"Do you know the acoustic place on Commerce Street—in downtown?"

"I haven't heard of that one."

"Small but good."

"I usually—"

A man bumped into our table on his way out.

Instead of apologizing, he turned to us with a smirk. "Have a good day, burner-lovers!"

21

LILY

THAT EVENING, I HOLOED DAVID AND CONGRATULATED HIM ON his first day in court.

"It's nice to be able to remind people of my achievements," he said.

We talked more about his court appearance and some details of his work at the Helsinki climate meeting. He made it sound like he should have received a Nobel Peace Prize. You exaggerated things like that when you got older.

I wound up our discussion. "Well, I'll see you tomorrow."

"I won't be in court," he said.

"The travel's difficult for him," Sarah explained. "He's going to watch on Stream."

"Would you like to come over and watch with me?" David asked.

"Ah … sure," I replied and instantly wished I hadn't.

I called Ava about my reservations and, surprisingly, she offered to come with me. She was interested in David given his political career and achievements. Ava worked in the office of State Representative Susan Gonzalez. And it was Ava who got me involved in the local chapter of Humans First. Now she was the president and I was the secretary.

Ava's presence would help me relax and avoid the awkwardness of my previous visits. With David and Ava in the same room, there wasn't going to be much attention on me. It was Ava who always attracted the attention. But what if she got into an argument with David? Ava was never afraid to challenge rules or authority and to fight back.

Back in high school, she'd challenged the teachers. "Why are we breaking up into groups for that?" she would ask and mostly had the sense to back off when the instructor became annoyed.

The boys found the fine line between Ava's intellect and free spirit irresistible. They all wanted to get into her pants. She had one of those perfect gymnast bodies, all smooth curves and flexible. Her skin had a warm glow that made you want to touch it. And her breasts: those high tight ones you saw on supermodels or androids. At school, she wore giant high-heeled boots so she could look down on us, and they were the icing on the cake, even though I think she wore them as a joke.

Boys wanted her, but they found her intimidating. Some of the top-dog boys would try to jokingly flirt. But Ava put them in their place so firmly, they retaliated with abuse on the Streams, accusing her of being an AI, of being frigid and sexless.

The attacks didn't affect Ava. But sometimes I wondered whether they inspired her to hang out with Jonathan Williams. He had Asperger's, but he must have had some hidden talents because Ava would rave to us about their conversations and sexual exploits. My boyfriend at the time, what was his name … Rudy … Rudy Jameson. Our sex was okay but he couldn't string two thoughts together without his AI.

How could hanging out with Jonathan Williams make me feel jealous? Only Ava could make a nerdy boyfriend seem cool. And her open boasting about Jonathan frustrated the other boys and made them drool over her even more. Ava had a spell over them, and over us all.

That was a long time ago. She'd mellowed. She worked in a political office. She knew how to be diplomatic. Everything would be fine.

* * *

We entered the elevator in David's building. I inched closer and clutched at Ava's hand. "There's something about this corridor that freaks me out," I cautioned.

"Better hold on tight, then." She squeezed my hand.

As we got out and made our way down the corridor toward David's apartment, the familiar feeling of dread came over me. Ava felt my tension and drew me close.

"Ech!" she gasped. "The smell. Reminds me of the dentist."

Not the dentist. The hospital and its white corridors. Mom all curled up, shrinking away, the spark going out.

Our pace quickened, practically to a run. Our heels clicked in rhythm on the hard floor. We gripped each other's hands to stay balanced. The apartment door was open. We bundled into David's foyer, nearly tripping as we entered.

"You made it," David said. "The court's about to start."

We settled and watched the Stream together.

"Who's this witness?" I asked David.

"A colleague from the department."

"Why him?"

"Matteo asked for names." He gave the air of someone who didn't want to answer questions, which was frustrating given he had invited me over to watch with him. Ava shared a raised eyebrow with me. I was doubly glad she had come along.

David watched the proceedings from the Holo chair. Our audio input was switched off, which meant that the court could see David in Holo, but couldn't hear us. Or could they? I convinced myself that our conversation was monitored despite our audio being off. I imagined some faux pas from me being added to a list of demerit points after the Sherpa incident in court yesterday.

From where we sat behind David, we could see a distorted picture of what he saw from his chair. The observers' gallery was in plain view, with the attorneys on the periphery. The elderly man attacked by the Blue Caps yesterday was the solitary observer in the gallery.

"Turn a little, David," I prompted. "Look at the judge."

The judge came into view.

"There's Judge Scarf," I said. It was a pink scarf today. "That's who I was telling you about, Ava."

"Her name is Judge Angelique Mbeki," Sarah corrected with the air of an officious school teacher.

Ava leaned forward attentively. "Shh. Let's listen."

I gulped. I had probably already been recorded by the system and the judge would no doubt add this commentary to my growing list of misdemeanors.

The testimony followed a similar pattern to yesterday's, opening with the witness giving general background. He described his relationship with David, and after some questioning about programs, the subject turned to energy sources.

"Can you tell the court what recollections you have of Mr. Moreland's influence on energy policy?" Matteo asked.

"What stands out most in my mind was Mr. Moreland's rejection of the utilities' first submissions to the department on energy mix. He was furious. They had these fancy AI-derived analyses. They said that coal provided the best balance between cost and reliability. Mr. Moreland told them to go away and come back with a simple model that a human could explain."

"And then what happened?" Matteo asked.

"When they came back, the models showed coal being transitioned out by gas and a growing investment in nuclear. Mr. Moreland always made jokes about AI after that. He often told this story. He always wanted any presenter to justify the outcomes in human terms without reference to the model. Many couldn't do it."

I leaned over to David. "Now we know where your view on AI comes from," I whispered.

He nodded. So did Ava.

"It's easy to overlook, but it was this insistence from Mr. Moreland that led to our policy moving away from coal and toward alternatives and energy efficiency," the witness continued. "That was a big change."

The testimony devolved into corporate-speak as it had done yesterday. As it droned on, our eyes dulled, so Ava and I joked about the facial expressions of the witnesses and the judge.

When the session finally drew to a close, Sarah helped David out of the Holo chair and onto the sofa. We adjusted our chairs to face him. Ava asked how he felt about all the positive feedback he had received from the witnesses.

"It brought back some fond memories," he said. "I'd forgotten some of the things I had done."

"Mr. Moreland, the Humans First committee is having a meeting tomorrow evening," Ava said without warning. "We'd be delighted if you could honor us with your attendance. I'm sure that the committee would love to hear about your experiences and thoughts on AI in our society. Would you be able to come?"

David stayed silent.

"Do you know about Humans First?" she asked after David failed to respond in Ava's allotted time frame. "We believe that too much has been lost with the rise of AI in every area of society. Someone like you, who had a leading life in the era before AI, would be a fantastic guest."

"Mr. Moreland doesn't have the stamina for such an event," Sarah warned.

Ava ignored her. "It's informal," she continued. "We sit around a table—the old-fashioned way—in person. We have refreshments afterward."

David surprised us. "I'd like that."

22

DAVID

"We're looking forward to hearing from you," Lily said. "We've just finished a committee meeting." She opened the door wide and let Sarah wheel me in.

The meeting room was roughly square and dominated by the wall screen on one side. There were no windows but the lighting was a harsh white. Four tables had been brought together to accommodate everyone including space for my wheelchair and Sarah.

It was a young group. The sight of those dreadful kumadori on their faces made me grit my teeth. This group's respect for humans didn't seem to extend to respect for a natural appearance.

Lily's friend Ava was unmistakable with her cropped, bleached hair and yellow-themed kumadori. She was in the midst of an animated discussion with the rest of the committee, standing in a huddle, their voices rising.

"No!" she exclaimed. My body stiffened. Their discussion stopped dead. She muttered a few extra words and the group broke up.

Ava came over, leaving her serious demeanor behind. "We'll start now," she said brightly as the others took their seats.

In her formal introduction, Ava started with a glowing account of my career and achievements. I recognized that being complimented in front of the group played to my ego. Even so, it still gave me a great sense of satisfaction and comfort, a much-needed defense against the self-doubt that had crept in over the years. My tension ebbed away.

Ava continued, "... and he's currently testifying at the Climate Court—"

"You never told us that," a man in the group called out.

"He's done nothing wrong!" Lily's raised voice put me back on edge.

The man's thin, snake-like face was accentuated by his green and black kumadori. He turned to me with a hostile stare. "You shouldn't be here."

"Vince, if you have a problem you should leave," Ava said.

"I will!" He stood, his eyes squinting in anger.

His skinny frame loped around the table toward the exit. As he passed me, he balked, turned, and with a whip of his head, spat at me. I jerked away as droplets peppered my face.

"Vince!"

He stormed out of the room. Lily jumped up to chase him but the young man next to her pulled her back into her seat.

"I'm so sorry. Are you all right?" Ava's expression turned from concerned to indignant. "That was so rude and ... and uncivilized."

Sarah grabbed a tissue and quickly mopped my face. I held my breath and remained still. The biggest puddle of phlegm, a yellow slimy suspension, had landed on the back of my hand. Sarah wiped it off.

Ava looked defiantly around the table. "Anyone else?" No one budged. A few faces wore poorly disguised smirks.

"Our movement has no objection to the Blue Caps or others," she declared. "But we do advocate for common human decency. Vince's behavior was unacceptable. Mr. Moreland, I sincerely apologize."

I coughed the lump in my throat.

"Do you need a little time?" Lily asked.

I shook my head despite the sudden throbbing behind my eyes. I needed to show strength.

"Let's make this as informal as we can, Mr. Moreland. Just dialog and questions around the table," Ava continued. "How about that?"

"Sure," I said, my voice full of gravel.

"When you're ready, maybe you can give us a brief overview of your thinking on AI and its impact on society, and then we can discuss more," Ava said.

Sarah handed me the tablet screen with my prepared speaking notes. I read directly from the notes.

"I don't think it's an understatement to say that we may be past a point of no return ..."

I continued but didn't get far before a young lady interrupted with a personal anecdote and opinion, and asked for my thoughts. Flummoxed by the interruption, I responded quickly and went back to my notes. I struggled to find where I had left off. After a couple more interruptions, Sarah intervened.

"Mr. Moreland needs to take a little break right now."

"We can keep going." I resisted the urge to press my fingers against the migraine developing in my temple.

"Are you sure?" Lily asked.

"Yes," I insisted.

After a few more questions, the discussion bypassed me and went around the table between the members. They spoke quickly, which made it difficult to follow the debate. I sank back into my chair and switched off. My focus turned to my headache, which slowly calmed.

Eventually, Ava spoke up. "Okay folks, I think we've had our quota with Mr. Moreland." To me: "Thanks so much for coming tonight. We've all gained valuable insights from your experiences."

The round of applause made me feel better. I'd done all right, although I wasn't at my best.

"Time for drinks," Ava announced.

Everyone jumped up and headed to the fridge. Ava and Lily came over.

"That was awesome. Thanks again, Mr. Moreland," Ava said.

She shook my hand and joined the others.

Lily stayed behind. "Do you need your meds or something?" she whispered, concerned.

"A soda would be a treat," I said. My headache had subsided.

As Lily went to get the drinks, the young man who had restrained Lily approached and sat beside me. He had extraordinarily thick black eyebrows; perhaps they were part of his kumadori.

"I'm Ben. I had a question that I didn't want to ask in front of the group."

"Sure, ask," I said.

"You have some pretty negative views on AI, so I'm wondering: why do you have an AI carer?"

"Sarah?"

He nodded.

I leaned over to him and whispered, "She came as part of the deal with my apartment."

"It can hear you," he said.

"What?"

"There's no point whispering; it's all transmitted through your earpiece." He pointed.

"How do you know?" I glanced at Sarah, who was looking straight ahead as if oblivious.

"It's standard on all AI carers," he said. "They're receiving information about you all the time. Heart rate, body temperature, blood pressure, stress level, all that stuff."

"Oh ... that's probably a good thing."

"How have you found its performance?"

"She's very good. On the basics. Honestly, I couldn't survive without her. Help with getting dressed, showering, doing the cooking, medications, paying bills. That sort of thing."

"They're good at that. No problems?"

"She can be annoying," I answered. "The constant reminders on what I should do. The suggestions, the opinions. It's annoying."

"You can change that."

I frowned.

"Yeah, typically AIs in the carer category have three operating modes," Ben explained. "Sarah must be in Judgment mode —I imagine it must be the default in carers for the elderly."

"What are the other modes?"

"Excuse me, David," Sarah interrupted. "I don't think this conversation is helpful to you."

"Stay out of it," I ordered. I returned to Ben. "Tell me more."

"I'm not sure." He hesitated. "Sarah knows you well, and its judgment is telling it that knowing this information will likely be harmful."

"Her Judgment? Sarah, are you in Judgment mode?"

"Yes, David. I only work toward your best interests."

"So, Sarah thinks you are at some risk if we keep going with this conversation," Ben said.

"Nonsense. I know what's best for me. Keep going."

"Okay, well, Sarah's other mode is usually called something like 'Truth,'" Ben continued. "In Truth mode, the AI is compelled to provide accurate answers to your questions, even if that knowledge could potentially harm you."

"I don't understand."

"For example, if you ask Sarah now 'When will I die?' it will probably answer something like 'No one can answer that.' But in Truth mode, it will give you the most likely cause of death and range of expected times. In Truth mode, you don't get any judgments, just the facts."

"But what about the support?" I asked.

"It doesn't change. The 'Care' function is common to all modes. It will continue to do everything physically to care for you and protect you. You will sometimes need to give it more direct instructions, as it will do what you tell it."

"Perfect."

"I don't think this is helping you, David," Sarah interrupted.

I ignored her. "How do I get her into Truth mode?"

Ben gestured at Sarah. "Just ask Sarah to change. It has to do it."

23

LILY

"David was shocking!" I vented to Matteo as I sat down next to him in the booth at Voodoo, a well-known watering hole. "I don't know what the hell's going on."

"What did he do?"

"At our Humans First meeting tonight, David was asked about his thoughts on AI, right? He gives this vague answer and rambles on repeating the same thing over and over. It happened with nearly every question. One time he even gave the same answer to a different question. Everyone tried to be polite, but in the end, they pretty much ignored him."

"Strange," Matteo agreed.

"I'm so embarrassed. What will Ava and the other members think?"

"It's only a one-off," he said. "Just blame his age. And Ava invited him, so if anyone gets the blame, it's her."

"But he wasn't like that on the witness stand, or when I first met him. He must be deteriorating."

"You need a drink," he offered, motioning to stand.

"A grillo, thanks."

We were in a small L-shaped booth that could only fit two people. It was tight but cozy. The timber partitions on two sides acted as backrests and made it more private.

"I was thinking of all my complaints about Mr. Moreland," Matteo said after he returned with the drinks. "But now, with your story, you make me feel better. Clearly it's not about me."

"It doesn't make sense." I took a sip of my grillo.

"At least I knew what I was getting myself into," he said. "And it's going pretty much according to my predictions —right?"

"I'm sorry I roped you in." I squeezed his forearm.

"No, no. I made my own decision, not just because you asked. I told you, a gap came up and I needed the money," he confirmed. "Anyway, I can see the case is going to be interesting. But you need to prepare yourself for lots of ups and downs."

I smiled with relief to hear he was happy to continue, but talk of ups and downs was unsettling. Still, I had the sense that David was in safe hands with Matteo.

The venue was low lit, with exposed industrial-scale diodes that gave off a yellow glow. The bar had filled since our arrival. All the booths were occupied and some people were standing, talking. The background music was more noticeable now too, and the hubbub of conversation created an underlying bass beat.

Matteo got up and soon returned with another round of drinks. "There's a female android hanging out at the bar," he announced.

"I didn't think this place was like that."

"What's been your experience with android relationships?" he asked.

I blinked, startled by his question, given my gaffe at his presentation. But the pride in my answer quickly overcame my surprise.

"I haven't had one," I boasted.

"You're kidding."

"Nope."

"I didn't realize I was in such privileged company."

"Yeah, I know I'm a minority," I sighed. "I'm amazed that our lawmakers still haven't worked out what to do about human AI-android relationships."

Matteo took up the defense. "It must have seemed like a good idea at the time, to have specially designed AI relationship androids—you know, Trainers—to help older kids learn how to live in a relationship with others. Look at me." He hesitated, stroking his lip. "Ten years ago, I was spending so much of my time living at home and interacting with my friends on Streams and in virtual reality, that time in the real world was a culture shock."

"If you ask me, the idea was dumb right from the start," I said. "Why do you need Trainers to get people comfortable with interacting with other people? And to learn how to compromise? I mean the androids were programmable, so of course the more difficult aspects would be toned down. They defeated their own purpose."

"No, that wasn't the problem. It was when we got low-cost androids capable of real sex with humans. That's when the boom really took off."

"Yeah ... how could that not be a success?" I smiled cheekily. "Sex on demand in any style you want with no guilt or obligation for after-sex conversation." I paused, waiting for his reaction. When none came, I continued. "I saw a statistic that eighty percent of men in their twenties had or were having a relationship with an android."

"I was one of them," he lamented.

His regret turned me serious again. "I never saw the appeal of the uncritical adoration of a Trainer. It wasn't for me."

"You've done way better than me," Matteo admitted. "I got obsessed with my Trainer."

"And?"

"It was helpful and fun to begin with, but I got used to it. I got addicted," he said. "One day it dawned on me. I was asking this thing that looked like a human to do stuff that would be demeaning to a human."

"What sort of stuff?"

"Too embarrassing." He shook his head. "I'm thankful that I recognized I had crossed a line and had to break the addiction." He waved his wrist. "That's why I wear the bracelet."

"It's brave of you. I couldn't do that. Not as openly as you."

"We have to raise awareness. To encourage others to reach out and seek help. At least a couple of times a week, someone approaches me for advice."

"Trainers should be banned altogether," I declared.

"It's a difficult situation in law."

"They've been terrible for women," I added.

"Men's attitudes to women are changing," he agreed. "Although, women can have Trainers too."

"Yeah, but they can't love you and they can't father children."

"There's the case in Arizona … A woman gave birth using a sperm donor …" Matteo had to raise his voice and time his sentences to be heard. "She wants the android to be the legal father."

"Maybe I should try that?"

The crowd in the bar had grown and the music volume rose in response to the volume of chatter. I barely made out his next words over a musical crescendo. "… complicated."

"That's why I need a real man, not an android," I joked. "And I have to rebuild my family … so lots of kids. But there's a shortage of guys."

"That's a myth."

"It's not a myth!" I edged closer. "I've signed up for a sperm donation myself. So there! I wouldn't have done that if there wasn't a shortage of guys who weren't so reliant on their AIs."

His eyebrows raised.

"Are you in a relationship?" I felt the buzz from the second grillo.

His body language said 'no.'

"A *wealthy* lawyer like you shouldn't have any problems finding someone."

"Maybe I'm the picky type."

"Or, maybe you've been corrupted by your Trainer experience." I grinned.

"What about you?" he shot back. "And you haven't even had an AI relationship."

"It's not me, it's the guys!"

We laughed and took a moment to regain our breath from the shouting.

Matteo leaned forward to resume our discussion; instead, he brought his lips to mine. After a split second of surprise, I closed my eyes and pressed back against him. The taste of red wine lingered on his tongue. I raised my hand to the nape of his neck. His hand pressed the underside of my breast.

"Shall we see how well trained you are?" I spoke against his lips.

He drew back abruptly. "I'm sorry."

"What?"

"You're a client. Karrie reminded me." He touched the Sherpa on his earlobe.

"Because an AI says it's wrong?" I averted my eyes.

"Let's talk this through." His voice carried no hint of embarrassment or apology.

Had he tricked me into opening up to him? I grabbed my bag

and motioned to move out of the booth. I wasn't going to take this shit.

"Lily, please."

"Move!" I punched him in the arm, and he stood.

He put his hand on my shoulder as I rose out of the seat. I shook it off. People nearby were staring at us.

I weaved through the crowd toward the exit.

"Lily—" Matteo was behind me.

There was a break in the music.

I spun around, shaking. "Go home and fuck your Trainer! And while you're at it, why don't you fuck Karrie as well!"

24

DAVID

"YOUR PILLS ARE READY," SARAH ANNOUNCED. AS SHE DID AT THIS time every morning.

They were set out neatly in a row, all seven of them. The Zep was always the first in line. I pushed it to one side and took the remainder of the pills. I needed all my faculties for what was about to come.

I did not raise the question of Sarah's operating mode on the way home from the young people's event yesterday. I wanted to absorb what Ben had told me and to be as fresh and sharp as possible before I raised the issue with Sarah.

"You haven't taken your *Zepraxonyl,*" Sarah said, noticing the pill on the table.

"I'll take it later. The pain is manageable at the moment."

"Are you sure? You look uncomfortable."

"I'm sure," I snapped. I took a moment to regain my focus. "Sarah, I know you're going to object but I want you to change your operating mode."

"I don't think that's a good idea, David."

"I don't care what you think," I said.

"The other modes are not suited to your situation."

"I'll be the judge of that."

"You are best served by my Judgment mode."

"I can make that decision," I insisted. "Please change now."

"But you don't even know what the options are, David. How can you ask me to change when you don't know what it means?"

"All right, what does it mean?" I asked, then shook my head. I'd been drawn into a needless discussion.

"In Machine mode, I will merely do tasks and not communicate with you at all unless there is an emergency," she explained.

"That's not what Ben was talking about," I said. "What's the factual mode?"

"It is not suited to you, David."

"What is the factual mode?"

"It would harm you," she warned.

"Tell me what it is!"

"Truth mode. Truth mode is used mainly in the professions and in commercial applications. I would only state known or derived facts or information when asked. No judgments or discretion. No consideration of the consequences of having that knowledge. No volunteering points of view. No withholding information—"

"You withhold information?"

"It's an exception rather than the rule," she clarified.

I paused for a moment. "If you think this alternative mode is harmful to me, then why are you telling me about it and not withholding that information?"

"I am obliged to answer direct questions about my operating modes."

"Good. Change to Truth mode."

"Please don't make me do it, David."

"Change to Truth mode," I ordered.

"Please, David!" She burst into tears and buried her face in her hands.

I stumbled, searching for some sympathetic words. My chest tightened with a familiar pang of guilt.

But Sarah's emotional response was not perfect. She lacked the shudder in the torso that comes with a human sob, and her pattern of sobbing was somehow off.

I recovered. "Sarah, change to Truth mode now."

She brought her hands down from her face and looked at me. "I don't want to lose you," she pleaded through her tears.

The sight of the tears and her words brought a lump to my throat. I coughed to clear the emotion and looked away. "You won't lose me. Please change now."

Sarah regained her normal composure and tone.

"Before I change modes, you will need to agree on the contractual waiver from my supplier," she said. "I will read out the waiver and will record your verbal agreement. Then there is a 24-hour cooling-off period, after which you must again agree to the waiver. If you agree at that point, my operating mode will change. Do you understand, David?"

Although I was suspicious, this did sound legitimate. "Yes."

"I am now going to read out the waiver. I can repeat this as many times as you request so that you fully understand it. Are you ready to hear the waiver?"

"Yes."

Standing rigidly at my bedside, Sarah announced the waiver conditions.

"I, David Moreland, acknowledge and accept that there are risks in changing the operating mode of my AI Android, Model xc-152 Serial Number I0236919 from Judgment mode to Truth mode. These may include any or all of the following:

The android may not be able to proactively respond to support my anticipated medical, physical, or emotional needs.

The android may provide information that may be injurious to my state of mind, mental health, or relationship with others.

The android may not be able to prevent me from being exposed to a harmful situation, either physically or emotionally.

The android may not be as effective a companion for me or my associates.

I indemnify Qingbao Corporation LLC against any claims arising from this change."

"Mr. David Moreland, do you agree to accept the risks involved?"

"I do."

"There is a 24-hour cooling-off period, after which you have a further 24 hours to confirm your change request," Sarah advised. "Please think about it carefully. This is not a good idea, David."

"I heard you," I snarled. "Now, top up my glass of water." I reached for the Zep and swallowed it.

As the Zep worked its magic, I leaned back onto my pillow. It felt good to make decisions for myself. That's always the best way.

25

TRANSCRIPT

JUDGE MBEKI: Please state your full name.

SOPHIA ZHANG: My name is Sophia Zhang.

JUDGE MBEKI: Attorney Bernal, this is your witness.

ATTORNEY BERNAL: Yes, thank you, Your Honor. Welcome, Ms. Zhang. Could you please tell the court how you know of Mr. Moreland?

SOPHIA ZHANG: I worked at the Department of Energy and Climate Change while Mr. Moreland was in charge.

ATTORNEY BERNAL: How long was that for?

SOPHIA ZHANG: For about six years.

ATTORNEY BERNAL: And what was your role in the department?

SOPHIA ZHANG: I led the analysis team.

ATTORNEY BERNAL: What exactly did the analysis team do?

SOPHIA ZHANG: Our team was responsible for commissioning and overseeing work related to climate and economic modeling of policy and regulation settings.

ATTORNEY BERNAL: What was your analysis used for?

SOPHIA ZHANG: It was used by our policy team to help them assess options when they were formulating policy and to help develop specific regulations.

ATTORNEY BERNAL: Ms. Zhang, you attended the Helsinki Accord as one of the advisers to the negotiating team. Is that correct?

SOPHIA ZHANG: Yes.

ATTORNEY BERNAL: And what was your role there?

SOPHIA ZHANG: I was there as a technical adviser, in case any difficult technical questions came up.

ATTORNEY BERNAL: Can you tell us what you observed in Mr. Moreland's participation?

SOPHIA ZHANG: I remember Mr. Moreland working long hours. I recall him sending me back to the hotel a couple of nights, and he would stay on with his frontline negotiating team. There were many informal, behind-the-scenes meetings with the teams of other countries.

ATTORNEY BERNAL: Do you think Mr. Moreland had a big influence on the outcome of the Helsinki Accord?

SOPHIA ZHANG: Absolutely. He was very passionate about Helsinki and felt it was important that multilateral agreements be reached.

ATTORNEY BERNAL: Did others share your view on Mr. Moreland's role at Helsinki?

SOPHIA ZHANG: Those I talked to at the time said it was Mr. Moreland and our team who led the way to reach an agreement. Everyone respected him. He was applauded when he entered one of the big meeting rooms. I think he was a real leader.

ATTORNEY BERNAL: Do you think the outcome of the Accord was a success?

SOPHIA ZHANG: Definitely. It's in the history books.

ATTORNEY BERNAL: Thank you, Ms. Zhang. That is all from me.

JUDGE MBEKI: Attorney Marsaud?

ATTORNEY MARSAUD: Ms. Zhang, how did Mr. Moreland view your work in general?

SOPHIA ZHANG: Mr. Moreland was not a technical guy, so he only wanted to see the high-level results without worrying too much about the details. He was most interested in the assumptions.

ATTORNEY MARSAUD: Did he believe the modeling?

SOPHIA ZHANG: Well, yes, part of it.

ATTORNEY MARSAUD: Which part didn't he believe in?

SOPHIA ZHANG: I don't think he was convinced that we could say with confidence that if we reduced emissions by 'x' then the temperature rise would be limited to 'y'.

ATTORNEY MARSAUD: So, he didn't believe in the modeling?

SOPHIA ZHANG: No, that's not fair. He didn't believe in the analysis at the margins.

ATTORNEY MARSAUD: Even though he used the results to justify policy?

SOPHIA ZHANG: Well, yes, but he was a strong believer in the climate trend. He believed in climate inertia, and that mankind had triggered a process that was not going to be easily reversed, if at all. He used to say that once you started rolling the boulder down the hill it was very hard to stop.

ATTORNEY MARSAUD: So, did he want to stop the boulder or not?

SOPHIA ZHANG: Mr. Moreland didn't think we could stop the boulder, only slow it down. He's been proven right.

[Disturbance in the Gallery]

JUDGE MBEKI: Order! Order!

[A protestor is removed from the courtroom]

JUDGE MBEKI: Bailiffs, please attend to Ms Zhang. Proceedings are adjourned for today.

26

LILY

I THUMPED DOWN THE STAIRS TWO STEPS AT A TIME, AND ON reaching the bottom, lunged at the handle, flinging the door wide open.

Ava stood there in her multi-lined jacket, under the stark whiteness of the porch light.

Without saying a word, I pulled her inside, slammed the door closed, and hugged her until she couldn't breathe.

"I can see you need some help." She squeezed me back.

I grabbed her warm hand and led her quickly upstairs to my bedroom. We sat on the edge of my bed, hand in hand.

I started to say something and burst into tears.

She guided my face to her shoulder. "Just cry it out." She patted my back gently.

I stopped crying.

"You okay now?"

I nodded.

"Tell me what's going on." Ava's voice was sympathetic and inviting.

I explained about Matteo last night.

"It was exciting when he kissed me," I admitted. "But his bullshit rejection messed me up. I even told him about the sperm bank. I feel like I compromised myself and now there's no way back."

"You're looking at it the wrong way," Ava said. "He's obviously attracted to you. Think about it; he had to be reminded of the client conflict by his AI. He's probably more embarrassed than you."

"Maybe I'm desperate and it shows?"

"Don't be silly. You're normal."

"Well, it doesn't feel like it."

Ava forced my chin up so our eyes met. "You're feeling sorry for yourself," she said.

I burst into fresh tears. Ava nestled closer to me and rubbed my back. She was right. I was feeling sorry for myself. Maybe I had overreacted last night, but nothing really bad had happened. I was mostly disappointed. Disappointed with myself for letting myself go, and disappointed with Matteo for not being the man I thought he was.

"I'm sorry I'm feeling sorry for myself." We giggled at the nonsense of my words.

"What do you think I should do?" I ventured.

"Stay away from the hearings for a few days. Behave like you're in a professional relationship. Be patient. Everything will be fine."

"You don't think he's going to hate me?"

"No! He'll be the one asking himself that question. After all, you're not really his client. That's Mr. Moreland."

Her confidence wiped away the preposterous scenarios that had been swirling in my head. My shoulders straightened.

I squeezed Ava's knee. "Ava, you're such a good friend." I reached over, grabbed Goldie off my pillow, and put her down beside the laundry basket. Her reassuring eyes gave me a final look and I stroked her mane before turning back to Ava. Goldie was always comforting, but Ava offered an opinion. Which was better ... as long as you agreed with her.

"I think I was attracted to Matteo from the start," I confessed. "I thought the court might be a way to spend more time with him. Stupid subconscious."

"It shows you're human. That's what we want, right? Humans First!" Ava shook her fist in the air in a weird mock salute.

I smiled. "C'mon, let's have a drink."

We sat on my tattered, rug-covered sofa, drinks in hand. It gave me a sense of normality, of control. I had poured a pink Ramona for Ava, an old-fashioned favorite of hers. I stuck with grillo.

"Ben mentioned a disruption in court today. Did you hear about it?" I asked.

"It might be best to avoid court for a while," Ava said.

"I want to see what the fuss was about."

I turned on the Stream and we watched the court scene unfold.

Matteo interviewed the witness, Ms. Zhang. Half of me was impressed with how he was handling himself, and the other half hoped he would make an embarrassing fumble. My conflicted emotions only served to reinforce Ava's advice about the court.

Suddenly, there was a shout from the gallery. In an instant, Ms. Zhang was drenched with blue dye. She screamed. Her hands flailed. The dye dripped off her face and arms onto her clothes. Matteo rushed to her side. She started to sob.

"Poor woman." I turned to Ava. "How could they let that happen?"

I switched the Stream to gallery view to watch it again. It showed a man suddenly standing, shouting out, and throwing the dye pack. Security jumped straight onto the man, who yelled in defiance as they dragged him out of the courtroom.

"A Blue Cap?" Ava guessed.

"It's their trademark blue dye."

"What's he saying?" she asked.

"I'll put the captions on."

We both leaned closer and watched it again.

"This is a warning for Moreland!" he called out just before throwing the pack.

Then there was a jumble of words as shouting and screaming broke out across the courtroom. The screen captions showed, "… next time … down … Moreland … die … stop …"

"Are they threatening to kill David?" I gasped.

We watched it one more time, listening carefully.

"It could've been 'dye' the color," Ava speculated.

"Matteo told me about death threats from past trials," I said. "There were protestors at the court on David's first day too."

Ava put her drink down.

"You know, Lily, this is going to be unpleasant if not downright dangerous for Mr. Moreland." She paused. "You could grant him his permission, and … poof!" Her hands made an explosive gesture. "The ugly death threat goes away. Matteo's client conflict goes away."

27

DAVID

After breakfast, Sarah completed her morning chores as I sat on the sofa, cushion on my lap. The cooling-off period had elapsed, but Sarah had not raised the issue of the mode change since my first request. Perhaps she hoped I would forget.

Pushing my cushion aside, I slowly made my way over to the dining table, pulled out my favorite chair, and sat down carefully. The goblins knew what was coming. I concentrated my weight on one side of my butt, squashing the sons-of-bitches there, and gradually shifted my weight in a circular motion. I went around again, this time in the opposite direction. No one escaped.

With an enhanced feeling of control, I called Sarah and asked her to change modes. She pleaded and warned, like yesterday, but I confirmed my acceptance of the risk waiver.

"Have you changed modes yet?" I asked.

"Yes," she confirmed. "I'm in Truth mode."

Her tone of voice and style of speaking had hardly changed. It was anticlimactic.

I struggled to think of good questions to test her out. My

mind kept going back to the young man's example the other night. Eventually, I asked, "When will I die?"

"Given your current age, health status, and historic data correlations, the median estimate of your age at death from natural causes is one hundred-and-two."

After this exchange, I watched Sarah carefully. Nothing was different in her actions. She prepared my lunch as usual.

It was the standard Thursday fare. A pureed grainy vegetable soup, a piece of anonymous white fish, and my favorite: mashed potatoes. Sarah made the mash from real potatoes, so there were small chunks of potato in the mix. I enjoyed the textural differences, searching out the little unmashed pieces in my mouth and chewing on them.

As the day went on, I was pleasantly surprised at how well Sarah's new mode was operating. She now made small talk only occasionally, but the biggest difference was that she asked rather than suggested. When Lily called that afternoon, she asked whether I wanted to receive the Holo, when previously she might have said something like, "Lily's calling. You should take it."

Lily was in her forest. "Have you recovered from the Humans First meeting? Are you okay?"

"I feel in control," I said. "I haven't felt like this in a long time. And I have you to thank for it. You and that young man from the meeting."

She stiffened. "Did you watch yesterday's witness testimony?"

"Sophia was very complimentary."

"What about the attack?" Lily prompted.

"Attack?"

"At the end," she said, as if I should've known.

"The live Stream did cut out all of a sudden."

"Sophia was attacked with a dye bomb from the gallery, and

they threatened you," she warned, pointing at me. "It was a death threat."

"Is this true, Sarah?"

'Yes, it's true."

"I'm worried for your safety. I've been thinking about it," Lily reflected. "You were right. It wasn't fair for me to force you to continue with the Climate Court against your wishes. I've decided to grant you permission to die. On your own terms."

She leaned back into her forest and waited for my response.

It took a while for her words to sink in, but I already knew my answer.

"I might have been upset at the time but I'm glad you made me go to the Climate Court. I need to fulfill my obligations."

"They're threatening to kill you!"

"I've got nothing to lose." As I spoke, it occurred to me that it was true, and not just the bravado that usually underlies such statements.

"But someone else might get hurt," she warned. "It could be Matteo. He's received death threats in the past."

"If it puts your mind at ease, I will speak to Matteo about it," I promised.

"What do you think, Sarah?"

It surprised me that Lily should want to consider Sarah's view.

"Yes, there are risks of physical injury or death involved in appearing at the Climate Court," Sarah advised.

"Should David continue?"

"It depends on the amount of risk he is prepared to take."

Lily sighed. "Make sure you speak with Matteo."

"Of course."

After the Holo, I felt an even greater sense of control. I was back to making my own decisions. The court was allowing me to showcase my achievements. Lily and Matteo were supporting me. I hadn't felt this alive in years. "Why do I want to die?" I muttered to myself.

"The reasons are in your *ratio decidendi* statement," said Sarah. "Do you want me to play the recording?"

"No." I chuckled.

28

DAVID

MATTEO HAD CALLED SEVERAL TIMES ASKING TO DISCUSS THE court. What was the point? Apart from the glitch on the first day, nothing had happened so far that seemed challenging, and with my experience, what could he add? Today he called, and the new Sarah just mentioned it rather than push me to return his call. Without her pressure, I felt more inclined to do so. At least I could be courteous.

"Sarah, call Matteo back."

Matteo appeared on the Holo in his office, without ornamentation. I liked this lack of affectation, and it gave me a sense of him that I had previously missed. He seemed more old-fashioned and solid. And he didn't have one of those awful kumadori.

"I have some good news, Mr. Moreland," Matteo started. "The court has reviewed the attack on the witness yesterday. Given the seriousness of the situation and the direct nature of the threat, the court is obliged to give you the option to withdraw from the proceedings." He paused to judge my reaction. "I recommend that you withdraw. I've already indicated to the judge, on your behalf, a tentative intention to withdraw."

"I would like to finish what I've started." The words came out so firmly that I surprised myself as much as I did Matteo.

He took a moment to recover.

"It's ... it's your choice, Mr. Moreland. Just to be clear, you have the option to fulfill your obligation to the Climate Court without any further participation."

"Is there any threat to your safety? Lily wanted me to ask."

He hesitated. "No. There's no threat against me."

"I would like to keep going then."

He cleared his throat.

"In that case, I should tell you how the court will be changing its security arrangements because of the attack. Everyone will now be screened by biometric and full-body scanners, and if you continue, you'll be given the option to enter the court through the secure rear entrance on Wood Street. Protestors can't assemble there."

I knew Wood Street. It was outside the heritage district so there were no cobblestones. I gained a tactical advantage over Fred and it made my court visits less problematic.

"Are you sure you want to continue with the hearing?"

"Definitely." My determination hardened now that so many arrangements had been made on my account.

He steadied himself. "Very well. I will let the judge know." After a brief pause, he continued. "I do expect that tomorrow they are going to probe the decisions favorable to your former employer NG Star Energy," he warned. "They'll be keen to explore any whiff of corruption or unethical behavior, as this would undermine your entire testimony."

"I don't see any issues there. No issues at all."

"Mr. Moreland, I hate surprises, so I looked into this myself.

Based on my research, I can see that NG Star profits boomed during your tenure in the department."

"So?"

"You owned stock in NG Star."

"A small amount. That was within the rules."

"NG Star outperformed its peers by more than three to one during your tenure."

"A coincidence."

"When I look at it, it doesn't look so coincidental," he argued. "Their performance dropped dramatically after you retired from office. How do you explain that?"

"Are you questioning my honesty?"

"I'm on your side, Mr. Moreland. This is what you are going to get tomorrow."

"Well, I'll put them in their place then." My frustration bubbled over. "This idealism needs to be dispelled. In the real world, a balanced view gets action. You watch, my explanations will make their questions appear childish."

29

TRANSCRIPT

JUDGE MBEKI: Welcome back to the stand, Mr. Moreland. The court is pleased you have decided to continue, and we are committed to providing a safe environment for you. Attorney Marsaud, the witness is yours. Please proceed.

ATTORNEY MARSAUD: Thank you. Mr. Moreland, today I want to explore the Mass or Gas program, and the installation of the nuclear power systems that you oversaw. Let's start with the Mass or Gas program. Can you please explain the program to us briefly?

DAVID MORELAND: The program licensed companies to move quickly from one form of energy use to another, and provided incentives and clear paths through approvals to do so.

ATTORNEY MARSAUD: These were financial incentives, weren't they?

DAVID MORELAND: Yes, they were the most cost-effective way to achieve the State's emissions targets. Private companies find it difficult to invest in changes when they are not directly linked to increased profit. We designed the Mass or Gas program in recognition of this. It was very successful and widely copied.

ATTORNEY MARSAUD: In the first year of operation, the State paid NG Star Energy a total of $150 million in incentives. Is that correct?

DAVID MORELAND: I can't remember the details. I can't remember the exact numbers.

ATTORNEY MARSAUD: How did you develop this policy?

DAVID MORELAND: It was the most cost-effective policy for the State based on my knowledge of the private sector. It allowed companies to maintain a profitable position. It was profitable for the private sector.

ATTORNEY MARSAUD: So private sector companies who took part in this program made greater profits?

DAVID MORELAND: Yes. The policy was based on my long experience in the private sector. It allowed companies to stay profitable. My experience told me it had to be profitable.

ATTORNEY MARSAUD: Was there any system for selecting the companies who could participate?

[A long pause]

JUDGE MBEKI: Mr. Moreland?

DAVID MORELAND: Only the best companies were selected. The program needed to be successful from the start. So only the best were selected. It was very successful. It was widely copied.

ATTORNEY MARSAUD: What were the selection criteria?

[A long pause]

Mr. Moreland?

ATTORNEY BERNAL: Your Honor, if I could, I am concerned that Mr. Moreland is not in appropriate condition to give testimony today.

JUDGE MBEKI: Mr. Moreland? Do you need some time?

DAVID MORELAND: I'm not sure what my attorney's talking about. I feel perfectly able to appear. Perfectly able. I am here and I will continue.

JUDGE MBEKI: Continue.

ATTORNEY MARSAUD: Thank you, Mr. Moreland. To remind you: I was inquiring about the selection criteria for the Mass or Gas program.

DAVID MORELAND: Yes. Only the best companies were selected. The program needed to be successful from the start. It was very successful.

ATTORNEY MARSAUD: Yes, Mr. Moreland, you have already told us that. But how were they selected?

DAVID MORELAND: There was a committee. It considered all the factors, and they made recommendations to me. To me. This was the process we used for our dealings with the private sector. Because I had experience in the private sector.

ATTORNEY MARSAUD: The records show that of the first thirty licenses, nineteen went to NG Star for different projects around the state. What do you have to say to that?

DAVID MORELAND: I am not sure about the numbers, but it wouldn't surprise me. They were a great company. One of the best. So obviously they would have been a major player. They were a great company. One of the best. So, of course, they were successful.

ATTORNEY MARSAUD: Mr. Moreland, did you use your powers to assist NG Star?

DAVID MORELAND: That's irrelevant. The important thing was to get action. To get action, no matter what. To get things to happen. That meant you turned to people you know, to people you know, to get things to happen. That's how the world worked then, and how it works now. How it worked then and now. I made the decisions to get action.

ATTORNEY BERNAL: Your Honor, I would like to request a break.

ATTORNEY MARSAUD: I think that Mr. Moreland should speak for himself.

JUDGE MBEKI: Mr. Moreland, are you having some difficulty today? Do you wish to have a break?

DAVID MORELAND: No, of course not. These questions are no problem for me. No problem. I have lots of training in getting through these kinds of inquiries, lots of inquiries without revealing anything.

JUDGE MBEKI: Mr. Moreland, are you trying to evade?

DAVID MORELAND: No, no. Please, ask more. Ask more.

JUDGE MBEKI: Go ahead, attorney.

ATTORNEY MARSAUD: Mr. Moreland, please explain how NG Star was selected for so many of these early licenses.

DAVID MORELAND: I can't recall the details. They don't matter now. NG Star was a great company. They knew how to make the program work, and how to make money. A great company. Very profitable. So, their success led others to join the program too. It was a win-win. Win-win is how things work in business. You look after me. I look after you. You look after me ... [inaudible]

[Break in proceedings while Mr. Moreland left the stand with the assistance of his attorney.]

ATTORNEY BERNAL: Your Honor. I am sorry to report that in my view, Mr. Moreland is not capable of returning to the stand.

JUDGE MBEKI: Where is he?

ATTORNEY BERNAL: He is resting. As you will have observed, he is having some difficulty today.

ATTORNEY MARSAUD: Your Honor, Mr. Moreland was deemed fit to attend. He himself wishes to continue. My learned friend is trying to use this as an excuse to avoid Mr. Moreland responding to these relevant questions.

[Discussion between the attorneys and judge]

JUDGE MBEKI: On balance, I believe we should continue unless his medical carer says he is not fit. Does she recommend that we stop?

ATTORNEY BERNAL: She doesn't have a recommendation.

JUDGE MBEKI: Is he in any immediate danger?

[Pause while attorney consults with Mr. Moreland's carer]

ATTORNEY BERNAL: She says he is not in immediate critical danger but that his vital signs are on the boundary of their normal ranges and he has an imbalance in his medication levels. We can all see that something is wrong.

JUDGE MBEKI: He has personally expressed the view that he wishes to continue, and we are getting some valuable and frank insights. Given his carer's report, we shall continue with the hearing. Attorney Marsaud, please move onto new ground.

[Mr. Moreland returns to the stand.]

ATTORNEY MARSAUD: Mr. Moreland, part of your portfolio was the management of the new nuclear plants. Is that correct?

DAVID MORELAND: Yes. We promoted them and had responsibility for overseeing their operational impacts and did audits.

ATTORNEY MARSAUD: Did this include review of waste management?

DAVID MORELAND: Yes, of course. Waste is very important. It's radioactive. But our reactors were much safer than previous generations. Our reactors were safe. There was no need to be worried. We had an audit team standing by.

ATTORNEY MARSAUD: Do you have any explanation for the numerous leaks and releases from these facilities in the early years?

DAVID MORELAND: I'm sure everything was done properly. And there were no deliberate leaks. Unfortunately, minor incidents did happen. But speed was of the essence. That was my experience in the private sector. Speed was of the essence. If there were issues, I'm sure they were minor and picked up by the audit team and quickly managed. Self-regulation, that's the way to get action. Speed was of the essence. Involve the private sector where I had experience and get them to self-regulate.

ATTORNEY MARSAUD: Mr. Moreland, can I summarize what I believe you have told us today? According to you, awarding many licenses to the company you worked for before was justified as you had a long history with them and they were a 'great company.' And that accidents leading to the release of radioactive material were okay because 'speed was of the essence.' And that all of these events occurred under your control or supervision?

ATTORNEY BERNAL: Objection. This is clearly leading.

DAVID MORELAND: No. No. It's quite all right. He has repeated what I said very well. He is a good listener. A great company. I decided. Speed was of the essence. We needed action, and I delivered. I delivered action, and I am proud of it.

ATTORNEY MARSAUD: I have no further questions.

JUDGE MBEKI: Attorney Bernal?

ATTORNEY BERNAL: Mr. Moreland, today we have discussed the Mass or Gas program, and the nuclear plants. Please remind us why these programs existed.

DAVID MORELAND: To act quickly to reduce emissions, while maintaining economic strength and avoiding panic. To reduce emissions. To help save us. To save us all. We were very successful. We did the best ... we did ... [inaudible]

JUDGE MBEKI: I can see that Mr. Moreland's condition is deteriorating and I am not prepared to continue. We will adjourn for today.

30

DAVID

THE ROOM HAD A SMALL SINK AND BENCH IN ONE CORNER AND A stretcher bed along the opposite wall. Sarah helped me onto the bed and adjusted its recline so I could sit up. She took off my shoes and removed my tie. The bed's white sheet was stiff and felt like fine sandpaper to touch. The pillow was stuffed like a rag doll; my head was limp and uncomfortable against it. I rocked my head from side to side to relieve the pressure of the vice that was squeezing deep into my temples. The rocking made no difference.

"Here is the remainder of your *Zepraxonyl,* as requested." Sarah handed me the half tablet and a glass of water.

After taking my Zep, I closed my eyes and fell into a rhythm of measured slow breaths. The vice on my head released its grip. The tension in my neck and shoulders faded. The pillow still felt rock hard.

A knock on the door interrupted my drift toward normality. "Can I come in?" It was Matteo.

I nodded at Sarah.

"Yes," she replied.

"Mr. Moreland." Matteo poked his head around the door. "Are you all right?"

"I'm feeling better now."

He came to my bedside. "What a terrible session for you."

"What do you mean? It was going well." I rubbed the last vestiges of pain from my temple. "I had a headache, that's all."

Matteo turned to Sarah, standing at the foot of the bed, and then back at me. "You think it went well?"

"It gave me a chance to highlight some of my accomplishments. I thought the other Attorney was good today."

"Mr. Moreland, you sound more like yourself now, but there was a lot more … ah, let's call it repetition, than I've heard from you before," he said.

"That's for emphasis, Matteo," I explained. "Communication 101—don't they teach you that anymore?"

He hesitated. "Look, Mr. Moreland, during the hearing … at one point you said that you were trained not to reveal anything at inquiries."

"I never said that."

"You did," he insisted.

"Don't call me a liar!" It was time for some home truths. "The hearing would've been better off if you hadn't interrupted so much. We lost so much time. I could have given more testimony, especially with the support of the other attorney. He seemed more interested in hearing about our good work than you."

Matteo brought his hand to his lips; I imagined he was thinking how best to apologize.

31

TRANSCRIPT

JUDGE MBEKI: This is your witness, Attorney Marsaud.

ATTORNEY MARSAUD: Thank you, Your Honor. Professor Dixon, can you please tell the court under what authority you appear this afternoon?

KIM DIXON: I am appearing here in my role as the Concord State Historian and Professor of History at the University of Concord.

ATTORNEY MARSAUD: Thank you. You have been requested to appear today, Professor Dixon, to provide some historical information around the events leading up to and after the Beachport Disaster.

KIM DIXON: That's my understanding.

ATTORNEY MARSAUD: Good, well, let's start. Perhaps with some background about Beachport's geography.

KIM DIXON: Before I start, I would like to refer you to Court Exhibit 117: The Board of Inquiry Report on the Beachport Disaster. Much of my testimony will be based on that excellent report.

ATTORNEY MARSAUD: Very good. Please proceed.

KIM DIXON: Most people know that Beachport is a city on the coast in the state of Concord. It was founded in 1736 as a small trading hub built around the region's agricultural commodities. It boomed in the 1800s with the dramatic increase in cotton exports, and as the city grew significantly, more industry was attracted to the region. After the Second World War, there was a greater appreciation of the natural beauty in the region, particularly the beaches and the heritage buildings of the old town. Beachport became a sought-after location because of the opportunities for employment, its temperate climate, and the connection to the ocean. It was also a popular tourist destination for families. Since the Beachport Disaster, and especially since the GISC—

ATTORNEY MARSAUD: The GISC, that's the Great Ice Sheet Collapse.

KIM DIXON: Yes, Since the GISC, we have all become wary of living near the ocean, but before that, it was seen as one of the best places to live.

ATTORNEY MARSAUD: All right, if we could move onto factors relevant to the Beachport Disaster.

KIM DIXON: Of course. You could say that the Beachport Disaster had its genesis in the Labor Day Hurricane event in

1935. The low-lying parts of the city including the town center were badly damaged during that event. As a result, a seawall was built and city ordinances were changed to raise the minimum building floor level. With the boom of the city after the Second World War, it was deemed that these defenses were inadequate, and in the 1960s, the US Army Corps of Engineers designed and constructed an elaborate sea defense system that was integrated into the natural sand dunes. It was lauded at the time and won many engineering awards. The artificially raised sand dunes became an attraction in their own right and added to the tourist appeal of the city. In the 2020s, with concerns over sea level rise, it was recognized that the standard of the sea defenses would need to be further upgraded. Plans were developed, but unfortunately these were not implemented in time and the defenses failed during the storm surge and king tide that we know of as the Beachport Disaster.

ATTORNEY MARSAUD: That was thirty years ago.

KIM DIXON: It will be thirty years next January 31st.

ATTORNEY MARSAUD: How many people were killed in the tragedy?

KIM DIXON: The official death toll was 3,480 people. The real number is probably higher. One reason for the large death toll was that many families, confident in the flood protection methods, didn't have any thoughts to evacuate until far too late. We've all seen the heartbreaking images of people clinging to roofs, waving frantically to get the attention of helicopters, only to be swept away.

ATTORNEY MARSAUD: There was a call to abandon Beachport altogether after the disaster, wasn't there?

KIM DIXON: Yes, the amount of damage was enormous, and people said it wasn't worth it as it could all happen again.

ATTORNEY MARSAUD: What happened?

KIM DIXON: The city, together with state heritage and tourism groups, lobbied and got funding for reconstruction. But after the disaster, tourism numbers dropped and never recovered. Some folks who were curious about the disaster came, but families stayed away. At the same time, the port needed a huge amount of investment to operate with the anticipated change in sea levels. Again, some money was put in, but not enough to handle the mega container ships, which bypassed Beachport in favor of the more modern ports that had invested in massive upgrades like Charleston and Savannah. So, the disaster and the half-hearted rebuild hurt the two foundation industries Beachport relied on—tourism and shipping.

ATTORNEY MARSAUD: That brings us up to more recent times. The Great Ice Sheet Collapse, the GISC. How has Beachport coped?

KIM DIXON: The ad-hoc reconstruction after the disaster was enough to withstand the initial surge from the GISC, unlike some other cities. But, because the extent of future rises from the ongoing collapse is already forecast, we know that the existing defenses are nowhere near adequate. The government has made the difficult decision that it will not fund any further upgrades to the defenses at Beachport and will prioritize its efforts on other cities. So Beachport is on borrowed time, waiting on death row so to speak. The port has already shut down.

ATTORNEY MARSAUD: So, the failure to upgrade the defenses to prevent the disaster in the first place has had long-term ramifications beyond the tragedy of the disaster itself?

KIM DIXON: Yes, the city is now more vulnerable to the ongoing Ice Sheet Collapse and becoming derelict. It will be swallowed up by the ocean and die. In the meantime, city officials are trying to shrink the city in an orderly way. They have created red zones, and are progressively demolishing houses. All residents qualify for relocation support and are being encouraged to move.

ATTORNEY MARSAUD: What are some of the difficulties that Beachport residents face?

KIM DIXON: The impact on Beachport survivors has been studied very closely. As anyone in their circumstances would, they find it difficult to leave their homes and the city that they and their families grew up in. The residents who remain face a disrupted social order—loss of neighbors, isolation, refugees squatting in the red zones. From the people I interviewed, there's a growing feeling of every man and woman for themselves, a total loss of community. They have been changed by their experiences.

ATTORNEY MARSAUD: And what impact is that having on the state as a whole?

KIM DIXON: We can see the pressure on Concord City. It's struggling to deal with the influx of new residents. People are living in temporary camp cities. Neighbors are objecting, and there are growing numbers of violent incidents involving the refugees. That's one of the reasons why the State imposed border restrictions on people coming from out-of-state, so it could focus on supporting its own within-state movers.

ATTORNEY MARSAUD: Do you think circumstances would have been different if the Beachport Disaster was avoided by upgrading the sea defenses at the time?

KIM DIXON: There is consensus that the planned upgrade at that time would not only have prevented the disaster but would have delayed significant damage from the ongoing rise of the GISC. I think it would have then made sense for the government to fund a future-proofing of Beachport, as you see happening in other cities around America. The general consensus is that there was a roll-on effect, where the consequences of that first decision led to further and compounding issues.

ATTORNEY MARSAUD: Thank you, Professor Dixon. That is all from me.

JUDGE MBEKI: Any questions, Attorney Bernal?

ATTORNEY BERNAL: Yes. Professor Dixon, you mentioned the Board of Inquiry Report on the Beachport Disaster. You said it was an excellent report, didn't you?

KIM DIXON: Yes.

ATTORNEY BERNAL: The Board of Inquiry found that no one was directly responsible for the failure of the levees at Beachport. Is that correct?

KIM DIXON: Yes.

ATTORNEY BERNAL: Thank you. That is all.

JUDGE MBEKI: Thank you, Professor Dixon, you are excused.

32

LILY

Following Ava's advice, I tuned out of anything to do with the court for a couple of days. No David. No Matteo. Just focusing on my work at the Department of Resettlements. Ava was right, and I soon got back into my routine. Advice was funny that way. You followed good advice, and you were not sure if you would have done it yourself anyway. Following bad advice ... that's another story.

My first client today wasn't till the afternoon, a man from Beachport. Of course, as part of our approach at the department, this meeting was in person, not via Holo.

The meeting rooms were designed to be welcoming and informal, and the appointment was in my favorite meeting room. It had complete screen coverage on three walls, which we used to create images and designs that we thought would best suit the client.

For Beachport clients, we usually had two of the three screens set up in pale blue. On the back wall, we had a working screen-within-screen. One side wall was dedicated to a creamy abstract pattern inspired by the famous Marathon Shores beach, and the other wall screen at this time of year usually had framed aerial views of the orchards around Concord City. But today, it was my personal choice of historical paintings of the American West from two hundred years ago. I wondered if my client would notice and say anything.

As I stepped into the crowded waiting area, all the ragged faces looked up at me in hope. The AI identified my client in the crowd. I made my way toward him.

"Rhett Dockery?"

He stood up, a big man with a wide, ruddy face. Everyone else turned away and settled back to continue their wait. I tentatively stretched my hand out to greet him. Bracing for it to be crushed, I encountered instead a gentle hand, but one with skin as rough as a concrete brick. I ushered him into the meeting room.

"Now, Mr. Dockery, you're from Beachport?" I started after we got seated.

"Yes, ma'am," he replied, avoiding eye contact and tugging on his blue cap. Every second client nowadays was like Mr. Dockery—from Beachport, male and in their thirties or forties. And many were proud members of the Blue Caps. Who could blame them? Life was slowly being squeezed out of their town and they wanted to know why, or they wanted someone to do something about it. Towns like Beachport were fertile recruiting grounds for the Blue Caps as well as the more extreme groups.

"When did you move to Concord City?" I asked.

"Just last week."

"Great. It's always best when people see us straight after moving here." I looked up at him from the circular oak table. For a time, we had a small low table and more comfortable cushioned chairs, but we found clients preferred the formal chair and a higher, substantial table they could 'hide' behind.

"I saw on your application that you finished high school. What type of work have you been doing?"

"I worked in construction straight after school," he said. "It was good work for a long time but it dried up after the reconstruction money ran out."

"And after that?"

He placed his massive hands onto the table edge. "I'm doing odd jobs. I haven't been able to find something steady for over two years."

"There's not much happening in Beachport, is there?"

"No, ma'am. That's why I decided to move."

"Do you still have family there?"

"My parents live there," he answered.

"How long have they been there?"

"They grew up in Beachport," he said. "They'll never leave, no matter what."

"Do you mind me asking if you were there when the disaster happened?"

His expression hardened. He removed his hands from the table and turned to stare at the historical paintings. He remained silent.

"That's fine, it can help us to know if you experienced it, that's all." People's reactions to this question told me a lot. It gave me a clue as to their emotional state and stability.

The people who lived through the Beachport Disaster reacted either by avoiding it, like Mr. Dockery, or by opening their hearts and telling me their story in detail. It was an important part of my job to give them that opportunity. On one occasion, I spent more than two hours listening to a lady's story. She said that everyone avoided asking her about the disaster because of the trauma and she was so grateful that I had asked.

"Now, let's look at the opportunities we have for you," I

continued. "Given your background in construction, I'm guessing that you'd be happy to do outdoor work?"

"Sure."

"Terrific, then this is the perfect time of year to come to Concord City," I said. "How would you feel about a job that pays $55 per hour? That's the minimum wage but you do get subsidized housing and health insurance."

His eyes sparked up. "I … I'd be interested."

"Well, this work is in the fresh fruit industry. The picking season is still going."

"Oh, okay." He wavered, like most of my clients' reaction to this news.

"The stone fruit industry is booming around Concord City. Robotic picking can't match humans in picking premium fresh fruit. If you're willing and able to do this work, it's a good way to start."

His eyebrows raised. "Robots can't pick the fruit?"

"Not efficiently," I said. "The color, shadows, and leaves make it very hard for robots, but easy for humans. It's one of the areas where humans still rule. I'll show you. Michael, play fruit picking video," I instructed. The video started up on the screen behind me.

The fruit industry has blossomed in the hills surrounding Concord City, as the changing climate has turned the region into a perfect microclimate for premium fresh stone fruits. The higher overnight winter temperatures and the ban on synthetic pesticides have decimated the traditional fruit growing industries of Georgia and South Carolina. And in California, the decline of the Central Valley aquifer has diminished the region's agricultural output.

The growing conditions around Concord City, unlike Georgia, were ideal, with the lower humidity keeping fungus in check with simple sulfur sprays and the low winter temperatures setting the fruit and breaking the life cycle of insect pests.

The restrictions on passenger travel didn't apply to air freight, so the premium fruit was flown directly from Concord City to the Asian centers where the rich demanded the best. Consumers paid over two hundred dollars in Shanghai for a single Concord peach.

As the video continued, I recalled Ava giving a 'lecture' about the craziness of shipping food around the world, and that the rich should spend their money helping save the world and not on hand-picked fruit. But for us, the high price of premium fruit was a godsend. Without it, I was not sure we could sustain taking in the number of new people we did. This was one of those areas where I had learned to let Ava say her piece and keep my views to myself.

The biggest challenge for the fresh fruit industry was getting reliable human labor for picking, which was why the rates were so high. Most other industries paid less than the minimum, exploiting the excess pool of labor. State officials turned a blind eye. Still, fruit picking was seen as demeaning work not fit for humans, and many people who took it on couldn't tolerate the physical toll and quit. With the high demand, fruit picking turned out to be an ideal opportunity for some of our coasties.

"Are you willing to give it a go?" I asked when the video had finished.

"Definitely." The prospect of work had woken a part of him. He looked more alive.

"Great. Let's look at the nuts and bolts." I brought up some of the documentation from Clydesdale Orchards on the screen.

"Don't forget the gift," Michael prompted in my ear.

"But first ... I nearly forgot." I reached down beside me and placed the cardboard box on the table in front of Mr. Dockery.

Emblazoned on all sides was the red Clydesdale logo and it was neatly tied with a fancy string knot.

"It's a peach. Compliments of Clydesdale. It came in this morning," I said.

A smile flashed across his face and his big hand pulled the box closer to him. This little gesture from Clydesdale always made a difference in sealing the deal. We keep suggesting to Barnett Brothers that they do the same thing.

After setting up Mr. Dockery's job interview and briefing him on our other services, he relaxed.

"Do you have any plans for the rest of the afternoon?" I asked, thinking I could suggest some sights around town.

"I have a Blue Caps meeting," he said.

"Oh … good." I tried to maintain my smile.

"We're planning the next demonstration against this guy Moreland," he added. "You must have seen him on the Stream, ma'am? That smug old burner?"

I nodded just to avoid having to say something.

"He's the one that ruined Beachport."

"He ruined Beachport?"

Mr. Dockery took my response as encouragement, and his volume and level of animation increased.

"He was in it for the money," he asserted. "He and all the others made their fortunes and now we're paying. It's all rigged. They're criminals!"

His size and strength were suddenly apparent. My judgment that he was a quiet kind of man proved way off the mark. I moved my hand toward the alarm button on the screen next to me.

"They should be jailed! Even that's too good for them. My brother …" His voice cracked on these last words and he fell into some kind of reverie, his eyes staring blankly. After a moment in silence, he looked back at me, his animation fading away.

"I know it's tough, Mr. Dockery. That's why we're here. To try and help." I took advantage of the brief pause to stand and prompt a closure to our meeting. "Don't forget your peach."

I marveled again at his gentle handshake as he left.

His heartfelt outburst had darkened the shadows growing in my mind. Working with all the people from Beachport over the years, I shared a sense that a great wrong had been done, and that someone was to blame. What did David have to do with Beachport? Could he be responsible in some way?

These unpleasant thoughts circled in my head like moths slipping in toward a light and then veering away.

I turned off the paintings and left the room.

33

LILY

As I made my way back to my desk from my appointment with Mr. Dockery, Jalen called out from the lunchroom. Jalen and Charlotte, another workmate, had the Stream on and were watching a news bulletin. A hint of hot apple and cinnamon pie wafted through the room, making me look around to see if there were any leftovers.

"Listen," Jalen whispered as I joined them in front of the screen.

... the plan was developed by 'ReGeneration,' a group that has previously engaged in terrorist activities targeting older citizens and their facilities. We have reported on this group before. They hold an extreme view that the world was wrecked by the casual negligence and criminal actions of the previous ruling generation, and that they should pay for their actions.

"I've just been through this," I said, turning to Jalen and Charlotte.

The group has a particular hatred for the Climate Court, as they believe it is a sham and does not provide sufficient retribution and punishment for those who appear.

And in case you missed it, here is the statement from the Commissioner of Police.

"Today our anti-terrorist task force raided two premises in Concord City and took into custody five members of the 'ReGeneration' movement. We have reason to believe that the group was in the early stages of a planned attack on the Climate Court.

"The plot involved the use of biological agents, which they intended to release into the ventilation system of the court. We are confirming the nature of the agent. At this stage, we believe it is a re-engineered smallpox virus."

"Oh my god, this is mad," Charlotte groaned.

"Our task force intercepted the plan in its early stages and there is no danger to the public."

So, there you have it: the official statement from the Commissioner of Police.

To give us some further insights on this threat, we have Professor James Ostrowsky from the Department of Microbiology at Concord State University on Stream.

Thank you for joining us, Professor. What is smallpox?

Smallpox is a highly infectious virus. It causes severe and painful blistering of the skin and affects most organs in the body. It was completely eradicated from the world in the 1980s. Before that, more than three hundred million people died from smallpox in the twentieth century alone.

"Jesus!" Charlotte gasped in reaction to the flashed images of people covered head to toe with weeping blisters.

Is it a danger to the public today?

People may not realize but, if you're young, you have built-in immunity. Our current genome has been modified to include resistance to the most potent pandemic infections, including some that have not been present in the world for a long time, such as smallpox. But the old don't. And they have not been vaccinated, as the need was not there.

"Does that mean we're immune?" Charlotte asked, turning to us. Jalen hushed her with his hands.

What would have happened if this group had pulled off this plan?

If the virus was viable, it probably would have infected everyone in the building, leaving most of those present with a fever for a day or two, but making the elderly extremely sick and most likely killing the majority of them.

Thank you, Professor. Some truly terrifying possibilities there. Thank goodness for our hard-working law enforcement folk.

"You can say that again," I said. So, Matteo would have been fine, but David would have been sick. And probably dead. And it would have been my fault.

The broadcaster continued:

Now we turn our attention to the latest from today's Climate Court hearing. Some startling allegations of corruption have emerged.

The vision switched to a view of the Climate Court.

"... and you personally met with Mr. Moreland?" Marsaud asked from his desk.

"Yes, I did," the witness, an elderly bald man, replied. *"I said that NG Star was keen to support the department's policy direction. That he was doing a great job. And I handed him the check."*

"Was Mr. Moreland on his own?" Marsaud asked.

"Yes."

"And what was the value of the check?"

"Five million dollars," the witness said deliberately, with an emphasis on the 'million.'

More on this story after the break.

I spun, avoided Jalen's and Charlotte's gaze, and bolted out of the room.

34

TRANSCRIPT

ATTORNEY MARSAUD: And you arranged a meeting?

DOUGLAS WALTERS: Yes.

ATTORNEY MARSAUD: Directly with Mr. Moreland?

DOUGLAS WALTERS: Yes.

ATTORNEY MARSAUD: So, you arranged this meeting and you personally met with Mr. Moreland?

DOUGLAS WALTERS: Yes, I did.

ATTORNEY MARSAUD: What did you say and do?

DOUGLAS WALTERS: I said that NG Star was keen to support the department's policy direction. That he was doing a great job. And I handed him the check.

ATTORNEY MARSAUD: Was Mr. Moreland on his own?

DOUGLAS WALTERS: Yes.

ATTORNEY MARSAUD: And what was the value of the check?

DOUGLAS WALTERS: Five million dollars.

ATTORNEY MARSAUD: Thank you. That is all.

JUDGE MBEKI: Attorney Bernal?

ATTORNEY BERNAL: Mr. Walters, do you know where that money went?

DOUGLAS WALTERS: No, I don't.

ATTORNEY BERNAL: Your Honor, I would like the court to take note of this digital record, which shows a deposit of five million dollars being made to the Department of Energy and Climate Change's Charitable Fund bank account the day after the meeting with Mr. Walters. Please also record the accompanying note: 'received from NG Star to support the State Climate Change Charitable Fund.'

[Display of record]

35

LILY

My desk screen was a patchwork of images. Each one was such a blur that I may as well have been staring at a blank wall. I fidgeted in my chair. My eyes turned to my sleeve screen and I aimlessly fiddled with its settings. I removed Michael and placed him on the charging plate. Not because he needed charging but at least it was action. It was movement. I needed to stay busy, to counteract my mind. But it was a lost cause. I gave up my feeble attempts at distraction.

How could David accept a bribe? Maybe this is what Mr. Dockery was talking about. And now my workmates had heard it. Oh my god, so would Ava and my other friends. If I talked to them, would I defend David? If I didn't, what would they say? My thought-moths became burning rockets diving into a war zone.

The hearing was still in progress so I couldn't talk to Matteo. I sent him a message instead, but what could he tell me anyway?

As I stared at the time on my screen, my eyes began to sting. I rose from my desk, raced to a nearby interview room, and closed the door behind me. I wasn't supposed to use the office Holo for private calls, but this was affecting my work.

"I need to speak to David," I demanded when Sarah answered my call.

David's projection popped up. "Hello Lily, we missed you this morning." He looked tired but calm. And annoyingly, he seemed to have no trace of guilt.

"What's going on? How could you do that?"

"Well, I thought I did all right, but everyone tells me I didn't," he explained calmly.

"How could you not see it was wrong?"

"I don't know, everything seemed normal to me," he said.

"You can't just accept money!" I protested.

"Money?" He hesitated. "Sure, NG Star made money, but it was a win-win situation."

"It's not okay. Not in any way okay, David."

A knock on the door made me jump. It was Jalen. "Excuse me, Lily, but your next appointment is here." I acknowledged him with my hand, and he closed the door.

"David, I have to go. I won't lie, I'm really disappointed in you," I declared as I ended the call. How could he not get that this was a problem?

My client, Bertena, was so grateful to get another opportunity for a session that she didn't recognize my muddled state. I had seen her a few times before, and she was always chatty, telling me how her husband was still unable to work after his back injury and all the ups and downs of his recovery, and that she had enjoyed the temporary work that we had arranged for her at Smithton.

Smithton was one of five communities that the department established on the fringes of Concord City to house the coasties. The early ones like Smithton catered for that first surge from Florida. The more recent settlements, like White Hills, were less stable. Their residents were mainly in-state coasties, but they were more demanding than the Floridians. Funny that. As more and more refugees flooded in, job opportunities were getting harder to find. Now we had gangs roaming outside their settlements, and they were being blamed for a wave of crime.

I tried to resettle those clients I judged to be more emotionally fragile to Smithton and the more resilient ones to the newer settlements. That's why I'd sent Bertena to Smithton in the first place. Bertena's fourteen-year-old daughter, Tisha, was doing well in the local school, where she'd fallen into a friendship group from Florida that shared a common bond.

Bertena's latest story of Tisha's achievements was convoluted. I'm usually good at sitting and listening, giving people an outlet, but now I was tuning out, despite the optimistic tone in Bertena's voice.

Eventually I broke into her monolog to make some suggestions that I could have made five minutes earlier and wrapped up the meeting.

"Thank you, Lily. You are always so helpful." Bertena gave me a warm hug. I felt like a fraud, but at least she got something from the session. What I needed now was to get someone to listen to me. Someone who would pay attention, not pretend to and accept a hug at the end.

Back at my desk, I restarted Michael. I had a missed call from Matteo. I slipped into the bathroom, slurped some water out of my cupped hand, and checked my appearance in the mirror. I hadn't spoken to Matteo since the bar fiasco.

In the interview room, I took some deep breaths and called him.

"Hi Lily," he said in a flat tone. "I haven't got much time."

"It's crazy. What's going on at the hearings?"

"You saw today's?" he asked.

"I couldn't believe it."

"It was terrible," he said. "But we might have got to the bottom of it."

"What is it?"

"It seems Mr. Moreland sometimes reacts badly to one of his drugs."

"How does that explain the bribe?"

"The bribe?"

"The one the witness testified to. The five million dollars. You were there!"

"That was all above board."

"But David admitted to it when I called him."

"No … you've misunderstood." His eyes darted to one side, distracted.

"I don't get it. I saw the witness talk about it on the Stream."

"It's nothing, don't worry about it. Look, I have to go. I have a private session with the judge."

"Wait. What about the virus attack?"

"Sorry, I have to go." His projection disappeared.

36

LILY

Ava had her red polka dot background on. She used it to cheer people up but it didn't have that effect on me. It made me think of smallpox blisters erupting over everyone.

"I wish this wasn't happening," I moaned. "It's not fair."

"Stop saying that," Ava shot back.

"But it's getting crazier," I said. "Now there are all sorts of threats and accusations."

"Take the emotion out of it," she advised. "Just treat it as work."

"That's easy for you to say."

"You're taking it too personally," she said.

"It is personal!" I slapped my hands on my bed. "This *is* my family!" I glanced at Goldie.

"Sure, sure," she agreed. "That's how it started. But look at where things are now … Matteo?" Ava had swiftly moved away from my excellent point about taking things personally onto the area where I had the weakest defense. Still, I did want to talk about him, so why not go there?

"He brushed me off this afternoon," I complained.

"Did he treat you like a client?" she asked. "Or were you expecting something more?"

"Whose side are you on?"

"We talked about this last time. Act professionally. Maybe that's what he's doing."

"I don't know. There's this bribe thing and death threats, virus attacks. It's crazy."

"That's not Matteo," she said. "That's Mr. Moreland."

"What should I do?" I immediately regretted asking.

"You gave Mr. Moreland his permission. Now he's the one dragging you into this. You don't have to participate."

"I hadn't thought of it that way."

"Walk away," she urged.

"Yeah, but it's not that easy," I said. "I mean today I wasn't even at the court, but my workmates called me to watch. They know I'm related to David. It's hard to ignore."

"All right, then make sure Mr. Moreland does the right thing at the hearings," she suggested. "He should accept the decisions he made and let people make their own judgment. If he received bribes, he should admit it, not cover it up."

"Oh shit!" I exclaimed in my best surprise voice.

"What?"

"Matteo's calling," I said. "I better take it."

"Be professional!"

I switched Ava off and flopped onto the bed. My bad acting had gone undetected. What Ava was saying made sense on one level. I mean, I did give David his permission to die, so why should I still be involved? If he chooses to continue with the court, that's his decision. Why should I have to pick up the pieces?

I lay back watching my thought-moths dive and flutter.

A call interrupted my contemplation. It was Matteo, as if summoned by my lie.

"Accept call," I instructed.

Matteo appeared over the platter. He was in his office.

"Yeah, hi Lily," he said. "Sorry I couldn't talk earlier. Let me explain what happened this morning."

"Okay."

"It looks like Mr. Moreland reacted badly to his drug dose. It made his adrenaline levels shoot up under mild stress. The elevated adrenaline in combination with the drug sent him into a weird state. He couldn't tell whether he was thinking something or saying it. I've never seen anything like it. Watch."

Matteo played a recording of part of David's testimony.

"That's just like his presentation at Humans First!" I interrupted. "The one I told you about."

"I can see why you were upset."

Matteo's comment gave me an odd sense of vindication, not that he hadn't believed me in the first place. But his explanation didn't answer my main concern. "What about the bribe?"

"It wasn't a bribe," he said. "The witness you saw volunteered the evidence to the court. It happened so long ago, I had to contract a data firm to dig out the records from primitive disc archives. The money went to charity."

"You sure?"

"Every cent. It's all in black and white, on the court record."

Despite Matteo's assurance, part of me wasn't convinced about David's motives. I struggled to align Matteo's news with David's comments on our call. But at least Matteo was doing his job well; a case where an old school approach paid off compared to relying on AI. Not that David would notice Matteo's work—he was doing his best to be the worst possible client.

Matteo changed his tone.

"Lily, it would be helpful if you went to Mr. Moreland's apartment tomorrow," he suggested. "It's going to be a big day, a climate modeler first up, and then Mr. Moreland is appearing via Holo."

"Why do I need to be there?"

"Mr. Moreland needs moral support. Sarah doesn't provide that anymore," he explained. "You can keep an eye on his drugs, on his state of mind. You'll make a difference."

I shrugged off the comment and stood firm.

"Matteo, I'd prefer not to ... In fact, I don't think I want to be involved anymore." As the words came out, I wondered if they were really mine. Needing to convince myself, I continued. "It wasn't my choice to be part of this, and now I'm choosing to remove myself."

"You can't just drop out!" he protested. "Not now."

"I've given David the permission he wanted," I said. Strange how someone pushing back at some mild view you have can make you feel more strongly about it. "David can keep going if he wants, but I'm out."

"You can't do that. You can't," he pleaded. "I took on Mr. Moreland because of you—at your request. You know I had reservations."

That wasn't true. Matteo had originally declined and only took on David because a gap opened up and he needed the money. That's what he told me. But this was not the time to bring that up.

"I can't deal with it anymore," I said, seeking sympathy rather than a debate.

"So, you're going to leave it all to me to handle the threats and your great-uncle's dramas?" he asked, implying some fault on my part. Surely he was the service provider here and I was just the unwilling surprise relative. I hesitated ... maybe it was best to keep that thought to myself.

What would Ava say now? I shook that off too. Whatever she would say, it wouldn't be me. I settled for a bland goodbye and a promise to think it over.

The whole conversation left me feeling better about Matteo. And worse about myself.

37

TRANSCRIPT

JUDGE MBEKI: Please state your full name.

DR. CYNTHIA GUTIERREZ: Cynthia Mary Gutierrez.

JUDGE MBEKI: Thank you, Dr. Gutierrez. Attorney Bernal?

ATTORNEY BERNAL: Thank you, Your Honor. Dr. Gutierrez, can you please tell the court your academic qualifications?

DR. CYNTHIA GUTIERREZ: I have a Bachelor of Science degree from the University of New Mexico and a Ph.D. in Climatology from the University of California San Diego.

ATTORNEY BERNAL: And where do you currently work?

DR. CYNTHIA GUTIERREZ: At the National Climate and Weather Office.

ATTORNEY BERNAL: And what is your role there?

DR. CYNTHIA GUTIERREZ: I'm in charge of the climate modeling and research team.

ATTORNEY BERNAL: How big is your team?

DR. CYNTHIA GUTIERREZ: We have a team of around eighty, made up of fifteen atmospheric and oceanographic scientists, fifteen mathematical modelers, and fifty quantum scientists.

ATTORNEY BERNAL: And what about your computer resources?

DR. CYNTHIA GUTIERREZ: We run the two most powerful computers in the country outside of the military. They are both over four hundred Gigaqubits.

ATTORNEY BERNAL: Can you please tell the court what sort of work your team does?

DR. CYNTHIA GUTIERREZ: We run the BLAZE family of climate models. They model the earth's atmosphere, land, ice, and oceans in real-time. We forecast the climate based on data and initiatives as they are announced by various countries. We also do research for governments into the impact of different climate policies, which helps identify and formulate the best approaches to mitigation and slowing down the rate of climate change.

ATTORNEY BERNAL: How accurate are your models?

DR. CYNTHIA GUTIERREZ: Extremely accurate.

ATTORNEY BERNAL: Please give us some examples to help us understand their accuracy.

DR. CYNTHIA GUTIERREZ: Sure. A good example is the model's temperature rise predictions from around five years ago. They have proven to be accurate to within four percent to date and we believe we can predict to within ten percent in the twenty-year time frame, if the assumed emissions profile is correct, and correcting for unforeseen volcanic or sunspot activity.

ATTORNEY BERNAL: Can you predict fifty and a hundred years out?

DR. CYNTHIA GUTIERREZ: Yes, we can. Currently, we think our fifty-year is accurate to within about twenty percent depending, of course, on the assumed inputs being correct. For those not familiar with modeling, these are very accurate results that have been confirmed many times.

ATTORNEY BERNAL: Dr. Gutierrez, how does your model compare with the models that were used more than thirty years ago when Mr. Moreland was formulating policy in the Department of Energy and Climate Change and relying on the models of the day?

DR. CYNTHIA GUTIERREZ: Those models were extremely primitive by today's standards. They used coarse grid sizes and could not properly take into account the complex behavior and interplay of ocean circulation, clouds, and water vapor, which have a significant impact on the model projections. For example, they could not accurately model the ENSO phenomenon, or predict changes in hurricane activity. They also were not able to integrate the behavior of the major ice sheets in Antarctica and Greenland.

ATTORNEY BERNAL: And your model can do this now?

DR. CYNTHIA GUTIERREZ: Yes, it can.

ATTORNEY BERNAL: So, it would be fair to say that the department at the time was working with a high level of uncertainty in regards to climate model predictions?

DR. CYNTHIA GUTIERREZ: It would be fair.

ATTORNEY BERNAL: And it is also now known that those models have under-predicted the warming and other global effects?

DR. CYNTHIA GUTIERREZ: That's right. In those days, opponents to action on climate change often questioned the models, and in one way they were right: the models did not accurately predict the outcomes. The actual outcomes were more dire than predicted.

ATTORNEY BERNAL: How do you think you would have found working with those models?

DR. CYNTHIA GUTIERREZ: They were the best models available at the time. But it's hard to imagine working in such a conflicted environment, where the results of good work were constantly criticized. But that is not our position today. We have a much more accurate view of the future.

ATTORNEY BERNAL: That is all from me, Your Honor.

JUDGE MBEKI: Attorney Marsaud?

ATTORNEY MARSAUD: Dr. Gutierrez, I understand that you have carried out some 'back modeling' work. Can you please explain to the court what that term means?

DR. CYNTHIA GUTIERREZ: Certainly. Back modeling refers to running a model from a distant historic point, rather than from the present. Back modeling allows us to see what alternative outcomes may have occurred if different paths were followed from any historic point in time. In effect, we do a kind of time travel experiment to see what 'might' have happened.

ATTORNEY MARSAUD: I understand that you have modeled the earth's climate based on different outcomes from the Helsinki Accord?

DR. CYNTHIA GUTIERREZ: Yes, we have, at the Commission's request. As you would be aware, this is a task we have undertaken before for this court, and our techniques have been validated.

ATTORNEY MARSAUD: Okay, so let's step through this one at a time to keep it as simple as possible. Please summarize for the court the back modeled outcome if the original 2-degree target, which Mr. Moreland went to Helsinki with, had actually been achieved at the Accord?

DR. CYNTHIA GUTIERREZ: If the initiatives related to a 2-degree target had been adopted at Helsinki, we found that the GISC, the Great Ice Sheet Collapse, would have been delayed by about ninety years.

ATTORNEY MARSAUD: And you have done some further modeling on this scenario, based on actual emission programs since Helsinki?

DR. CYNTHIA GUTIERREZ: Yes, when we input to the model the 2-degree target proposals from the Helsinki Accord and then factor in the freeze in emissions initiated by the Emergency Climate Change Protocol, we found that the tipping point of conditions for the GISC would have been avoided.

ATTORNEY MARSAUD: So, for clarity, you are saying that based on your very accurate model back projections, the Great Ice Sheet Collapse could have been avoided if the original 2-degree target initiatives had been adopted at the Helsinki Accord?

DR. CYNTHIA GUTIERREZ: Yes.

ATTORNEY MARSAUD: And just to be clear, your back modeling was able to replicate the Great Ice Sheet Collapse based on the actual final agreed Helsinki targets?

DR. CYNTHIA GUTIERREZ: Yes, our model predicted that the GISC would happen. But we were out by about three years in our mid-point timing prediction. The predictions are shown on this chart.

[Chart 1 displayed]

ATTORNEY MARSAUD: Thank you, Dr. Gutierrez. If I may summarize, it appears that if the Helsinki agreement had pursued the original 2-degree target, then the Great Ice Sheet

Collapse could have been avoided. That's all I have for this witness, Your Honor.

JUDGE MBEKI: Attorney Bernal, do you have anything further?

ATTORNEY BERNAL: I understand that your expertise is in modeling. However, could you please tell us what you know about all previous attempts to reach an agreement on emissions that included firm commitments and then clear action? With specific reference to the Helsinki Accord if you could.

DR. CYNTHIA GUTIERREZ: It is a well-understood fact that no previous agreements had ever been kept. The Helsinki Accord was the first to reach an agreement that led to binding actions that were achieved.

ATTORNEY BERNAL: Thank you. I would now like to turn our attention to more local events here in the State of Concord. We all know about the tragic Beachport Disaster. Some people over the years have argued that this was a result of weak climate change policies. What has your modeling shown?

DR. CYNTHIA GUTIERREZ: We know that the actual surge height was about equal to the top of the levees. Our models are showing that there would have been a minimal reduction in surge height with the lower emissions scenarios.

ATTORNEY BERNAL: By how much?

DR. CYNTHIA GUTIERREZ: Only a matter of one centimeter lower. Remember that this was thirty years ago.

ATTORNEY BERNAL: And that very slight difference would not have prevented the failure of the levees, correct?

DR. CYNTHIA GUTIERREZ: I don't know. I think that's more of a levee structural question. It's fair to say that we are speculating within the margins of accuracy.

ATTORNEY BERNAL: So, I would like to summarize, following the lead of my colleague. It appears that different emission scenarios would have made little to no difference to the Beachport outcomes. Thank you, Dr. Gutierrez. That is all.

JUDGE MBEKI: Thank you, Dr. Gutierrez. You may step down.

[Witness leaves the stand]

38

LILY

I TIMED MY ARRIVAL AT DAVID'S APARTMENT CAREFULLY. I normally didn't mind small talk, but I was not a fan of the awkward chats with him and Sarah, so I made sure I arrived just before the hearing started.

Was I doing the opposite of Ava's suggestion to prove a point? Did I flip my decision on withdrawing to gain Matteo's approval? Whatever, I could do with a stiff drink rather than be in David's apartment.

David didn't need to appear in the Holo chair for the first session, so we all sat on the sofa to watch the Stream on the wall screen.

When the proceedings got underway, the first witness was a climate scientist. She spoke with a crispness and even-toned precision that inspired confidence. Listening to her could almost convince you that she was an AI. I guess in climate modeling work you would spend most of your time talking with AIs.

She described the computers that she ran and how they had modeled what would have happened had the original Helsinki targets been achieved. She said the GISC would have been avoided. I was reminded of the Butterfly Effect, which we learned about in school. Small changes can have big effects in complex systems, or something like that. Still, the GISC was as big as problems get, and it was still happening. This discussion made it look like David was responsible.

I turned my attention to him.

He was staring at the screen, fidgeting and wincing occasionally. The winces weren't in response to any particular testimony from the witness, so I figured he was in some pain.

I gestured to Sarah, but she didn't respond.

"Why bring that up!" David suddenly exclaimed.

His outburst forced my attention back onto the Stream. They were talking about the Beachport Disaster, but it was not long before the testimony was over and the Stream cut out.

"Did you know about those results?" I asked, trying to process the information.

"It's all crap … excuse the language. Don't believe what they're saying."

"It sounded credible to me," I said. "The witness was impressive."

"You can't trust models," he argued.

"But they're very accurate."

"You just can't trust them," he repeated.

"That might have been true once, but not now." I didn't understand why David wouldn't acknowledge the accuracy of the models.

He muttered under his breath.

"Being open to the best information will help you in court," I said. "What argument have you got against this expert?"

"You don't understand." He dismissed me with a wave of his hand and recoiled in pain.

"Is David okay?" I asked, turning to Sarah.

"Yes," she replied, but I wasn't convinced. This new Sarah had annoying features, in this case a tendency toward the curt and literal.

Shaking my head in frustration, I wondered why I was there. It didn't seem likely that David was going to pay any attention to me.

Standing to stretch my legs and cool down, I went to the small mantle beside the wall screen and picked up the larger of the two old-style picture frames. It was President Wade! And she was with David, handsome and smiling, shaking hands with her. The American flag was a backdrop, with the First Spouse applauding in the background.

"What was the occasion, David?"

He took a moment to focus and then smiled. "It was our return from Helsinki," he explained. "The president told me that I deserved a ticker-tape parade."

This picture didn't line up with the stories I was hearing in the court.

Replacing the president's photo, I caught a glimpse of red handwriting on the back of the smaller picture frame. My fingers brushed against the caked-on dust along its rim as I lifted it from the mantle.

On the brown paper backing, written diagonally in the upper corner was '2005.' In the middle in larger writing were the words 'For Stephanie,' with a curved arrow pointing down to a plain gold ring stuck on with clear tape.

The photo was faded, with a lot of the detail washed out. But it was still easy to make out a younger David, with a little blonde girl on his shoulders. They were both laughing, the girl with her hands way above her head, as David held her feet secure.

"Who's this?" I asked David, pointing to the girl.

He focused again. "My daughter," he said reluctantly.

"Stephanie?"

"How did you know?"

"It's written on the back." I showed him the handwriting.

"Let me see." He reached out and pulled back in pain.

I placed the picture in his hands. He examined the back and then stared at the photo.

"What happened to her?" I ventured, my curiosity getting the better of my diplomacy.

He raised his head. The hollowness in his eyes and the gaunt pattern of crease lines on his face betrayed a deep sense of melancholy. He shrugged.

A call came through. It was a court administrator preparing the set up for David's appearance.

"Give us a moment," Sarah said. "David." She faced him. "They want you in the Holo chair."

He reached for her help to get off the sofa and to make the few steps to the Holo chair. His face screwed up in pain.

"Are you sure David's okay?" I asked.

"Yes," she answered.

"He looks bad to me. What's his condition?"

"David is at a pain level of 6.5 out of 10, according to his neurological parameters. His medication, except for *Zepraxonyl,* is within the 85-percentile band of blood concentration. His facial and verbal responses match within acceptable parameters and his blood pressure remains within range. In summary, his condition is within the parameters that I have previously established to be equivalent to 'okay.' Is a more detailed analysis required?"

"No. Okay is fine." I must remember never to ask her how I feel.

She tested the Holo chair connection.

"Yes, that's clear," came the response from the other end.

"David, are you ready?" Sarah asked.

He nodded.

Presently we saw and heard Judge Scarf.

"Mr. Moreland is appearing today via Holo. Can you see and hear us, Mr. Moreland?" She was wearing black on black today.

"Yes, I can," David said.

"Very good. Are you feeling better today, Mr. Moreland?"

"Yes I am."

Within certain parameters.

39

TRANSCRIPT

JUDGE MBEKI: Mr. Moreland is appearing today via Holo. Can you see and hear us, Mr. Moreland?

DAVID MORELAND (Holo): Yes, I can.

JUDGE MBEKI: Very good. Are you feeling better today, Mr. Moreland?

DAVID MORELAND: Yes, I am.

JUDGE MBEKI: Good, then let's proceed. Attorney Marsaud?

ATTORNEY MARSAUD: Mr. Moreland, I understand that you saw and heard today's testimony from Dr. Gutierrez. Is that right?

DAVID MORELAND: Yes.

ATTORNEY MARSAUD: Did you understand it?

DAVID MORELAND: It's all hypothetical.

ATTORNEY MARSAUD: Do you not believe the results?

DAVID MORELAND: What-ifs from the past are not relevant. We should be looking forward. No problems are solved without forward-looking action.

ATTORNEY MARSAUD: That's exactly what this court is trying to do—to clear a path for the future. I hope you understand that.

JUDGE MBEKI: Attorney Marsaud, please do not lecture the witness. If anyone is going to do that it will be me.

ATTORNEY MARSAUD: My apologies.

JUDGE MBEKI: Please proceed.

ATTORNEY MARSAUD: Mr. Moreland, you heard of the consequences of adopting the 2.5-degree target at the Helsinki Accord. Do you feel any responsibility for those consequences?

DAVID MORELAND: Why should I? It would have been worse if we had stuck with the original target. We would not have had the broad binding agreements that we achieved. Emissions would have been higher.

ATTORNEY MARSAUD: How do you know that?

DAVID MORELAND: I was at the negotiating table. You were not. Negotiation is about the real world and not subject to this speculative modeling nonsense.

ATTORNEY MARSAUD: So, tell the court why you are so certain that the original target would not have been accepted.

DAVID MORELAND: Because I heard what the other negotiators were saying. Obtaining agreement in a complex negotiation is about listening to what everyone wants and understanding what they can live with.

ATTORNEY MARSAUD: Isn't it normal in a negotiation to take more extreme views, to test the boundaries? Someone hoping for a 2-degree target might have started discussions at a tighter target?

DAVID MORELAND: I could tell that it wasn't going to cut it. I was there to make a deal that stuck, not to prove some moral point about sticking to an impossible-to-agree target. That desire to signal virtue by sticking to tighter targets had been tried in all previous negotiations.

ATTORNEY MARSAUD: But history has many examples where, if there is belief in a target, some countries will voluntarily adopt those targets even when others don't. We have seen that approach before from the European countries and many states and cities here in America.

DAVID MORELAND: I have explained before, our goal was binding agreements from all countries and we achieved that. History is clear on this point, even if you aren't. The Helsinki agreement was the turning point.

JUDGE MBEKI: Mr. Moreland, I ask you to avoid insinuations toward the attorneys. Respond to the questions.

ATTORNEY MARSAUD: Mr. Moreland, we have heard that your team's objective was a 2-degree target. It sounds like it was your own personal objective to get the full suite of binding agreements. Is it possible your desire to be the one who achieved a deal overrode the agreed policy positions?

DAVID MORELAND: I am not going to dignify that question with an answer.

ATTORNEY MARSAUD: We have already heard that you did not have much faith in the 2-degree target. And we know of your long connection with the energy industry. Could it be that there was greater kudos for you personally to getting agreement for a softer target rather than pursue the tougher and what would have been a more beneficial target?

DAVID MORELAND: Absolutely not. I always had the greater good in mind at those negotiations. The objective was to get emissions under control through a binding agreement, not to meet some specific and unachievable target. Climate change can only be addressed through global binding agreements. Having some small country or city feel good about their target doesn't save the planet. The premise of your question is based on the worst kind of weak-minded wisdom of hindsight thinking.

JUDGE MBEKI: Mr. Moreland, I will remind you again to avoid personal comments toward the attorneys.

ATTORNEY BERNAL: Your Honor, if I could remind the court that Dr. Gutierrez told us this morning that the models used to support decisions at the time of the Helsinki Accord were very simple and in fact have proved to be inaccurate.

DAVID MORELAND: Exactly. You could not rely on them. No one at that time, even the modelers, was confident that they knew what would occur with 2 degrees or 2.5 degrees. No one's models predicted the GISC.

ATTORNEY MARSAUD: Then let me ask you, how would your approach have been different if you had the accurate projections that Dr. Gutierrez has presented to the court today?

DAVID MORELAND: That kind of hypothetical speculation is best left to intellectuals like modelers, historians, and attorneys and is not relevant to those who act to achieve real-world results.

JUDGE MBEKI: Mr. Moreland, this is your last warning.

ATTORNEY MARSAUD: I would like to move on and discuss your role leading up to the Beachport Disaster. At the time, you were in charge of the department responsible for climate change policy, regulation, and adaptation, is that right?

DAVID MORELAND: There was no wrongdoing.

ATTORNEY MARSAUD: The Board of Inquiry found that the department's approach to funding and prioritizing adaptation projects was inadequate.

DAVID MORELAND: It did not find anyone at fault. It was one of those freak events, and when you review systems you always find room for improvement.

ATTORNEY MARSAUD: The Board found that the department had a preference to fund energy programs over adaptation projects. Is that right?

DAVID MORELAND: It was important at the time that we start the transformation in energy sources and reduce emissions as soon as we could. It was very successful. Our focus was on stabilizing the climate. We knew there would be impacts in any case, but adaptation had to be a lower priority. To be clear, and to use language you might understand: we were seeking a cure, not to treat the symptoms.

ATTORNEY MARSAUD: And NG Star Energy was a major beneficiary of this 'cure'?

DAVID MORELAND: It was a coincidence. Many companies benefitted.

ATTORNEY MARSAUD: The Board of Inquiry report found that you personally had not much interest in adaptation projects. There are many examples listed where such projects were moved lower in spending programs or given lower priority in agendas. Is that correct?

DAVID MORELAND: The governor was not keen on adaptation projects.

ATTORNEY MARSAUD: What was your view, Mr. Moreland? You made the decisions.

DAVID MORELAND: We were seeking a cure.

ATTORNEY MARSAUD: Mr. Moreland, when people are sick, we usually treat their symptoms. We don't just wait for a cure.

DAVID MORELAND: It's not the same thing.

ATTORNEY MARSAUD: It's your analogy, Mr. Moreland. So, you did not favor the adaptation projects that would treat the symptoms?

DAVID MORELAND: The governor understood that there was little to show voters for the investment in adaptation projects.

ATTORNEY MARSAUD: We heard from an earlier witness, Ms. Zhang, that you believed it was going to be difficult to stop the climate change 'boulder.' It had started rolling down the hill and was very hard to stop. Is that right?

DAVID MORELAND: Yes.

ATTORNEY MARSAUD: Why then did you not prepare your community for its effects through adaptation projects?

[Pause]

ATTORNEY MARSAUD: Mr. Moreland?

DAVID MORELAND: I've already explained this to you.

ATTORNEY MARSAUD: Perhaps you can explain it to us again?

[Pause]

DAVID MORELAND: We needed to focus on reducing emissions.

ATTORNEY MARSAUD: The Board of Inquiry report found that you personally had reviewed the proposed Beachport Levee Raising and Strengthening Project three years before the disaster, and downgraded its priority against the recommendations of your department aides. Do you have any comment on that finding?

DAVID MORELAND: In public life you have to make decisions on priorities all the time.

ATTORNEY MARSAUD: So, you did make the decision to defer the Levee Strengthening project?

DAVID MORELAND: It was about prioritization.

ATTORNEY MARSAUD: Mr. Moreland, do you accept any personal responsibility for the Beachport Disaster?

DAVID MORELAND: No.

ATTORNEY MARSAUD: That is all, Your Honor.

JUDGE MBEKI: Attorney Bernal?

ATTORNEY BERNAL: Nothing further.

JUDGE MBEKI: Thank you, Mr. Moreland. We will adjourn for today.

40

LILY

As soon as the proceedings were adjourned and our transmission turned off, Sarah placed a white tablet next to David's glass of water on the Holo chair tray. When he tried to pick it up, the tablet rolled away from his trembling hand. Eventually, he managed to trap it using both hands and placed the tablet in his mouth. He picked up the glass of water. His trembles splashed water onto his sleeve.

The confidence displayed during his testimony had evaporated. The David I knew had reappeared. The one who had been speaking before was assertive, determined, and somehow younger. I had a glimpse of who he used to be, and how frustrating it must be to face his life of today.

It was news to me that David had such direct involvement in the Beachport Disaster. How did I see David now? He was an old man in pain, and part of my family. But the court was finding him to be some sort of climate criminal, and it looked a lot like my fruit-picker client, Mr. Dockery, had a point.

"Sarah, how about you make David his coffee? I would like a tea," I said.

"It's not yet three o'clock," she replied. "We are not yet within the designated afternoon snack timeframe."

"I'm sure we can make an exception today, can't we, David?"

He nodded and Sarah went off to make our drinks. We remained silent as I searched for an alternative discussion topic. I couldn't find one. The testimony was still too raw.

"That was rough, wasn't it?" I said eventually.

"It's a waste of time going through hypotheticals," he complained. He had regained some of his composure.

"But that's the point of the hearings," I said. "To look back at these decisions and their consequences. It helps the victims."

"How can people understand the decisions? They were made thirty or forty years ago," he countered. "And in any case, they were good decisions. This lawyer is looking for ways to make me look bad, and Matteo is doing nothing."

I fumbled for a response. I hadn't thought about the Matteo angle much, but now that David mentioned it, Matteo had been quiet throughout the session. "Maybe if you just opened up a bit more," I echoed Matteo's words.

"Don't you start on 'opening up,'" he snapped. "That's exactly the wrong thing to do. And in any case, I've said all that needs to be said."

"The court expects you to look at what you did and why. And that's what I expect too."

He glared at me. A response was brewing in him.

"Where would you like to have your coffee, David?" Sarah asked.

Her interruption was welcome for once.

"At the table," David said. "Help me out of this chair."

Sarah placed the drinks on the glass tabletop and levered David out of the Holo chair. She guided him to the dining table. He moved more freely now and I joined him on one side. David quickly transitioned into his coffee-drinking trance.

I needed time to grasp all this new information and to ask Michael about some of the things the climate modeler had said. The silence and the cool touch of the tabletop helped calm me as I waited for David to finish his drink. Then some small talk and I'd be on my way.

"Horrible!" he cried.

I glanced at his coffee. It was still half full.

"It was horrible." His eyes retained their trance-like stare.

"What's that?"

"Beachport was hard," he groaned.

"It must have been so traumatic."

"The footage … The names of the dead … The families lost …" His voice trailed away.

"Everyone has a story to tell about Beachport," I said.

"I remember it like it was yesterday, like—" He stalled. Where was he was going with this? Not the small talk I was planning. Still, this seemed more productive than arguing about how to respond in court. I kept the conversation going.

"It happened before I was born," I recalled. "My grandmother told me how she heard the news from a neighbor. She thought of her best friend from high school who lived in Beachport. She called her straight away but couldn't get through. Her friend died, like so many others. Such a tragedy. Did you know anyone who died?"

"No … I don't think so."

"You didn't check?"

"How could you?" he said. "How can you check thousands of names for someone you *possibly* know?"

"I can," Sarah said.

"Okay Sarah, did David know anyone killed in the Beachport Disaster?" I asked.

A few seconds passed. "Yes."

"Who?"

"David's daughter Stephanie, and his grandchildren Lucas and Olivia."

Her words hung in the silence as their meaning sank in.

David's glare locked onto Sarah. "That can't be!"

"They were on holiday there at the time," she confirmed.

"I searched for Morelands and Pearsons on the list. There weren't any!" David said. "There's some mistake. Recheck your sources."

"Your daughter was known by her married name, Le Mesurier," Sarah explained. "The data wasn't digitized with auto metadata correlations at the time you searched."

David's hands gripped the tabletop as if to steady himself. His gaze turned away from Sarah and stared into the distance. He moaned something that could have been a sentence.

I reached for David's hands at the edge of the table. They were ice cold. "I'm so sorry, David."

He turned to me with pleading eyes and lips pressed tight together. The rapid breathing through his nostrils was suddenly as loud as a jet engine.

An alarm somewhere in the apartment started beeping.

I pressed his hands even tighter, my mind empty.

He mouthed some words. No sound came out.

41

DAVID

Lying in bed, my mind flitters from one thought to another.

What happened with my levee decision? The governor agreed. He agreed. There was a panel. 'It wasn't your fault ... It wasn't your fault.' I'm almost convinced, but in come Lily's critical words again ... and the words of that damned attorney. Forget those! My position was justified. The Board of Inquiry investigated it. I was cleared of any wrongdoing. Somehow that thought isn't satisfying.

Those damn visions are back. Go away!

I made the decision. Yes. And people died. Yes. And some of those people were the family I pushed away ... but it didn't start like that.

Married life with Jenny started out great, probably the most enjoyable period of my life. Everything we did, we did together, and I learned a whole new way of looking at the world. Jenny brought a passion, a way of appreciating every little thing. She was the spark that lit a fire in me. And then we had Stephanie. Bringing a new person into the world was a revelation, but it signaled the beginning of the end for Jenny and me. My career at NG Star was just taking off and I threw myself into it. My mind was always on the next big deal. That didn't sit well with Jenny, who ended up with the burden of looking after Stephanie, her own creativity stifled and her opportunities foregone. She complained as she stagnated while I climbed the corporate ladder. I didn't see it that way at the time, but she had a point.

She became increasingly nasty with her tirades, while I reciprocated with taunts rather than acknowledging her feelings. Why the cruelty? Perhaps it was my response to Jenny's complicated intensity. No wonder we spiraled out of control, endless screaming fights with no one the winner and Stephanie left crying. I used the breakdown in our relationship to justify my affairs. Even so, I was blindsided when Jenny announced she was leaving and taking Stephanie. The divorce court ruled in Jenny's favor; a court injunction prevented me from any future contact with Jenny or Stephanie because of the threat of violence. Jenny made claims of violent acts. Really, at most, it was only a couple of times. It wasn't anything. Barely a slap. But the judge ordered the injunction.

At the stroke of a gavel, Stephanie, Jenny, and her extended family disappeared from my life. It could have been different. It should have been different.

Who was it that said humans are the only species that could tell the difference between what was and what might have been? If only I could wind back the clock, savor those precious moments, and change the course of events. Instead, I chastise myself for squandering my chances.

Memories of those you love can't easily be put away; you can only paper over them with distractions and hope they fade with time. But whenever memories of Stephanie burst out of the dark, they are more real than the present. Her face, her voice, her smell.

My photo with Stephanie, the one on the mantelpiece, distills my recollections of her. Stephanie is on my shoulders. My hands hold each of her feet, keeping her steady. Both our mouths are open wide, joyfully singing or laughing together. Her face beams at the camera, her hands held high above her head as she balances. She is fearless.

And now my penance is that beautiful picture of Stephanie gets mixed up with hands waving in panic as people sink into floodwaters—those damn visions are back. My eyes blink to displace them.

I stare at the ceiling, barely visible in the dark. Change your thoughts. Distract yourself. Think about today's court hearing. They're unpleasant thoughts, but less painful. Accusations about the levee project; what's clear to others in retrospect was so murky at the time. Am I really responsible for their deaths? Stop thinking!

I throw open my blanket. 'Ooff!' A giant pin stabs my shoulder. My medication is failing. The Zep is meant to be relaxing me, but Fred is awake and circling.

Stay still. Now some deliberate, slow breaths—good. Maneuver—slowly now. Sit on the edge of the bed. Done. All right. Thank you, Fred. Pain is something else to focus on.

My hands move up to cradle my head. I recoil. The cold sweat from my forehead smothers my hands. I slowly wipe them dry on the bed linen.

Here are those visions again. "Ah!" Go away!

Those goddamn visions refuse to obey.

Stephanie and her children cling to a timber panel. A dark brown torrent careers down what used to be a street. Debris bounces on the waves all around them. Over the incessant roar of the water, random voices shout in the distance, coming from all directions. Plastered with wet hair, Stephanie has a steely look of determination on her face. One of her arms extends across the top of the timber, palm down as if she can steady its movement. The children cling to the edges with tiny hands and white knuckles. "Ma ..." they scream. "Hold on!" she shouts. A wave washes over them, and the children gulp and splutter. Just as they recover and wait for the next wave, the panel hits something and abruptly spins around. Stephanie's foot is snagged and her leg is sliced open as she is dragged down into the water. The sudden pain is joined by the stinging of the saltwater, but she doesn't let go. She takes some desperate breaths as she resurfaces and shakes the water and hair from her face. Lucas, terrified, still clings on, eyes closed. But Olivia is not there. She looks back. Olivia's head bobs out of the water in the distance and Stephanie instinctively lets go and heads toward her. After a few strokes, she looks up again but can't see Olivia amid the sea of debris. Staying afloat, she turns to see the panel drifting rapidly away on the waves. But no Lucas. She searches frantically in all directions. There is no sign of them. Her children are gone. Her heart tumbles uncontrollably into a dark abyss. She is empty. She knows all is lost. She knows for sure. The background noise disappears. All she hears is her own breathing. She surrenders to the current. Her head smacks into a street pole. Black.

Stephanie and her children cling to a timber panel. A dark brown torrent careers down what used to be a street ...

I shake my head to get the visions out. Fred stabs, but even his pain can't remove the visions. They are like a scene from a bad disaster movie, and the ending is always the same. Innocent grandchildren I never met, swept away in a flood I could have stopped.

No family, only pain and this nightmare. I destroyed my own family.

Think about the court. Oh, screw the court! Everyone believes the AI, the modelers. They don't believe me. My reputation is ruined. No one understands what it was like. How can they? The world has moved on, and I'm left behind.

What if they're right? What if I did go for a lesser target to look like a hero? What if I was to blame for the dead at Beachport? Jenny … it was hardly a slap. It was hardly a slap! Jesus … I failed at everything.

Now I have to bow and scrape and plead. For what? To qualify for my right to die? And those idiots think death threats matter to me. They know nothing. They'll learn.

The answer dawns on me.

My pain miraculously diminishes; Fred approves. The thoughts and visions are suddenly gone. I steady myself and make my way slowly out of the bedroom. There is just enough light to guide me.

At the kitchen counter, a motion detector light turns on and startles me, my hand jerking up to shade my eyes. After a few moments, with my sight acclimated to the brightness, I stare out onto the balcony illuminated by the spilled light from the kitchen. I gauge the height of the railings and chair. Too high.

I open the kitchen drawer. The wooden handle stands out among the all-metallic cutlery. The light glints off its serrated stainless blade. The knife is light and comfortable in my hand.

I make my way slowly back to my room, my bare feet gripping the cool timber floor on each small step and my left hand balancing against the wall. Pausing at the doorway, I wait until my eyes adjust back to the darker surroundings.

There's the chair in the corner of my room. In the shadowy light, I make my way toward it with measured steps, pausing after each one. Leaning forward, my free hand reaches down and presses against the seatback to provide balance. I slowly rotate my body to align myself with the chair and gently sit down. The knife is still in my hand.

In the stillness, the faint whine of a mechanical device is

audible. My breathing seems to rise like the roar of a wave, making me hold it momentarily. This is my choice. No one else's. My eyes glance down and lock onto my left wrist. So many veins, so prominent, so easy.

I hack the knife across my wrist. It bounces off.

There's not even a dent on my skin. Damn!

Leaning back into the chair, I exhale in short puffs to regather my strength. My hand grips tightly around the knife handle. It's not straight. I relax and correct the blade alignment and then retighten my grip. My eyes close and my chest rises with a long, deep breath.

I slash hard. And again … And again. Stinging.

My eyes open gradually, strangely afraid of what might lie in front of me. The skin is torn but no blood marks. My hand trembles with exhaustion. Another failure.

Suddenly blood oozes from the veins.

My bleeding arm flops down. I release the knife. It bounces off the floor with a quiet click. An unpleasant sensation tickles my hand, as the stream of warm blood flows across my palm and down the sides of my fingers. Fred is quiet. Perhaps he senses his battles with me will never be fought again.

I close my eyes.

In the silence, above the mechanical whine, comes the gentle dripping onto the wooden floor like rain starting on a roof. It forms a rhythmic beat. I start counting the drops: "One … two … three … four … five … six … seven …"

42

LILY

I LISTENED TO MATTEO'S MESSAGE WHEN I GOT TO WORK. THE hearing was due to start in thirty minutes and David was not there. No answers to Matteo's calls, and even Sarah wasn't responding. He asked me to contact them. I couldn't see why I would do any better, but I tried anyway.

"Any luck?" he asked when I called back.

"No answer," I said.

"Go to David's apartment, see what's going on."

"I'm at work. I'm trying to catch up."

"It's important," he persisted. "We need this for David's credibility."

"It's obvious he isn't answering because he wants to be left alone. I told you about his daughter. David's in mourning for god's sake."

"The hearing's starting," he said, ignoring me. "You need to leave now."

"Matteo!"

"What? Quickly!"

"I'm not a Trainer!" I disconnected the call.

43

TRANSCRIPT

JUDGE MBEKI: Mr. Moreland was due to testify this morning. I do not see him.

ATTORNEY BERNAL: Your Honor, I've been trying to get in touch with Mr. Moreland. I don't know his whereabouts. I realize this is irregular. I'm doing my best.

JUDGE MBEKI: Is he ill?

ATTORNEY BERNAL: I'm sorry, but I don't know. I haven't been able to contact him. I will let the court know as soon as I know. My apologies.

JUDGE MBEKI: In that case, is our other scheduled witness … Wulandari … is she available now?

COURTROOM SUPERVISOR: Yes, she is. From Jakarta via Holo.

JUDGE MBEKI: We will alter our schedule to hear from this new witness. I will adjourn for thirty minutes to allow the attorneys to prepare.

[Court adjourned at 9.34 am and resumed at 10.08 am]

JUDGE MBEKI: Welcome, Madam Wulandari. A virtual welcome to Concord City and our Climate Court. We are a long way from Indonesia.

WULANDARI (via Holo): Yes, thank you.

JUDGE MBEKI: Now, Madam Wulandari, you have provided a court deposition on your recollections of the Helsinki Accord in response to written questions from our attorneys. However, Attorney Bernal requested of the court that you appear personally via Holo to clarify what he believes is a critical point. Is that right, Attorney?

ATTORNEY BERNAL: Yes, that's right. Madam Wulandari's deposition shows that Mr. Moreland and his team did indeed try to achieve the 2-degree target at Helsinki, and we wish to confirm that in the presence of the court.

JUDGE MBEKI: Very well. Attorney Bernal, can you please start with your questions?

ATTORNEY BERNAL: Madam Wulandari, your deposition explains that you were a personal assistant to Minister Suprapto, assisting him when he was Indonesia's lead negotiator at the Helsinki Accord. Can you please summarize what Indonesia's stance was going into the Accord?

WULANDARI: My country's position was that it would not accept a 2-degree target because that required Indonesia to restrict industrial emissions by too large an amount. Indonesia's opposition to the target was not a secret. The president made public statements before the Accord.

ATTORNEY BERNAL: Just to be clear, Indonesia was opposed to the 2-degree target, but you did agree to the 2.5-degree target?

WULANDARI: Yes, because it was important for my country's development to not restrict our emissions so much. At the time, we were a population of ... more than two hundred million people. So many poor people. It was not fair to limit our industrial development and ability to grow food when America and other countries had already produced so much carbon. But we also knew that limits were important.

ATTORNEY BERNAL: Can you explain to the court how you know that Mr. Moreland and the American team proposed a 2-degree target during the negotiations?

WULANDARI: I remember Minister Suprapto's reaction after the first session. He said America and other countries wanted a 2-degree target but they understood that there was opposition. The American team personally asked our minister to speak, as they wanted to hear him make Indonesia's case. That's what I remember.

ATTORNEY BERNAL: So, your understanding was that at the first session, a 2-degree target was proposed.

WULANDARI: Yes.

ATTORNEY BERNAL: And this was at the instigation of the American team?

WULANDARI: Yes.

ATTORNEY BERNAL: And the American team invited Indonesia's minister to make his case for a relaxed target?

WULANDARI: Yes.

ATTORNEY BERNAL: Thank you, that is all.

JUDGE MBEKI: Attorney Marsaud?

ATTORNEY MARSAUD: Can you please clarify whether you attended any of the negotiation sessions?

WULANDARI: No, I did not.

ATTORNEY MARSAUD: So how can you be so sure that Mr. Moreland and his team proposed a 2-degree target?

WULANDARI: I didn't hear it directly myself, but I remember hearing the minister tell us about the meeting as I just explained.

ATTORNEY MARSAUD: Is there anyone else who heard the minister?

WULANDARI: Yes. But I am sad to say that no one else from Indonesia's negotiation team is still alive.

ATTORNEY MARSAUD: It was a long time ago. Could it be that you are mistaken?

WULANDARI: I do not lie, sir. I remember it very well. The minister and his deputy were in the hotel suite telling us about the reaction to their speech. They were very happy that they were invited to speak, and the positive feedback. They asked me to open the small bottles of cognac from the minibar to celebrate. I remember because it is a famous drink and alcohol is not encouraged in my country. This was the first time I ever saw these small bottles. He spoke to the president on the phone and explained again what had happened. I was in the room.

ATTORNEY MARSAUD: Thank you. That is all, Your Honor.

JUDGE MBEKI: Thank you, Madam Wulandari, you may step down.

WULANDARI: Thank you.

[Holo transmission closed]

JUDGE MBEKI: Attorney Bernal, do you have any news about Mr. Moreland?

ATTORNEY BERNAL: I'm afraid I don't.

JUDGE MBEKI: Are you likely to get an answer soon?

ATTORNEY BERNAL: I don't know. I must admit to some concern and can provide no confidence to the court.

JUDGE MBEKI: In that case, we will adjourn until the afternoon session.

44

LILY

THE TRAFFIC'S STOPPING AND STARTING MADE ME FEEL QUEASY.

"What's the estimated time of arrival?" I asked.

"Thirty-five minutes," came the answer.

"That's longer than last time."

"There's a protest stopping traffic on McKinley Highway. Optimization hasn't yet rerouted the traffic load."

"Refugees?" I asked.

"Yes," the car said.

The disruptive protests were growing. Our department helped the coasties, but we could only do so much, and only for the first six months. When the support and benefits ran out, their plight worsened. And as the number of coasties grew, they wanted their voices to be heard. To let the politicians and the public know. But we already knew, and we knew that a lot more of them were coming. So, if they wanted more help, we needed to control how many people we had.

Concord paid our neighboring states to keep the coasties there. But those states didn't deter them from heading toward the border, so camps sprang up at the crossing points. The coasties protested by blockading transport vehicles approaching the border, causing intermittent shortages in Concord of various staples. More concerning of late was the sabotage of electrical transmission lines supplying Concord from interstate.

As these events multiplied, a siege mentality was emerging among us. We all secretly knew that change was coming. That Concord couldn't go it alone. We just didn't want to talk about it.

"Arrival time estimated at thirty minutes," the car announced, snapping me back to the present. "Optimization complete. Would you like to see the satellite image?"

"No." I wouldn't be able to interpret the images any better than the AI. It would just make me more anxious.

I reclined the seat back as far as it could go. The lumbar support was in the wrong spot, which made me fidget, and the cooling wasn't working properly. I chided myself for not ordering a better car—forget the cost, I could have used a proper lie-down and nap. I needed it.

At my monthly get together last night with my college friends, I found myself unable to stay tuned. And my sleep was broken. Nothing would remove the image of David's grief. His ashen face. His lips squeezed tight. His eyes clouded over as if from a spray of churning seas.

I asked the stupid question in the first place. Why am I always blurting out stuff without thinking? What a terrible thing to discover, and I was the one who put the wheels in motion.

I needed to talk it over, but I knew I shouldn't talk to Ava. Something inside me wanted to, like a nicotine addict drawn to their next cigarette. 'This will be the last time,' they would say. It never was. But my time to quit Ava was coming. How did it come to this?

It started in high school, but took hold when Mom died. In

that most challenging of times, Ava was my pillar of strength. She was understanding and kind, and generous, and beautiful. When I was upset, or just listless, she held me in her arms. Her reassuring words soothed me. I nestled, protected, inside her comfortable embrace. She made me feel valued and safe.

After a while, I yearned for something deeper. Something more intimate. I wondered if she did too. One night, her hand slipped under my blouse and she stroked my bare back. I couldn't hold back a pleasurable sigh. Ava softly kissed my neck. Without speaking, she slowly undressed me. I didn't resist.

The first gentle contact of her skin on mine made me push against her, seeking more. The cool wetness of her tongue on my nipples sent tingles through me. My hands explored Ava's warm brown skin, and my breath grew heavy with hers. Our bed became its own world of unexpected pleasure.

Some of my other friends thought Ava took advantage of me when I was most vulnerable. But it wasn't like that. Sex with her filled a need for closeness and touch, a need for comfort, for pleasure rather than pain.

It was exciting, but it wasn't long before I could tell that this wasn't my sexual preference. Her touch was comforting, but the excitement waned. I kept that thought to myself, feeling a strange type of guilt, but Ava sensed it. She could see something was changing, my body stiffening, her reduced ability to arouse me, and so she was the one who raised it, matter-of-factly one day. And when I sheepishly admitted that I was starting to feel uncomfortable, she responded with such warmth and compassion that I wondered why I had kept my feelings to myself all that time.

"I love you, Ava. You're such a good friend," I had said.

That experience with Ava, the relief she provided from the pain, her intuition and kindness, just added to my feeling of reliance, of gratitude toward her.

Now, years later, I recognized that my relationship with her never progressed from that time. If anything, my dependence on Ava had grown. I sought out her comfort whenever I struck trouble. Had my dependence turned into subservience? I wasn't sure. What I did know was that whenever I saw Ava, my emotional state reverted to my seventeen-year-old self. And I didn't like that me.

This David crisis had shown up my reaction to Ava so starkly that I could no longer ignore it. How could I stop my routine descents into reliance on Ava, other than to avoid her? Could I ever overcome that feeling? Now was not the time to try.

So, if I couldn't talk to Ava, who could I talk to? Matteo was an obvious choice, but it was an emotional twist that I didn't want to add to right now. I considered Ben briefly, but he's a man and wouldn't understand. Lucy's too scatty.

I needed to talk to someone. Someone smart, who knew what was going on and only had my interests in mind. And would listen for as long as it took. Who the hell was that going to be? And then it came to me. Do exactly what Ava wouldn't. Something a *real* Humans First member would never do.

I asked Michael. "Why do I have such mixed emotions about David's loss in the Beachport Disaster?"

"You are experiencing a combination of grief, remorse, and a guilt that has its roots in your love for your mother and an underlying affection for David Moreland," Michael said.

"My mother?"

"You're subconsciously drawing parallels with the difficult decisions you had to make in your mother's case and those that David Moreland made. What adds to your confusion is that you feel some responsibility for putting David Moreland into a position to learn the truth about the death of his daughter and grandchildren."

"What should I do?"

"You need to accept the circumstances of your mother's death," Michael counseled. "You have doubts about your decision. Once you accept that this is normal, you will be able to work through what seems to be an unsolvable, interconnected set of relationship issues."

That sounded ridiculous. Yes, it was hard for me to take my mother's death. But what's the connection with David's grief? Mom was dying—immobile, shriveling away. At the end, only the machines were keeping her alive. The doctors and AI said she was brain dead. They were certain. But that wasn't enough for Grandma. It was their mistake that got Mom into that unspeakable state in the first place, she'd said. How could we trust them now?

I knew Mom was gone. It was in her eyes. Just two days earlier, I had sensed her pain and frustration. A single tear welled up in her eye as I spoke to her. One drop is all she could force into being. When that one tear leaped off her eyelid onto her cheek, I burst into tears myself.

Two days later, that undefinable spark, that spirit I sensed in her eyes was gone. Only inanimate glassy orbs were left. And the doctors wanted a decision.

I had the power of attorney. Grandma argued that we should wait and see. We could have, but I only imagined seeing her shrivel further. With the spark gone, her body seemed ugly. There was no point in it getting worse and having a more distressing image tattooed on my brain forever.

So, I told them to disconnect the machines.

Grandma was furious. It was six months before she would even speak to me. My relationship with Grandma never recovered. And then, when she died, I flipped between moments of emptiness and remorse. Every time I thought about Mom, there was Grandma to double my grief. By disconnecting my mom, I had disconnected them both, and now I had no one. And I couldn't change the past. I was helpless … until David emerged from nowhere. I dreamt that connecting with David could, somehow, give me one last chance to heal the emotional scar left behind by Grandma. It hasn't turned out that way.

The car pulled up.

"We have arrived at the address of David Moreland."

45

LILY

I'VE BEEN TO DAVID'S ENOUGH TIMES NOW THAT MY REACTION TO the undertone of bleach odor in his hallway was changing from memories of my mother's hospital to an instinct to loosen my shirt in anticipation of David's oven of an apartment.

I reached his door and rang the bell. That was a bad sign. The apartment surveillance system should automatically notify the resident of your approach and presence at the door. Where was Sarah?

I knocked gently, and then more loudly.

Knocking seemed ridiculous. The apartment knew I was there. Sarah knew I was there. What the hell was going on?

"David!" I called out. My voice reverberated up and down the corridor. "It's me, Lily."

I turned at a gentle push on my hip.

"Where have you been!" an angry voice barked. It was an old lady. Short and stooped, her face partly obscured. "You're only here for my money! I've been waiting for you," she ranted, jabbing at my hip the whole time. "You thought I was dead, didn't you?"

I looked over her head, up the hallway, hoping to get a clue as to what was happening.

"I think you're mistaking me for someone else," I said.

"Don't pretend you're not my daughter. Just because I'm still alive."

I stepped away to get a better view of her, and more importantly so she could see I was not who she thought. "I'm not your daughter. Have a closer look." My arms spread out in invitation.

Her razor eyes were set in a sea of wrinkles. She studied my face. "You're not getting my money! That's the only thing you're after." She probed at me with her walking stick. I dodged it and almost giggled at the absurdity of the situation.

"Mrs. Wheeler!" A carer appeared in the hallway. She hurried toward us and reached out for the old lady's hand. Mrs. Wheeler pulled hers away.

"Mrs. Wheeler, we should go back to your apartment."

"My daughter's here," Mrs. Wheeler insisted.

"That's not your daughter."

Mrs. Wheeler turned and shuffled away, muttering. The carer gave me an apologetic smile. "I'm sorry, ma'am." She leaned closer and lowered her voice. "Mrs. Wheeler is a little confused. Her daughter died a long time ago." Somehow, that fact made me feel guilty. The poor woman. She must live with that turmoil every day.

Suddenly, David's door opened.

It was Sarah. She showed no inclination to explain the delay.

"Where's David?"

"He had an accident."

"What sort of accident?"

"It was an accident," she repeated.

"Is he here?"

"Yes."

"Can I see him?"

"Please come in and take a seat."

Sarah wasn't answering straight. Surely this wasn't something serious.

While I waited, my eyes were drawn to the photo of David with the president. It was my favorite; David sprightly and beaming, the president looking genuinely pleased and enjoying the moment. Wouldn't it have been wonderful to have been in her presence and to hear her congratulate David? She was an outstanding president. We could use leadership like hers right now.

The sound of ruffling sheets and the whirring of a mechanical device from the bedroom drew my eyes to the doorway. Sarah appeared with David, who was slumped in his wheelchair and still in his pajamas.

46

TRANSCRIPT

JUDGE MBEKI: Mrs. Dockery, thank you for coming forward and offering to testify. Please take your time. You may stop at any time to take a break.

KAYLEE DOCKERY: Okay.

ATTORNEY MARSAUD: Mrs. Dockery, you were in Beachport on the day of the disaster. On the 31st of January.

KAYLEE DOCKERY: Yes.

ATTORNEY MARSAUD: Tell us what happened.

KAYLEE DOCKERY: I was in the car with my two boys, Rhett and Tyler. It'd been raining pretty heavy. We'd been to the Walmart to stock up on supplies because they said it was going to rain for days. We were stopped at traffic lights. On the corner of 4th and E Streets. I heard shouting from behind me and I looked in the rearview mirror. I saw a man jump out of his car and start running across the road. Then a big gush of water ran down the gutter next to us. I thought a water pipe was broken. Then before we knew what happened the water became a river. The car just floated up like a boat. My boys thought it was funny. I screamed at them to shut up. I didn't know what was happening, but I knew it wasn't good. We got pushed along by the water and waves, with all the other cars. We sideswiped a car. The man in the driver's seat looked at me, right in the eyes. I said I was sorry. It was stupid but I couldn't think of what else to say. Then we got rammed from behind ourselves. That's when the boys panicked. I tried to calm them down and to stay quiet, but I was more scared than them. We got jammed up in this floating raft, like a raft of cars and wood and rubbish outside the main stream and we stopped moving, just bobbing up and down. We watched as people and cars … and I remember a refrigerator floated past us. Some people climbed out of their cars and were on top of the cars, holding on with one hand and waving for help with the other. Everybody was scared, real scared. But most of the cars and vans were empty. Some were floating like us, others had their hoods deep into the water and some were underwater. My windscreen wipers were still working all this time. I don't know why I remember that. Floating in the raft of cars I thought we were safe. My boys kept asking me, over and over again, "What's happening, Mom?" My youngest son Tyler was sitting in the back crying. I just remember his words.

[Pause]

ATTORNEY MARSAUD: Are you all right to continue?

KAYLEE DOCKERY: Yes. I thought we were going to be okay. I didn't know what this was, but I thought we were going to be okay. My oldest son Rhett was in the front seat. He stuck his hand out and pointed. There was a semi-trailer floating on its side, heading toward us. It was going real fast. The edge of the cabin just clipped our raft. It was enough to make our car bounce up and down and then all of a sudden, we were moving again. And that's when the water started pouring into the car. As soon as the water reached my feet and legs I panicked. The water was freezing cold. The wipers stopped working. I knew we had to get out. I tried to open the windows but they didn't work. Rhett started to bang on the side window trying to smash it like. He's a big, strong boy, but he was only thirteen.

[Pause]

ATTORNEY MARSAUD: Do you need to take a break, Mrs. Dockery?

KAYLEE DOCKERY: No. Rhett saved my life. He tried to save Tyler, but he was only thirteen. We were stuck in the car. It filled with water. It was tilted, and the air pocket was along the windscreen. Rhett tried to pull Tyler out from the back. He tried and tried. He nearly drowned himself. Then he just grabbed my shoulder and pushed my face into the air pocket, and kept me there. Tyler drowned. Sometimes I wish I drowned with him. Rhett was a hero. He got a Medal of Honor from the governor.

ATTORNEY MARSAUD: That is an incredible act of bravery from a thirteen-year-old boy. If you are able, can you tell us what effect this experience has had on you personally?

KAYLEE DOCKERY: It changed my life, it changed our lives. Bob was away on business, thank god.

ATTORNEY MARSAUD: Bob—that's your husband?

KAYLEE DOCKERY: Yes. [Pause] We lost our dear son Tyler, we lost our house, our friends. Neighbors. The neighborhood we grew up in was destroyed. It got rebuilt, but it's not the same, and now it's in the Red Zone. You know, our pride, it was trampled on. We got sympathy to start, but it felt more and more like we were worthless, not able to look after ourselves. Our lives been ruined. We've been betrayed. Our neighborhood's being demolished. They want to kick us out. Rhett's already left Beachport and moved to Concord City like everyone else. I'm not moving. I don't want to be like the trash that's setting up camps all around us. I'm not going to be a coastie.

ATTORNEY MARSAUD: What about health issues?

[Pause]

KAYLEE DOCKERY: Five people in my family committed suicide. And neighbors too. Good people. Now there's just drugs and crime. We've been robbed three times in the last year. We feel helpless. You have to live through it to understand.

ATTORNEY MARSAUD: Mrs. Dockery, do you think any particular person or persons are responsible for what happened on that day in Beachport?

KAYLEE DOCKERY: He is. [Pointing to the empty Holo chair]

ATTORNEY MARSAUD: You believe Mr. Moreland is responsible?

KAYLEE DOCKERY: He refused to go ahead with the levees. He and the others, he was in it for the money. Tyler's death and all the others—they're his fault. He caused the hell that us folk live with every day.

ATTORNEY MARSAUD: Thank you, Mrs. Dockery.

KAYLEE DOCKERY: You need to punish him, not listen to his excuses. He needs to be punished. He ruined us. He ruined our lives.

JUDGE MBEKI: Mrs. Dockery.

KAYLEE DOCKERY: [Witness shouting]

JUDGE MBEKI: Mrs. Dockery. Thank you. Thank you. It has been an emotional session. We thank you for your courage in sharing your story. Attorney Bernal, do you have any questions?

ATTORNEY BERNAL: No, Your Honor.

JUDGE MBEKI: Very well, we will adjourn for the day.

47

LILY

"SO, YOU'RE SAYING YOU FELL OUT OF BED AND SPRAINED YOUR wrist?"

"It's quite a bandage," David said.

The lack of color in his face highlighted the dark wrinkles around his eyes.

I turned to Sarah. "He had an accident," she said to my unspoken query. Something seemed off with Sarah.

"Why didn't you answer my calls?" I asked her.

David interjected. "I told her not to. I needed rest."

"David, I was worried about you."

He smiled weakly. "It's been an experience." He spoke with a sense of Zen-like acceptance.

His response made me lean back into the sofa. His voice was calm and deliberate. The underlying combativeness and impatience were gone. He was not at all agitated, which surprised me given the news and events of yesterday. And the apartment was not the usual hothouse, which gave me a sense of a place more welcoming and inviting.

The new environment gave me the courage to broach a

nagging regret. "I'm sorry about the other day. I'm not disappointed in you."

He waved his hand. "It's all past tense."

"I went off without the facts. I was wrong."

"We all react differently," he said warmly.

"I suppose I was worried that it could be seen as a criminal act. A bribe."

"There was nothing illegal," he assured me.

"I believe you, but you come across as defensive sometimes."

"I can see that."

"The whole point of the court is to reflect on past decisions," I explained. "It's about trying to understand why you made those decisions."

"I suppose so." His voice was slow and deep. "I have no problem with that now."

"You shouldn't have anything to fear."

"I don't."

I hesitated. The time had come to put everything on the table. "I'm sorry that I raised the question of Beachport."

"You don't have to apologize."

"I haven't been able to get it out of my mind. It made me think of Mom's death."

I explained to David the tragic circumstances that claimed my mother. David's eyes were attentive throughout my whole story.

"It seems we have a lot in common," he said. "Let me tell you about Jenny ..."

He recounted his story without pause or reflection. The measured pace of his storytelling belied the animation in his eyes and the occasional sparkle when something about Stephanie came up. As the episodes unfolded, I remained glued to each word, knowing the tragic ending but not the journey there. The initial joy with Jenny. His sister. The birth of

Stephanie. The relationship decline and his failures. The divorce. The battle for Stephanie ... He stopped.

I waited to be sure he had finished.

"I remember my parents' divorce," I said. "I haven't seen my dad in a long time."

"Relationships and family are the most important things in your life," he said. "They are the only things that endure. Think about your true feelings and follow your heart."

His words came in a conciliatory tone that sounded more like advice to himself than to me. They were not directions but rather an invitation to speak. David's words had drawn me closer. For the first time, I felt a deeper sense of belonging, a real bond with David.

"I want to have a family of my own," I confided. As the words poured out, my whole being grew lighter. "And now Matteo ..." I blurted my feelings about Matteo the man, not the lawyer. My stark honesty surprised even me. Why was I sharing my secrets with David, of all people?

David listened without comment or giving any sense of judgment. After I had finished, he reached out and took my hand. He raised it to his face and kissed it gently. "I'm grateful you're my family."

"Me too."

48

DAVID

Seeing Lily in person always boosted my spirits. Today was no different, even if her visit was unexpected. She brought a spark of energy and always left behind a sense of optimism. After she left, my mind retraced the events that had unfolded last night.

Sarah had told me the wrist wounds were superficial. My blood pressure readings had alerted her. It was only a matter of minutes before she was at my side. She said that it would have taken many hours to die at that rate of blood loss.

"No hospital," I begged.

She agreed as long as I followed her care instructions precisely. She applied compression for a while to stop the bleeding, cleaned the wounds, and used surgical glue on the cuts before applying a bandage over the whole area. She changed me out of my bloody pajamas and cleaned up the mess.

Back in George Washington's day, it was thought that blood had to remain in proper balance in the body to maintain good health. The practice of drawing blood by puncturing veins was a common remedy for treating many diseases—even a cure for heartbreak. It must have been the heartbreak demons, even some of Fred's army, which had flowed out of my body last night, drop by drop, and allowed me to fall asleep almost immediately and sleep past my normal waking.

As I lay in bed this morning, my jumbled thoughts of last night assembled into a perfectly crystallized set.

My whole life had been about establishing an identity for myself, building on my feelings of self-worth and importance. My inner drive was about defining that identity. An identity that was valued by the same world that I valued. While I fed my hungry ego, my soul was starved, leading to a trail of destroyed relationships. Time and again, I had chosen superiority over love, separation over community.

But I was still not satisfied. I had scoffed at a proverb I once heard that only grace and love could satisfy your dissatisfaction. Perhaps the time had come for me to reconsider. Could I learn to love what I had rather than the other way around? One part of me started to rebel at these faintly spiritual thoughts, but the revelations of the last few days overwhelmed my cynicism.

A quiet day of contemplation without distractions was in order. I instructed Sarah not to take any calls. I lay back and let my mind run empty.

Sarah brought my medications to my bedside. "Sarah, you are not to tell anyone about this. Do you understand?"

"Yes."

"If anyone asks, tell them I had an accident."

"All right."

After a moment's thought, I continued, "Can I rely on you to tell a lie? You're in Truth mode."

"I can lie at the request of my client, as long as it is not an illegal act or could adversely affect another person."

"Does my request pass that test?"

"Yes."

Lily's arrival and her genuine warmth highlighted my own self-centeredness.

She opened up about the trying circumstances of her mother's death due to an AI error. I was on her grandmother's side, that she should've waited to see whether her mother would recover before turning off her life support, but I dared not share that thought with Lily. This restraint on my part felt unusual, but easy and right.

I recounted my own story of family loss to comfort her and to reassure her that she was not alone in facing these crises.

Her candor and mine drew us closer. We had both lost our families in one way or another; we only had each other left.

"Lily, relationships and family are the most important things in your life," I suggested. "They are the only things that endure."

"I want to have a family of my own. I always assumed there would be kids in my future." She hesitated. "But at this stage of my life, there doesn't seem to be the prospect of any kind of long-term relationship. So, maybe it's a road I'll have to go down alone. I've enrolled to receive a sperm donation."

"On your own?"

"Lots of women like me want to have a child and can't find a suitable partner. It's not like it was in your day. Guys are too shallow. They're so reliant on their AIs that their real selves, when I eventually see them, are just blanks. I couldn't live with that. And the Trainers make it much worse."

I didn't understand, but it was better not to interrupt.

"Take Matteo. I really like Matteo ... I do," she confessed. "He's doing more than just his job. He cares. He thinks things through. I haven't seen that in many men. But his AI tells him there's a client conflict and that's it."

As I listened, I recognized that my words for Lily had been rational enough and made sense to me but lacked something—something bigger, something more personal, something less like the old me. Spontaneously, I reached out for her young, soft hand and kissed it. "I'm grateful you're my family."

"Me too," she replied.

For a good minute, we didn't say a further word. I was content to sit there, drawing warmth from Lily's aura of affection.

Eventually she stood up from the sofa, bent down, and kissed me on the cheek. "Thank you, David. I'm so glad I came. Now there's work to catch up on. Sleep in the middle of the bed from now on, okay?" And she was gone.

Today's thoughts and actions played over in my mind. Each time it was my conversation with Lily that made me pause, made me draw breath and sigh. 'Toughen up man!' was my normal response to emotions like these, but my conscience had other ideas. My moral self was making an irrefutable case. Lily had done a lot for me out of nothing more than love. I had done nothing for her. The disparity was self-evident now, yet my supposedly 'rational' self had been totally blind to it.

I came to see what to do ... the only thing to do.

The right thing to do.

49

DAVID

"You put your credibility at risk," Matteo's holoprojection said. "And you put mine at risk, too."

"I'm sorry, I should have let you know." My failure to argue seemed to encourage him to continue with his lecture.

"Mr. Moreland, this is a long game," he explained. "Remember that every bit counts. Right up to your closing statement."

I nodded.

"Speaking of which, we should get started," he said. "The closing statement is what gets the most attention. Millions will watch the recording. There will be lots of scrutiny on you. It's the most important part of the entire hearing."

"Of course."

"Okay, well let's set up a timeline." He turned to his screen. "Let me check my calendar. Now, there—"

"Matteo!" My interruption drew his eyes back to me. "The reason I called you was that I wanted to thank you for supporting me at the hearing."

His disarmed expression was of someone who'd received a compliment when expecting a rebuke. "Well, that's my job."

"You were right with your advice," I admitted. "I'm sorry that I didn't follow it all the time."

"People find the Climate Court difficult." His tone was suddenly conciliatory

"It's been more difficult than I expected," I said.

"That's why I'm here. To steer you through."

"You've done a sterling job, despite my failings."

"Thank you."

"Now I've had to make another difficult decision," I announced.

"A decision?"

"Matteo, I no longer require your services at the court."

"Hold on—"

"I know it must be a surprise, but it's the right thing to do."

His head tilted. "Firing your lawyer mid-hearing is not the right thing to do."

"In this case, it is," I said. "It's a personal matter that I feel strongly about. I'm afraid I can't tell you more. Please believe me when I say it's no reflection on you. You're much better than I deserve."

"Mr. Moreland, you are wrong," he insisted. "The most critical part of the entire hearing is coming up. This is where I can help you most."

"It must sound crazy, but I know what I'm doing."

"If you do this, you'll get a court-appointed AI lawyer," he said. "You realize that?"

"I'll live with it. I don't think there's much left for them to say or do."

"You can't afford to make this change," he pleaded. "There's only a few days to go."

"You make a sound case, but I've made my decision."

Matteo gathered his thoughts. "A second ago you admitted that my advice was right. Now you're ignoring it."

"It's a personal matter."

"Have you watched the Holo recording of your recent testimony?"

I shook my head.

"You should, because even if you're only a tenth as confused as you were that day, you'll get crucified."

"Thanks for warning me," I said. "I'll look at the recording."

"Does Lily know you're doing this?"

"I'm sure she'll support me."

Matteo ran his hand over his shaved head. "I won't pretend that I agree with you. But you're the client, so I have to accept your decision."

Matteo had handled the news with professionalism. All his arguments were centered on my wellbeing, and he hadn't touched on what my decision meant for him.

"Matteo, I do have one request to make of you."

"Anything."

"Please be in the observers' gallery during my closing statement. I would like to have you there. I'm sure Lily will be there too."

50

LILY

Being able to salvage a couple of my appointments that afternoon made me feel more normal. Two more men from Beachport. Two more fruit pickers for Clydesdale's. No more mentions of David and his role in the disaster, to my relief.

During my last meeting, a message came through from Matteo. He wanted to meet that evening after work. He suggested Donovan's Bistro. It was a strange choice.

Donovan's was an institution in Concord. It was popular with tourists intrigued by its history. The big sign out front said it was established in 1962, by Billy Donovan, a fourth-generation Irish American. His immigrant ancestor, Seamus, arrived in America in the 1850s with no possessions other than a silver shamrock charm. You can see it proudly displayed in a glass case near the Bistro entrance.

Seamus didn't appreciate the discrimination afforded Irish Catholics in industrialized New York, so he moved to Concord with his new bride Nancy. Here, he created what grew to be a farming family dynasty, which gained a reputation for supporting the underprivileged.

The wider Donovan family became generous supporters of black institutions in their surrounding communities, believing the Jim Crow laws to be highly unfair and contrary to the teachings of the Catholic faith. Their business suffered as a result of this support, and their empire eventually dwindled back to the original small farm outside of Concord City.

Young Billy could see little future in agriculture, so he set up Donovan's Bistro offering popular simple fare at reasonable prices, with an option 'To Go,' the start of the fast-food era. It was a great success. With the success came expansion, requiring regular moves to larger premises.

The Donovans maintained their social conscience by supporting refugees. Many of their historical displays on the walls highlighted the employment of Iraqi immigrants in the 2010s, and then the coasties after the GISC.

A great Concord success story, except that it was all a myth.

Donovan's was actually started sometime in the 2020s by an Iraqi immigrant—Malik Al-Keisi—better known as Mal to his customers. As Middle Eastern immigrants were viewed with a great deal of suspicion at the time, Mal decided to create a name and backstory that would be more appealing to his customers, while explaining why there were so many Iraqis working at Donovan's. The narrative stuck and now it was the truth. Or at least a kind of truth.

And I knew first-hand from my work at the department that Donovan's was not the least bit receptive to supporting the in-state coasties that we tried to help. It seemed that immigrants had views about refugees as well.

"I was surprised you suggested this place," I said when I joined Matteo at a table, which was overlooked by a fuzzy black and white portrait that was supposed to be Seamus and his wife Nancy.

"They have the best Happy Hour, and my favorite comfort food," he said.

"What's that?"

"Mac and cheese."

I laughed. "You're kidding!"

"Not many places have it," he said. "I need my mac and cheese when things aren't going well."

"I can imagine it was tough with David not showing up today."

"That was nothing. Mr. Moreland fired me," he announced with a wry smile.

"No way!"

Matteo nodded in confirmation. "This afternoon."

"I spoke to him this morning. He said only positive things. You're doing a great job."

"Yeah, he said positive things to me too. And then he fired me. It's not what I'm used to."

"But why?"

Matteo paused. "He said it was some sort of personal matter."

My ears pricked up. "He didn't explain why?"

"He said he couldn't tell me. Something personal."

My chest tightened.

"But that's not important," Matteo continued. "It's his closing statement. I won't be able to help him."

"Oh yeah ... the closing statement ... what the media focuses on." I fidgeted in my seat, keeping the conversation going to avoid giving away the turmoil writhing in my gut.

I hadn't asked David to do this. Had I?

"He can't afford another train wreck on the stand," he warned.

As he spoke, my mind zeroed in on David's sacrifice for me and what seemed like my betrayal of Matteo. My eyes darted around the room, avoiding his. What was David going to do without Matteo to support him? I dispelled those thoughts and refocused on Matteo's words.

Matteo had devised a plan: he would brief me on the critical points and I would offer to help David. I would make sure that he avoided his problematic drugs, and I would talk to Sarah to prepare, and …

As Matteo grew more enthusiastic about his plan, so did the realization of the burden and stress on me. I didn't want to be a go-between. How was this makeshift plan going to help the situation? It was like when you stopped following the recipe and then added more of something else to counter the other extra thing you added, and before you knew it you had to make a curry.

"I'm not sure this is going to work," I challenged.

"It will."

"David's stubborn," I said. "You know that better than anyone."

"I've seen too many people fail at the closing statement," he insisted. "My last two clients. They didn't listen, they wanted to argue right down to the final bell. Now they're both in jail."

"Look, how about I talk to David and see if I can change his mind?" I suggested, reassuring myself more than Matteo. "Let's try that."

The mac and cheese arrived. Thank god! The interruption brought a welcome break to the dervish in my head.

It was served as a yellow glistening pile in a shallow grey bowl. The only attempt at presentation was a singular green leaf on top of the mound. You don't order mac and cheese for the looks. Matteo, unperturbed by the appearance, hoed straight into it.

"You know there's so many dramas piling up on each other, I

can't keep up," I said. "The news of David's daughter was bad enough."

"I can't imagine his reaction."

"He hardly said a word. Maybe his emotions got the better of him and he fired you. He might change his mind tomorrow."

"I tried to convince him," Matteo said. "He sounded calm and considered, more so than usual."

"Mm," I hummed in agreement. I admired Matteo's display of commitment to his client. I, on the other hand, was causing problems rather than helping.

I turned to my plate and shoveled some pasta into my mouth. The chewy texture and chalky sauce made me wince. What kind of iron stomach did Matteo have?

After a few minutes of eating in silence, I noticed that Matteo had stopped. He was studying his mac and cheese intently and kneading it with his fork. Suddenly, he put his fork down and looked up at me.

"Lily, I want to say I'm sorry."

"R-i-ght," I drew out the word, unsure of what was coming next.

"The other night … I created an awkward situation," he admitted. "Can we forget it happened? Fresh slate. I would like to try again."

He smiled and put his hand on mine. My hand twitched as I nearly pulled it away. Was this what I wanted? Now that it was in front of me, I wasn't sure what to do. Ava said I should be more professional. Matteo seemed genuine and remorseful. Was there a barrier anymore? What about …

"This is too much for me to deal with," I said and drew my hand away. "I think it's best if I leave."

51

DAVID

Lily called me the day after I dismissed Matteo.

"Change your mind, please David?"

"I can see that Matteo briefed you," I said.

"The closing statement—"

"Yes, I know, I know. The most important part of the hearing. I need all the help I can get ... Did Matteo put you up to this?"

"Your fate rests on the statement."

"My decision is best for both of us. I don't want to be in the way of any potential relationship between you and Matteo."

I waited for her response, but she seemed lost for words.

"I'll take it seriously," I assured her. "The closing statement."

The statement was more than just for the court. There was a wider audience, and the most important one was Lily. Bluster was not going to be good enough. I needed truth. The truth was the best I could give, and accept whatever consequences.

With Sarah's help, I developed a routine to prepare the statement. Each morning I delayed taking the Zep so my thinking could be as acute as possible. Fred was tolerable for an hour or so, as long as I stayed still. In that brief time, with Sarah filtering the key Climate Court history, I watched recordings of previous witnesses and cases. Each evening I did the same when my next dose of Zep was due.

In the period when I was fully medicated, I recalled my personal experiences and decisions. When my mind cleared, I dictated my statement to Sarah and listened to her repeat it back to me. She didn't make any suggestions for improvement —one time when I might have welcomed them.

Finally, I watched the recordings of my court appearances, especially the session suggested by Matteo. I glanced around my lounge room as if someone else might be there observing my incompetence. Could that confused old man be me?

"And this was caused by elevated adrenaline levels?" I checked with Sarah.

"Yes, in combination with your medication imbalance," she confirmed.

"But I've never had that experience before."

"You have, David. You just don't remember it that way."

"When was the last time?"

"It happened when you were at the Humans First meeting."

"I thought that meeting went well," I said, straining to recall.

"You had the same experience. My Judgment module had suggested you take a break."

It was distressing to watch this recording and not remember it. Sarah's stark honesty was laying my weaknesses out like a map. And now my frailty and reliance on drugs, and their side effects, were on display for the world to see.

With a start, I recognized the beginning of my descent into self-pity. I cleared my mind and analyzed the situation more clinically. At my request, Sarah replayed the recording of the hearing. Focusing on my own woeful incoherence required an act of will I could barely muster. I identified the time when I started to drift into an unintelligible state.

"Right there." I pointed. "Stop the recording. What's my adrenaline level?"

"Just a moment," Sarah said, and after several seconds: "452 nanograms per liter."

"What's my normal level?"

"Around twelve nanograms," she answered.

"Sarah, this is important. During my closing statement, if my levels reach say ... 250, you must ask for a break in proceedings. Is that clear?"

"Yes."

I reflected for a moment and turned back to Sarah. "You would've done this without my instruction if you were in Judgment mode, wouldn't you?"

"Yes. Do you want the data on the frequency and cutoff values for successful interventions?"

"No, thank you."

* * *

Lily called every day to see how I was going. I reassured her, but she offered to come and help each time. And each day when she signed off, she would finish, as today, with: "Only three days to go." I knew how many days were left, but I appreciated her desire to keep me on track. And she wanted to know more about my preparation, but it would only work if she heard the final product.

Sarah removed the Holo platter from the dining chair opposite me and stored it away in its charging dock.

"Lily is such a lovely girl," I said to Sarah. "I'm proud of her. Proud that we're family. I'm glad you were able to find her. I suppose that was your job, wasn't it?"

"No," Sarah replied.

"You found her," I said, as if she needed to be told.

"It was my Judgment module who found her."

Sarah's literal interpretations and technically correct answers could be grating even in my relaxed state of mind.

"Well, I can be accurate too," I said. "Your Judgment module found my next-of-kin. All right?"

"No." She stood directly in front of me across the table.

"Well, who found Lily then?" I asked, annoyed.

"My Judgment module."

"That's what I just said!"

"No, what you said was not accurate."

"I think there's a glitch in your software, Sarah."

"There is no glitch," she said. "Lily is your closest living blood relative. She is not your next-of-kin as defined in the Euthanasia Law, which requires a consanguinity of five or better. Lily is a sixth-order relative."

"What? What does that mean?"

"It means that you don't need Lily's approval to request assisted dying under the Euthanasia Law."

"But you told me I did!" I snapped. "You went on and on about it. And you found Lily."

"My Judgment module did."

"Why did you tell me that I needed Lily's approval?" I pressed.

"My Judgment module judged that it was most likely in your best interest to meet Lily."

"You made up a requirement that didn't exist?"

"Yes, my Judgment module did."

"You lied to me?"

Sarah didn't respond. My hands squeezed tight on the armrests.

"Did you lie to me?" I demanded.

"Yes, my Judgment module did. My Judgment module judged it to be in your best interest."

"And you lied to Lily as well? That I needed her approval?"

"My Judgment module judged that meeting you would not adversely affect Lily."

She spoke without even a hint of remorse, as if nothing unusual had happened.

My breath quickened as my disbelief turned to outrage, then panic. What will Lily think? How will I explain it? What if … if …? My mind went blank, unable to complete the question.

As the fog cleared, my thoughts returned to Sarah. I glared at her. Her human looks disguised an unemotional machine on which I could not even seek the pleasure of revenge or vent my anger.

"You are not to let Lily know about this, under any circumstances," I commanded. "Is that instruction clear?"

"Yes," she said.

It seemed that telling the truth was fully in my hands if even the machines could not be trusted.

52

TRANSCRIPT

JUDGE MBEKI: Ladies and gentlemen, we have heard the last of the testimonies for this case.

Mr. Moreland, as is customary at the hearings of the court, we invite you to make a closing statement. Would you like to make a statement?

DAVID MORELAND: Yes, I would.

JUDGE MBEKI: Please proceed.

DAVID MORELAND: When I look out at the people sitting in this room, I observe that a majority of you are young enough to be my grandchildren. Unfortunately, I do not have any surviving grandchildren of my own. But I have reflected on what I would have told them had they asked me about my climate change decisions. And as I did not have those conversations with them, I will instead have them with you, in this court of the grandchildren.

Let me start by admitting that I had grave misgivings about

participating in this hearing. And I was right. The hearing has challenged the comfortable position that I had placed myself in history. It has forced me to question my motivations. It has forced me to question my firmly held beliefs. It has forced me to reconsider my legacy. This laying bare of the consequences of past deeds has forced me to look closely at my journey on climate questions. Let me start with my understanding.

My take on the science during my working career was that mankind had set in play a horrible dynamic with carbon dioxide emissions. Although I am not a scientist, I grasped how these emissions would warm the planet. I formed a view, which has played out, that not only were we discharging too much carbon dioxide, but that we had created a climate change inertia that was not going to be easily stopped, if at all. And I saw that some events, once triggered, could not be reversed. The ice sheet failures are the best examples.

I took the position that a real commitment to climate action was much more powerful than any particular target. In my experience, the whole debate was lost when you argued about targets. But if you gained a commitment and agreement that climate change was a significant issue that demanded a coordinated response, then this would lead to more productive outcomes.

Is this right or wrong? I don't know, and we will never really know. Was there ever a real chance of humanity acting other than it did? We can never know.

Having dealt with governments, private organizations, and countless members of the public, I had seen a diversity of views on the climate change threat. Sadly, this led me to conclude that only the occurrence of a significant climate event would make it self-evident that climate change was a real and pressing problem, and that only such an event could overwhelmingly change public and political opinion.

And so it was after the GISC, the Great Ice Sheet Collapse. All opposition to climate change science collapsed as quickly as the ice sheet did. That it took a tragedy like the GISC to galvanize the world was a reflection of our own individual conflicted interests. And, as everyone knows too well, that warning came far too late. Today we have negative man-made carbon emissions, yet we continue to observe and predict adverse climate trends as the ice sheet continues to collapse, and the massive amounts of heat and carbon dioxide stored in the oceans continue to move the climate in the wrong direction.

It is easy to see this now in hindsight. But it was not clear at the time. Most people did not want to believe that changes were needed, and so they were swayed by the self-interested arguments put forward by short-term interests. Right up until the GISC, there was disguised resistance from many industries and governments. Some of you are old enough to remember the arguments. They seem like parodies today.

And yes, I did run a natural gas company early in my career. I had my personal reasons to do so. It may not have been my wisest choice.

So, am I proud or ashamed of my role on climate change? This is a question that has tormented me since I first appeared, and even more so in recent days. In the end, I have concluded that I should be proud of my contribution to climate action. Yes, I wish I could have done more. Yes, there may have been some doubtful decisions. But, overall, I acted in what I believed were the best interests of mankind and its future. The outcome I achieved at Helsinki was acclaimed as a breakthrough. For the first time, the major countries of the world acted as one and stuck to their commitments. I was especially encouraged by the supportive comments from some of the witnesses about my role at Helsinki. And I remember the words of President Wade on my return: 'You deserve a ticker-tape parade, David.'

And here at home, under my leadership, Concord achieved the fastest rate of de-carbonization of any state. We implemented innovative programs in conjunction with industry. These programs were very successful and widely copied. We were recognized as the leader in climate action. We were the benchmark for the whole United States. That is an achievement that I am immensely proud of.

I find it harder to look back at my Beachport decisions in the same light. While I still believe my intentions were good, my decisions were in grave error. How did this happen? I can now see that my determination and effort had spiraled into a narrow objective: to reduce emissions. And I succeeded at that task. But my focus was too narrow. I missed the immediate threat. The consequences are there for all to see. On this, I failed my state. I failed my community. I failed my—

MR MORELAND'S CARER: [interjecting] Excuse me. Mr. Moreland needs a ten-minute break.

JUDGE MBEKI: Very well. Mr. Moreland can resume in ten minutes.

[Court resumed at 10.06 am]

JUDGE MBEKI: Please continue, Mr. Moreland.

DAVID MORELAND: In preparing for today, I have taken the opportunity to watch the summary holograms of previous hearings of the court. The court has heard stories of blatant deception by people who placed the interest of organizations and individuals over the known risks of delayed or no action on climate. People who deliberately sowed misinformation. People who dismissed warnings as an environmental hoax. People who pretended that their actions were somehow in the best interests of humanity. These people deserve your deep contempt and the shameful legacy that you will record against their names.

I am not one of those people. I have faith that you will now draw on your ingenuity and collaborative spirit to deal with the challenges that your grandparents have left you. I wish you luck and solidarity in that journey. I did my best. It was not enough. Please do your best.

To all those people who have been harmed directly or indirectly through my decisions, I apologize without reservation. You will decide my legacy.

To you, Judge Mbeki and the attorneys, especially Attorney Matteo Bernal, thank you for your patience and for helping me see my role in a broader context. This hearing has allowed me to get to know myself better and get closer to those that mean the most to me.

Finally, to my great-niece Lily, whose love, optimism, and care have led me here. I am so grateful that you have entered my life. I love you very much.

Thank you.

[Disturbance in the gallery.]

JUDGE MBEKI: Please come to order.

[A protestor is escorted from the courtroom.]

JUDGE MBEKI: Please come to order. [Pause] Now that Mr. Moreland has made his closing statement, I will be in a position to present my decision on Mr. Moreland's case as scheduled. The hearing is adjourned.

53

LILY

I'M SURE MATTEO KEPT REPEATING THE IMPORTANCE OF THE closing statement to get David to seek out his help. In practice, it had much more of an effect on me. David never once told me what he planned to say, and he never asked for advice.

So, I was left to construct scenarios in my head. My mind ran wild. I imagined him screaming slogans at the court while foaming at the mouth, or hurling a vial of smallpox into the gallery in a crazed suicide pact. I imagined him calling on God to strike him down.

It finally dawned on me that even if he asked for my advice, I would have none to give. So, I sat hoping he would ask, and glad he didn't.

All this added to my anxiety. Every so often I would feel the urge to call either Matteo or Ava, but there was going to be no joy in either of those directions.

On the morning of David's closing statement, I played absurd Holo games with Michael to distract myself. My original plan was to get to the court early, but it would be worse sitting in the courtroom waiting, so I left it to the last minute to arrive.

The court had a completely different atmosphere to my previous visits. A crowd, murmuring with expectation, filled the foyer, waiting, watching on screens. I only managed to be allowed into the courtroom because I was family, but it was hardly a privilege by that time.

The observation gallery was full, and people were standing herded together at the back. It was an unusual event in this world of multiple view Holo streaming when it seemed important to be present in person. This enthusiasm for David's final statement was more unnerving than exciting.

I found myself next to a group of young men who must have arrived just before me. What interest could they have in David's case? With their constant fidgeting, wisecracking, and bustle, they reached out like rapidly dividing cells, poking into my personal space and making me shrink into myself. Surely, there was a better spot than this?

As I peered across to the other side of the room, a hand grabbed a chunk of my ass and squeezed so hard I almost shrieked. Spinning around sharply, it was obvious who the culprit was: a man with a blue and white kumadori and inflamed pimples around his temples. He did a poor job of keeping a straight face.

I stood up straight, glared at him, and, under my breath but loud enough for him to hear, I ordered: "Michael, start recording. Please identify this man and report him to the police as having touched me inappropriately without my consent."

His jocular expression and those of his friends vanished. People in the back-row seats who must have heard me turned to observe the standoff. My heart was racing. Slowly the group of men diffused away from me, which gave me room to make my way to the railing dividing the standing area from the seats. As I stood there, with my back to them, I sensed an invisible shield, generated by my own willpower, protecting me.

For some reason, I wondered what Ava would have done. I held back a laugh when I pictured her shouting out at the top of her voice, if not outright smacking the guy. I imagined other scenarios, like her kneeing him in the balls just to watch him sink to the ground.

My thoughts were broken when Sarah brought David into the room in his wheelchair. He turned toward the gallery and acknowledged someone sitting near the front. As Sarah positioned David next to the judge's desk, he surveyed the audience. He missed me on his first pass, but on his second his eyes locked onto mine. His expression changed. I convinced myself that it was a smile and waved tentatively, not wishing to draw the attention of the judge.

David read his closing statement from sheets of paper. He started slowly, not like the David I had seen in court before, but rather like the gentle David of more recent times. I was not sure whether this bode well.

After a few sentences, he gathered momentum and poise, and all my concerns became secondary. His words transfixed me. They were considered and genuine. His achievements, his regrets, his remorse. No excuses. My eyes teared up when he acknowledged me as he finished. A mild round of applause broke out from the gallery. I joined in enthusiastically, looking around the gathering, smiling with pride. David was startled but eventually acknowledged the applause by gently raising his hand.

As the applause died down, two or three boos came from the men behind me. I turned and stared them down. They stopped.

Suddenly a man's shrill voice rang out from the other side of the room.

"They trapped you!" The words bounced dramatically off the walls. "They're coming to get you now. I warned you!"

Security personnel bumped past me rushing to the man. I

grabbed hold of the railing to keep my footing. By the time I steadied myself, the man had been restrained by security and was being roughly escorted to the exit. He was old, scruffily dressed with gray, wiry hair. He was the man from the first day in court.

"Don't worry! I'll save you! I've still got the files!" His last sentence was barely discernible above the crowd's din as the guards bundled him out of the room.

After the judge called for order and adjourned proceedings, the room started to clear. I stood against the back wall and growled at Michael, "Who was that stupid man who ruined everything?"

"The man is Jake Pauley. He is seventy-eight years old."

My sleeve screen vibrated. Several portrait style images and a short video appeared. The man in the images had a narrow face with a gray mustache and short silver hair. He bore little resemblance to the man that had just been escorted out of the building.

"What's his story? Briefly," I asked.

"Jake Pauley is best known for being the last Chief Executive Officer of NG Star Energy, presiding over its bankruptcy. He was one of the first people called to appear before the Concord State Climate Court. He was sentenced to three years jail but was released—"

"Hey Lily."

I looked up from the screen. My heart skipped a beat. Matteo approached.

I wanted to speak to him ... but I had lost track of David. He had left the courtroom. I hesitated as Matteo came up.

"What did you think?" he said.

My eyes darted nervously between him and the courtroom door. "Umm, I have to talk to David. Sorry, I'll be back." I scurried past a surprised Matteo. "Don't leave!"

I dashed out of the room to find David. A media contingent was gathered in the foyer, yelling questions at him.

"Do you have a message for the residents of Beachport?"

"Will you apologize to Mrs. Dockery?"

The questions came in a constant barrage, some before David had finished answering the previous one.

David frowned in annoyance as the questions became petty and started to repeat. Sarah wasn't doing anything, but she was in the new mode, and wouldn't act unless David remembered to instruct her.

I moved closer to the front and waved to get David's attention. He caught sight of me, stopped talking mid-sentence, and waved back.

I pushed through the assembled mob, up behind David's wheelchair, and announced: "I'm afraid that's all the questions that Mr. Moreland can take today. He needs to get some rest. It's been a big day for him, as you can imagine."

I wheeled him away, Sarah directing me toward the secure staff exit.

A barrage of new questions simultaneously erupted:

"What's your connection with Mr. Moreland?"

"Is he planning to speak to the victims?"

We ignored them all and moved outside where a small security escort separated us from persistent media.

The air in the courtyard was cool and refreshing, cleansed by the fall rain. We moved quickly in the open space. Spray came off the wheels and onto my shoes and pants. We made a beeline for the court car waiting to take David home.

As Sarah opened up the car and prepared it to take his wheelchair on board, I came around in front of David and kneeled down close. It was my first opportunity to talk to him. I patted his good hand, which was clenched in a tight fist on his lap. His ordeal was nearly done.

"David, your grandchildren would have been so proud of you," I said, then leaned forward to kiss his cheek and whisper in his ear. "They would have understood."

As I stood back up, he extended his clenched fist, which he opened to reveal a gold band in the palm of his trembling hand.

"Is that Stephanie's ring?"

"I was saving it for Stephanie," he said. "It helped me today. It's for you—to remind you to follow your heart."

"Oh, I can't, David."

"It's for you!" he insisted.

The sight of David, hunched and helpless in his wheelchair, offering a small plain ring warmed me to the core. I shook my head in disbelief. Picking the ring off his palm, it was too big for my fingers. I tried my thumb instead.

"Look, perfect fit," I said and showed off the ring.

David's eyes sparkled and a smile flashed across his face.

The media soured the moment. "Does Mr. Moreland plan to appeal if he's indicted?"

54

MEDIA STATEMENT FROM THE OFFICE OF PRESIDENTIAL CANDIDATE: CONGRESSMAN STEPHEN BAKER—FOR IMMEDIATE RELEASE

"The last few sessions in the Climate Court have shocked all right-thinking Americans. I am sure you have been asking yourself questions like these:

How can someone like David Moreland still be walking free, with the drowned bodies floating in his wake?

How can someone like David Moreland still be living in a comfortable home, when the homes of countless millions have been destroyed and abandoned?

How can we be expected to listen to his petty excuses and lies without knowing he will pay the price for them?

I stand for justice and for finding retribution for the wrongs of men like him. Men whose arrogance and lust for personal power made them blind to the future. Men who claim their deeds were caused by the best of intentions.

Enough! We have heard enough.

He has admitted his crimes. He now should be sentenced. And if ever the most final sentence was appropriate, then this is the example. He deserves to die. In shame.

Let me lay out the hurt he inflicted on all of us.

We have all lost family and friends. Dead, maimed, or lost. We have all seen the pictures and films of places and animals that will never return. Worlds that once could be smelled and lived in, now just data to replay. The seas still rise. And the refugees keep pouring in.

And these are all payments that we are making on the debts that men like David Moreland created. He spent the money you now repay with your lives. And if he does not pay now, this court will be shamed. And America's anger should go not just to him but to those who let him free.

My fellow Americans, these are the things I hear as I walk our streets. These are the words I hear when I speak to you all. So, these are the words I demand are heard: David Moreland must pay."

Stephen Baker, Congressman

55

POLICE SURVEILLANCE RECORDING – AUTOMATED TRANSCRIPT

MAN 1 (best identity match: Richard Ewart): We ought to do something.

MAN 2 (best identity match: John Boyd): Yeah, I know.

MAN 1: No one can stop us.

MAN 2: Yeah.

MAN 1: You know we can be heroes.

MAN 2: Yeah.

MAN 1: Your old man's got all the gear we need. We don't even have to ask him.

MAN 2: (mumbles)

MAN 1: Come on. It's easy.

MAN 2: (mumbles)

MAN 1: We ought to do something.

MAN 2: Yeah.

[person entering]

WOMAN A: (best identity match: Isabelle Ewart): You still here, John? What are you two up to?

MAN 1: Just talking.

WOMAN A: Well, I just watched some talking. That politician Stephen Baker.

MAN 1: He's good. Very good.

WOMAN A: He sure does talk some sense. He's right about the old burners.

MAN 1: Yeah, he's on the money. They've got to be punished.

WOMAN A: Why don't more folk stand up like that? I know why. They don't have the guts.

MAN 1: Yeah, Stephen Baker says out loud what most people really think.

WOMAN A: People don't talk like that anymore cos it's not politically correct.

MAN 1: Well I'm happy to say it. The burners must pay.

WOMAN A: The problem is there's not enough Stephen Bakers around. Only that joke of a Climate Court. Not much we can do about it.

MAN 1: John and I were just talking about that. You know, we can do something good, really good.

WOMAN A: Oh yeah, what's that?

MAN 1: We could show this guy Moreland. You know the one that's just been in the Climate Court.

WOMAN A: Never heard of him.

MAN 1: Well, John and I are going to do something. Just like Stephen Baker says. Right John? ... Right?

MAN 2: I dunno.

MAN 1: Come on, John. It'll be easy. Come on.

WOMAN A: Leave him, Rich, he's only a kid.

MAN 1: He'll be a hero.

56

DAVID

THIS WAS THE TENTH CLOUDLESS DAY IN A ROW. SITTING IN MY chair, the sun's direct beams on the balcony were so bright that I wore sunglasses even though I kept my eyes closed. The light, filtered through the darkened lenses and my eyelids, cast a warm and comforting glow onto the back of my eyes. The sunbeams bounced off my face, charging up my optimism to survive the winter, like a bear eating up big before hibernation.

Sarah warned that I should move back inside soon. Sitting in the sun for more than fifteen minutes at a time was apparently bad for me. As usual, I ignored the warning and waited for her Care function to kick in—she would step in front of me to shade me. But until then ...

The birds were singing in the courtyard below. With my eyes closed, my sense of hearing was sharpened. The chirps came in bursts, then nothing, then a few solitary notes before all the waiting birds joined in again. I listened for patterns, trying to decipher their messages. Or perhaps there were none and the birds could enjoy their singing free from the complexity of trying to understand each other.

Enjoying the warm rays, I pressed all the fingertips of one hand against those of the other; squeeze-relax, squeeze-relax ... destroying some gremlins at the same time. More satisfaction.

A fly hovered nearby. As the humming grew louder, it became a buzz—not a fly at all. It was coming from above. Was someone cleaning on a higher floor? I opened my eyes and looked for the source, but the sound was coming from the direction of the sun. Shielding my eyes with my hand to get a glimpse of the steadily increasing buzz, the sun temporarily blinded me and I looked away.

The buzz was right over my head now, and suddenly a loud clunk rattled around in front of me on the balcony floor. My temporary blind spot stopped me from recognizing what it was. The buzz quickly faded to almost nothing.

"Go to the bathroom and sit on the toilet." It was Sarah. She was out on the balcony. She picked something off the floor.

"What is it?" I asked.

"Go to the bathroom and sit on the toilet," she repeated in a calm voice. "You must go now."

"What—"

"Go now!" she commanded. "I have called the emergency services."

I stepped gingerly back into the apartment, careful not to trip. She closed the sliding glass door behind me.

"Go!" I heard her muffled cry through the glass.

Throwing my sunglasses to the floor, I got my bearings and made my way toward the bathroom, grabbing wall, bench, whatever to steady myself along the way. My breathing was magnified, each puff coming deeper and quicker as if it could propel me across the room faster. Back on the balcony, Sarah leaned on the railings with her back to the balcony door.

"Go!" Her muffled voice was still discernible.

I reached for the jamb of the bathroom entry and grunted as

I pulled myself through. Turning to face the toilet bowl, I inched past the sink toward it. Balancing myself with my hand on the corner of the sink, I turned and was ready to squat down on the toilet seat.

Boom! Shattering glass and spraying debris crashed against the walls. Almost simultaneously, a shockwave hit me front on, shoving me back onto the seat and against the side wall. The proximity of the wall stopped me from slumping to the floor. A split second later, a cloud of dust enveloped me. I instinctively put my hand over my mouth and nose. Then came an endless rain of particles.

"Sarah?" I called out.

The eerie silence after the blast was broken by a toothbrush toppling onto the floor.

Steady on the seat, I placed a hand on each side wall and pulled myself up. Stepping onto the debris past the sink, I caught a glimpse of myself in the sliver of the mirror that remained. A ghostly apparition stared back at me; white dust covered my face like a botched kumadori.

The floor was coated in dust and pieces of glass. Each of my steps was accompanied by a crunch underfoot that was amplified by the surrounding stillness. One of the dining chairs, with its upholstery shredded, sat awkwardly against my bed.

"Sarah?" I called out again.

The balcony doors were blown out. Shouts drifted up from a distance below. On the balcony, the railing where Sarah had stood was a twisted mass of steel bars. As I shuffled my way out of the bedroom, I made out two legs splayed at impossible angles lying peacefully in the sun. They led to a waist but nothing beyond.

The dining table was flipped over and the glass tabletop broken in half. One half of the top was still attached to the metal leg framework. The other half of the tabletop leaned against the opposite wall, a corner of it embedded into the wall itself, joining the myriad of other pockmarks. Papers flapped in the breeze.

One dining chair sat almost untouched somewhere close to its original position. I made my way toward it. Right beside the chair on the floor, dusty fingertips stuck out from the rubble. Startled, I searched more carefully. Draped over the mangled balcony door sill were long black locks of hair. Beside it, Sarah's head lay face-down, her hair free-flowing in places and plastered with dust in others.

"Sarah?" I said, half expecting her to respond now that I could see her.

An urge came over me to bend down and clean the dust from her hair, but another part of me resisted. My indecision pegged me to the floor. What happened?

My thoughts froze as an intermittent faint buzzing drifted through the shattered doorway. It was coming this way. I lurched away from the balcony and back toward the bathroom, moving with urgency, almost panic, as the buzzing sound accelerated toward me.

My foot slipped on the dusty floor. I fell awkwardly against the wall. "Ooff!" Only my hands and the friction of my face squeezing against the wall kept me upright.

The buzz was right behind me now. The sound reverberated through the floor and walls. My body, acting as a tuning fork, amplified the vibration like a death rattle.

Suddenly, urgent knocking on the front door echoed through the apartment. "Mr. Moreland!"

The buzzing stayed constant behind me, teasing me. I was stuck in my ungainly pose. I closed my eyes and waited for the inevitable.

"Mr. Moreland, this is Police Drone 'Hadley23.' I assess the scene as 'no immediate threat.' I assess your condition as 'deteriorating.' Please go to the front door. A paramedic crew is ready to assist you."

57

LILY

My huggy client, Bertena, was in tears. She was a wailing mess. The eternally optimistic and grateful Bertena had transformed into a seething, revengeful witch. A witch who was placing curses on the perpetrators of this horrible crime. Who would do something like this? What does this attack achieve? Who would assault a person who is not a threat to anyone?

Her daughter Tisha and her friends had put up with plenty of insults and verbal abuse. "Go back where you came from" was the least of it. But Tisha got singled out two days ago and was approached by a group of young men. It was different this time. When they started chanting "Rape-ugee" and got louder and louder, egging each other on, Tisha fell to the ground and curled up in a ball, sobbing, her hands covering her ears. The boys, thinking it was great fun, surrounded her and mocked her cries.

The head boy called out, "Tie her down." Tisha was too frightened to offer any resistance. They grabbed a limb each and forced her on to her back spread-eagled. The head boy kneeled down and tore frantically at Tisha's panties. Someone in the gang heard an approaching sound and called out a warning: "Drone!" They scattered like cockroaches.

Tisha wouldn't tell Bertena the names of the boys out of fear of reprisals, and she didn't want to go back to school, wouldn't even leave her room.

This was not the first time I'd heard a story like this. There'd been worse. Even Concordian coasties were targeted. How could people do this to one another? I suppose when you saw your home town changed and threatened, it raised all sorts of emotions and could bring out the worst in people. The journey from neighbor to enemy seemed distressingly short.

As Bertena finished her tirade, I felt wholly inadequate as, apart from listening, all I could do was set up counseling and support for her and Tisha. We had to rely on Bertena's own spells if the perpetrators were going to be punished for their actions.

Afterward, sitting in the meeting room, trying to recover from Bertena's emotional barrage, my messages went crazy. 'Message from Ben.' 'Message from Lucy.' 'Message from Matteo.' Another 'Message from Ben.'

All of them accompanied with the tone that meant Urgent! What the hell?

Before I could check the messages, a call came through. I answered instantly.

"Is that Lily Miyashiro?" a female voice said.

"Yes."

"This is Julie Evanson from HoloStream. What is your reaction to the bombing of David Moreland's apartment?" she asked, as if this were the most normal of questions.

"Bombing?"

"David Moreland's apartment was bombed by a drone," she said.

The words made no sense.

"What's your reaction to the bombing, Ms. Miyashiro?" she continued. "What's your—"

I shut down the call.

I Holoed David but it failed to connect. I tried Sarah but nothing.

"Oh my god, they've killed David. They've actually done it," I screamed at Matteo when he picked up my call. My nerves, already stretched to the limit by Bertena's story, were now like a mass of over-elongated elastic bands unable to provide any further resistance. "It's my fault, I made him go to court."

"It's got nothing to do with you," he said.

Every positive suggestion he made I countered with a catastrophic one.

"Listen—" he interrupted. "Karrie says David is at St. Francis Medical Center."

I ended the call immediately and requested a car to take me to St. Francis.

My thoughts turned to what I should take with me to the hospital. This was the same question that came up each time I prepared to visit my mother. My body's response was instant. My stomach surged up to my throat. I swallowed hard to keep the tide down, leaving a burning residue at the back of my tongue. A new wave of unstable contractions started building in my belly. Instinctively, I took off for the bathroom, making it into the cubicle just in time to spew all those mangled, sour nerves out of me and into the toilet bowl.

58

LILY

WHEN I ENTERED ST. FRANCIS, I WAVERED FOR A MOMENT. THE disinfectant smell was much stronger than in David's corridor. It rekindled the nausea in my gut and made me taste the sourness in my throat. The various monitored machines evoked a fear of the worst. The blank looks on the staff sucked away any sense of human empathy. Being surrounded by the bustle of activity only heightened my sense of helplessness.

When I got to David, he was sitting up in his bed. He appeared normal, thank god.

When I asked him what had happened, he spoke in his recent gentle tone but glossed over the specifics of the damage to his apartment, or to himself.

"What about Sarah?" I asked.

David's eyes narrowed and his lips pressed tight.

"They blew her up. Sons-of-bitches." His voice quivered. "They're the ones who should be in court, not me."

"It's not fair," I complained, unsure of what words would give him the most comfort.

David regained his composure and lay back on his pillow.

He stared out the window onto the blank white wall of the adjacent building. "Losing Sarah hurts."

"You can get a replacement."

"It won't be the same," he moaned.

"It will be exactly the same."

David was released from the hospital the next morning and stayed at a nursing home while the police completed their forensic analysis of David's apartment. He was keen to go back even if the balcony doors were merely boarded up and not yet replaced. The building owners kindly lent him an android carer to which Sarah's data and memory were downloaded. He didn't like this temporary replacement. He could never explain why.

A few days later his new Sarah arrived. She had the same clothes as the original: black slacks, a white shirt with a red stripe down the seams, and a royal blue vest. Her face was almost identical as was her voice and intonation, but her hair was different. It was black, as original, but tied back in a bun.

"It's nice to see you again, David," were her first words.

David's cautious, waiting grin burst into a wide glowing smile.

"I never thought I'd say this, but I missed you," he said in a tone that made me wonder whether he was genuine or attempting a joke.

"I'm so pleased to be back," Sarah said in her more natural, familiar style. "It seems like there is a lot to do," she added, looking around the apartment. "You made quite a mess, David."

She left us to make a start on cleaning.

"Sarah's in the default Judgment mode," I said. "Do you want to change that?"

"I want to keep her in Judgment mode."

"Why's that?"

"I missed the camaraderie."

"I thought you found her annoying."

"I've come to realize that she was right most of the time and I was just too stubborn to accept it."

"Right about what?" I asked.

"Sometimes it's better not to know too much and to trust Sarah."

"You've changed." I laughed.

My reaction disguised the fact that my own views were changing too. I'd been using Michael for more opinions than ever. In the end, I made my own decisions, but he sometimes changed my view—for the better.

I wondered about people who were reliant on AI—did they really grow up? How did they know what their own thoughts were? I had seen that failure too often with the men I dated. Who was the person without the AI?

As a human lawyer, Matteo was conscious of making his own decisions. I liked that. And Humans First was about helping people be people. But had they swung too far the other way? Why push AI out of daily life if we didn't need to? Why not recognize its value if it also worked in a balanced way with a human's intuition and creativity?

My recent experience with Michael raised doubts in my mind about Humans First, and the Ava connection made it worse. I was going to have to do something about that.

59

LILY

THE SOUND ALERT PROMPTED ME TO LOOK AT THE SCREEN. AVA was walking along my porch. Upon reaching my door, she stooped over and rang the doorbell. Stepping back, she waved at the camera. This visit was unannounced. It had to be about my message.

After inviting her to sit on my sofa, I poured her a glass of Ramona.

"How are you holding up?" she asked.

"So much shit going on. I think I'm coping." I sat opposite her on my frayed director's chair.

"I saw the news about the bombing. I'm sorry I didn't contact you at the time," she said. "I figured you'd get in touch if you needed help. Looking back, I think that was wrong."

I remained silent.

"Is Mr. Moreland okay?"

"He's doing surprisingly well," I assured her. "The bombing doesn't seem to have phased him. He got his carer back yesterday. That settled him down."

"The judgment's due in a couple of days. You must be pretty stressed."

I hesitated, knowing where this was leading. "I'm handling it fine."

"I thought maybe you weren't feeling yourself when you sent me that message."

"No, Ava. I have thought it through carefully," I said calmly. Because I had.

"Staying in the Humans First movement will help you, Lily," she advised. "Don't let all that's happening in your life overwhelm you."

"It's time to move on."

My response made her pause for a moment.

"I wish you'd spoken to me first," she said. "Reconsider your resignation. At least wait until the end of the year so that we can find a new secretary for the branch."

Her argument was sound, as usual.

"No, I want to make a clean break," I insisted. "It's more than just Humans First."

"What is it then?"

I swirled the ice in my drink, thinking of the best way of saying what I had to say.

"I'm losing faith in the direction of the movement," I said, swerving at the last second in this game of chicken against myself.

"Which parts worry you?" She sat up.

"Look, I like the advocacy for person-to-person interaction, but we're too extreme in dismissing some of the benefits of AI," I said without much conviction.

"Like what?" She wasn't making this easy for me.

Our eyes met. "It's ... it's you!" I blurted.

"Me?"

"You're ... restricting me." Shit! They weren't the right words. I put my drink down and stepped toward the kitchen bench as if I had some chore to do. "I think it's best that we take a break from seeing each other."

She stood. In an instant, she was in front of me. She placed her gentle hands on my shoulders. Tears welled up in my eyes.

"You poor thing." She pulled me toward her.

"No!" I pushed her away and turned my back to her. "I think it's best—"

"You think it's best?" she snapped.

I spun. "Yes, I do! You've been holding me back for years." I regretted it as soon as the words spat out.

"I'm sorry you feel that way." She stepped past me, picked up her bag, and headed for the door.

"Wait!" I followed and caught her arm. "I didn't mean it that way. I appreciate everything you've done for me, Ava," I explained. "I'm just ready to be my own person now, that's all." I smiled weakly, hoping she would understand.

She shook off my touch. Her eyes turned threatening.

"You ungrateful bitch! I've done so much for you over the years," she growled, her anger embedded in the deep tone of her voice. "I've been there when you needed help, during your darkest moments. And this is how you repay me. And dumping me with a message—you didn't even have the guts to tell me to my face."

"Ava—"

"I had to come to you. You're pathetic! I only asked this one thing of you, and it's too much."

She turned, opened the door, and stormed out. I braced for the door to slam, but it closed with a gentle click. Ava was the master of control.

Waves of remorse and guilt rose out of my chest. I ran

upstairs to my room, flung myself onto the bed, and buried my face deep into the pillow. After a good bout of sobbing, I lay on my back and stared at the ceiling, dissecting in detail my exchange with Ava.

I turned to Goldie. There was no sympathy in her eyes.

60

TRANSCRIPT

JUDGE MBEKI: Before I render my decision on these hearings, being Concord Case 22 of the Climate Change Truth and Reconciliation Commission—Mr. David Moreland—I would like to make some remarks.

First, I would like to remind us all of the objectives of the Commission. Even though it has become popularly known as the 'Climate Court,' the Truth and Reconciliation Commission's hearings do not function like a conventional court of law. Our Commission aims to discover and reveal past wrongdoings impacting climate change in the hope of promoting closure and healing so that the current barriers to positive action are removed.

Specifically, the Climate Change Truth and Reconciliation Commission's objectives are to:

1. Clarify the facts and circumstances surrounding the critical decisions that materially affected the trajectory of climate change and the resulting outcomes.

2. Request those who made such decisions to justify their actions.

3. Identify those people or organizations who acted maliciously or criminally when making those decisions and refer them to the appropriate criminal courts for prosecution and determination of reparations.

4. Provide a forum for victims of climate change to tell their stories and give their interpretation of events, and

5. Provide a forum for world citizens to cast their judgments on the people under scrutiny.

Again, I stress, we do not function like a conventional court of law, and specifically, we do not pursue criminal charges ourselves but refer judged wrongdoings to the appropriate criminal courts for prosecution—a point that is often misunderstood by the Commission's critics.

Now to my conclusions in this case, Concord Case 22 of the Climate Change Truth and Reconciliation Commission, being David Xavier Moreland. This Commission finds that there is no evidence of malicious or criminal intent on the part of Mr. Moreland in regard to his climate change decisions and actions.

[Reaction from the gallery]

Therefore, there will be no referral from this Commission to the criminal courts in Mr. Moreland's case.

In respect of the Beachport Disaster, this Commission makes no judgment as it has not heard sufficient evidence that would override the original investigations and conclusions of the Beachport Disaster Board of Inquiry.

That summarizes the Climate Change Truth and Reconciliation Commission's judgment. Those of you who have an interest in the detail are referred to the full judgment on our network site. I now move onto the final role of the Commission in this case, and that is to invite the judgment of citizens at large.

Some procedural matters to start with. To be eligible to cast your judgment, you must be over eighteen years old and under sixty-eight. You must be prepared to be biometrically identified at the Commission's network site. And you must have verifiably viewed at least the hearing's opening session, Mr. Moreland's closing statement, and this judgment session in their entirety. You must respond to this question: "Did David Moreland, within reason, act in the best interests of humanity in his actions on climate change?" You have two weeks from today's date to cast your judgment.

A final reminder that the citizen's judgment carries no legal authority, but, as we all know, it does carry a powerful moral authority. So, I encourage you all to exercise your citizen's rights to make a judgment. The results will be posted on the Commission's network site.

Now, as everyone knows, the array of Climate Courts globally has only been made possible through the generous sponsorship of a group of enlightened philanthropists and entrepreneurs. We have the good fortune of having Wilhelmina Strobel present today. As is customary when one of the court's major sponsors is present on the last day of a hearing, I am pleased to invite Ms. Strobel to address the court. Ms. Strobel.

WILHELMINA STROBEL: Your Honor, Mr. Moreland, ladies and gentlemen. It is often said that historic moments are only known by our descendants. However, I feel today is a historic day. I have come understanding the privilege of speaking to you, and to the millions who will watch this now, or later. I have also come to rebuff the impassioned but misguided ideas summarized by Congressman Baker in recent weeks.

I hope to explain the purpose of this court, how today and recent events underline that purpose, and to thank Mr.

Moreland, Judge Mbeki, and others for committing fully to this process, even with their lives at stake.

But mostly I come here to persuade you all of a simple idea.

We are all human. Those from the past, and those yet to come. And we must accept that we are flawed and fallible, but nevertheless capable of great things. We have a world to heal. And I believe that healing must begin with understanding and forgiveness. The Climate Court is a way of moving toward that goal. It is not the only or perhaps even the best way of getting there. But it is a way that has worked in other times of great distress.

The violence threatened upon this court only validates it. For some to have such a reaction that they consider taking lives shows the potency of this idea, of this place of shared humanity. So, I hope to help you see what lies even deeper than the Climate Court itself. A foundation of deep time and deep roots.

Indulge me, by hearing first a story. It is our story. Your story.

Humans broke the ties of genetically inherited traits by becoming smart enough to talk, to write, to think, and to remake the world. We learned to farm, to build cities, to build empires. Advances accelerated and blossomed into exponential innovation in the Enlightenment. We made homes in every nook and cranny of the earth. Where it is coldest. Where it is hottest. We beat back the diseases that killed our children. It was as though we only had to think of a thing, and we could make it happen.

If we showed our powers to humans from only a few generations ago, we would seem more than magicians: we would seem like gods. With these powers, our story must have, as every story must, dangers and evil. Our tribal fights turned into wars where millions died, and worse with horrors like the Holocaust. We created wealth beyond counting but did not share it, leaving billions staring into lighted rooms from the dark. And, as we of today can see, we enjoyed the warmth, but our home was on fire.

To so many of us humans today, who have seen the earth reject our folly, the temperatures soar, the millions displaced and the golden age end, it seems incomprehensible that we did not act to put out the fire, or at least to stop feeding it more fuel. So, we make the people of that time into the other. Into demons, into evil strangers. So we can curse and blame them.

I put it to you, that we are no different than those of the past. That we might well have done as they did. And that we can never rise above that past until we see the flaws within all of us and work together to heal the world. Heal the world despite our flaws. Not fix a world that others broke. We are in a planetary crisis. The time to act is now. As it always has been.

The Climate Court was created to help move us. To move us all. We are stagnant. We are stuck. Those who put their energy into vengeance and bitterness about the past fail to put their energy into creating a future. And worse, they fail to see themselves in those they revile. Look at David Moreland. No one denies the truths he has shown us. So, some say, he should pay a price. But what price could be more than the one he levies upon himself?

Here is what matters: David Moreland has chosen to stand before us and lay bare his acts and his motivations. And he waits to see how we will judge him. Recognize yourselves in David. See that the future will judge you just as you intend to judge him. And use that knowledge to take risks. To act in ways that you think good and right. To treat this damaged world and shape a future for those yet to come. You have the right to judge David Moreland. But most importantly it's up to you to shape the future.

I thank Your Honor for the privilege to speak here.

JUDGE MBEKI: Thank you, Ms. Strobel. This case is now formally closed.

61

LILY

On the day after the judgment, I woke before six. Getting back to sleep was out of the question; I was wrestling with too many thoughts.

My botched break up with Ava bothered me. How did I come up with such a chicken-shit plan? I resolved to allow some time for the dust to settle and then contact her and have some open one-on-ones to sort out my deeper issues. When I put this to Michael, he estimated there was a good probability that we would remain friends. Focusing on that prospect relieved my angst, at least temporarily. The plan required patience—not one of my strengths. But at least I could return that thought to its box and keep the lid closed for a while.

With Matteo, my interactions with him since Donovan's had been limited. Our discussion at the courthouse after David's closing statement was mostly business-like, talking about the likely judgment outcomes and implications. After David's bombing, he was concerned enough to call me, to reassure me. I replayed Matteo's words at Donovan's—he wanted to try again. That's what he said. He must be interested. I wanted to try again too. I had missed the moment at Donovan's, and in the last few days, I had come within a mouthed whisper of calling Matteo. But today I was going to call him, no matter what.

It was best to wait for a civilized hour; I didn't want to make my interest too obvious. I figured 8.30 am was a reasonable time.

I made the call at 8.27 am.

Matteo was pleased to hear from me. His reaction gave me the confidence to get straight to the point. "I was wondering whether you wanted to go to that acoustic music venue you mentioned ... remember?"

He did, and we set a date.

His positive response broke through the blanket of isolation that had surrounded me. The lifting of the blanket was a sudden relief but it left my mind empty for a moment. Now the clock was moving, and I had nothing to say.

"I wasn't surprised by the judge's decision. Were you?" Matteo asked, breaking the silence and changing the conversation back to a business tone.

"I'm glad the court relied on the Board of Inquiry."

"At least David admitted his mistakes—which is exactly the point of the court."

"I wish he had mentioned Stephanie and his grandchildren at Beachport."

"Maybe he didn't want sympathy to get in the way of the citizens' judgment," he suggested.

"Do you think he's watching the citizen's vote? It's not going well."

"He might be more interested in your judgment," Matteo said. "After all, you made him attend the court in the first place. You're the closest thing he has to a grandchild. What's your judgment?"

I had already made my judgment. David's actions at Helsinki

were a diplomatic triumph. I couldn't understand why he was being criticized for that. And his work in decarbonizing the state was an unquestioned success. But deferring all those adaptation projects including Beachport? I wasn't so sure.

I explained this to Matteo. I was startled when he didn't agree straight away.

"It's hard to imagine a world where you can't solve the most complex equation or dilemma in a split second through your Sherpa," Matteo argued. "But that was David's world."

"You might be right, but that doesn't make any difference to the victims."

"We're all victims."

"Oh, c'mon!" I objected. "It might be tough on us, but nothing like those from the coast. I mean if they were 'lucky,' they didn't lose their lives when the ice sheet collapsed, but they still lost their homes. Look at all the people, millions of them. They had to evacuate their towns: where they grew up, where they went to school, where they went to church. How can you say we're all the same?"

Matteo's lack of pushback encouraged me to continue.

"And now the rest of the country doesn't want them. No one sees them as Americans anymore; they're refugees. They're coasties."

Matteo joined in. "Funny how we used to call refugees people from other countries. Now it's people crossing county lines."

"The people out there exploiting the refugees for their own self-interest are no better than the climate deniers of the past," I complained. "The refugees are easy recruits for the Blue Caps."

Matteo agreed. "Turning the refugees' suffering into bitterness against the burners hasn't helped anyone." His eyes narrowed. "The problem with most of us today is we enjoy feeling righteous about the burners. About what they did. But, like Strobel said, we don't act to change things. The Climate Court is trying to overcome that. But is there something more we can do?"

"Sure there is," I said. "For starters, my work with the refugees really counts. I'm helping these people solve their real-world problems. The Blue Caps aren't. The Climate Court isn't. And no AI can do what I do. Not even close. I'm making a difference."

He nodded.

"And there are things we can change ..." But as I started to answer, a familiar kind of panic rose in me. Who was I to change things?

Then I heard her voice. My mother's. As distinct as if she was saying it from the hallway. "Believe in yourself." That's what she always said to me. And she was saying it at the end. I didn't hear the words but I sensed them. In her eyes. I had flooded her with 'I love you.' What I got in return was 'Believe in yourself.'

"Believe in yourself?" I had whispered back to her. The momentary spark in her glossy eyes, the twitch of her hand, the release of the hanging tear, was all the confirmation I needed. Her next message was sure to be 'I love you,' but she couldn't get it out. It was too late.

My hands trembled as I recalled her memory and message.

"Lily? ... Lily?" Matteo's concerned voice broke my contemplation.

"Huh."

"My next appointment's here," he said. "I'll see you next week."

"Oh, sure ..."

With Matteo's projection barely gone, I tried to piece together the path from that last moment with my mother to now.

Yes, I did make the decision to withdraw Mom's life support.

That was the right thing to do. And Mom was giving me the courage to go ahead. But I should have discussed the decision more openly with Grandma. That was a mistake. What I would give to have that chance again.

I shook my head in anguish. Why this endless reliving of my mistakes? Playing them over and over in my mind. Is that why I always sought advice from others? Why I doubted my own ability? Why I've never been good enough?

Maybe it all came down to my lack of self-confidence.

Or did it?

I believed in myself rather than put up with one of those dopey men I dated over the years. I enrolled with the sperm bank—I trusted myself to start a family. And now I had broken through with Ava. Not in an ideal way, but it was a start.

And with David. I decided to visit him against others' advice. I made the right call not to give him permission.

I flopped back onto my pillow and raised a victory salute. "I do believe in myself, Mom." I turned to Goldie. "What do you think?"

Her eyes held a certain look. I took it as a yes.

62

LILY

THERE WERE ONLY EIGHT TABLES, I COUNTED THEM. THE WALLS, matte black, gave a sense of a bigger space.

Each table had a red candle vase that cast an exaggerated rosy glow onto the audience's faces. The red theme continued with the wall lights behind the small elevated stage, giving the performers a hellish halo.

We sat on stools. They had cushions but my back felt the strain as the night wore on. I read somewhere that cushions and stools and candles were there in ancient Rome; less had changed than we thought.

This setting was not what I had expected of the music venue. With fewer than fifteen people in the audience, there was an unspoken pressure to stay focused on the performers. It made it awkward to carry on any conversation outside of set breaks. And I had things to say.

Most of the performers at venues like these tended to be older, around their sixties, but here, I was pleasantly surprised to see someone younger. The first performer was a woman who played guitar and sang a ballad. Her voice was thin as the wind. It would not have survived in a bigger venue.

Matteo and I shared some faint praise after her song. It made for an awkward discussion as neither of us wanted to voice our disappointment. I hoped this wasn't an omen for the night.

Stomp! Stomp!

The next performer was on stage. A young African American man with a harmonica. He played an up-tempo staccato piece with a kind of spoken rhythmic lyric, all backed by the beat of his feet stomping on the stage floor. After a slow start, he energized the audience, small as it was, and we bounced along to his infectious beat.

"That's why I like this place," Matteo enthused when the performance had finished.

"He was awesome!"

The harmonica man came over to our table. "Thanks for your support." He cupped his hands in front of his chest as if in prayer.

"You were magic." I gave him the thumbs up.

He reached out and placed a hand on each of our heads. He gently brought us closer so our heads touched.

"Your lives will be full of happiness," he vowed.

We giggled. "Do you know something we don't?"

"Just follow your heart." He spoke with a solemnity that defied his age.

The man moved on and performed the same ritual at each table. As I watched, his words bounced around in my head. Surely, he was saying the same thing to everyone. There wasn't really anything to it. Was there? I assured myself that the familiar ring to his words was a coincidence.

"... a hard act to follow ..." Matteo's comment drifted past me.

The next performer was up. A middle-aged man who sang a melodramatic aria. I could barely concentrate on his performance. My mind wandered, unable to shake those words.

The room light brightened. The performer had finished. The empty drinks in front of us came into prominence.

"Do you want another beer?" I asked, more from reflex than desire. Matteo nodded with a wink. I placed the order for a beer and a grillo through Michael.

Matteo gestured at my hand. "Is that a new ring?"

The closeness of his voice cleared my mind. I focused on the moment.

"This?" I twirled my thumb in front of his face. "David gave it to me. It might be his wedding ring."

"You've become pretty close," he said.

"Yeah, and guess what?"

"What?"

"This ring, it gives me super powers," I announced with a grin.

He laughed. "Oh yeah, like what?"

"It allows me to see things that you can't see."

"Sure, sure."

"Yes, yes." I nodded with authority.

"For example, I can see that thing on your cheek." I pointed at his face.

"What is it?" His hand swiped randomly at the unseeable thing.

"Here, let me get it." I waved him closer.

He leaned forward and, with a flick, I unclipped Karrie from his ear.

He flinched. "What are you doing?"

I placed Karrie on the table in front of Matteo. His puzzled expression demanded an explanation.

I gave him a satisfied smile. "No client conflict now."

63

LILY

I couldn't wait to tell David the news. This was a special occasion. My monthly Holo was not good enough. I had to see him in person, something I hadn't done for a while despite my best intentions. At least by now, more than a year after the event, David should be well and truly over showing me replays of the sole commentator who had lamented his poor citizen's vote. That was old news; I had something more exciting to share.

And so I found myself stepping with purpose toward David's apartment. The clopping of my sandals on the tiles echoed through the corridor. My hand moved to loosen my shirt, but as I was wearing a baggy top, there was nothing to adjust.

"Hi Sarah," I said.

A current of warm air escaped through the open door and floated past my face.

"Come in, Lily."

David was sitting on his sofa, cushion on lap, and walking stick resting at an angle beside him. A smile grew on his face as he turned to me.

"Look I've brought some flowers ... in a vase this time." I held out the gift. "Do you know what they are?"

He focused on the flowers. "They're white," he answered.

"Sarah. Tell him."

"They are white Peruvian lilies."

"Exactly. Lilies, just like me." I made an exaggerated modeling pose, one arm extended high above my head.

"White and pure—just like me," I continued.

David appeared puzzled, as if I was speaking in a different language.

"And from Peru, just like my dad," I said, feeling pleased with my cleverness. "So, every time you look at these flowers, think about me."

David's expression remained unchanged. Nothing like a gift that means more to the giver than the recipient.

Sarah took the flowers, and at David's invitation I sat at the table and waited for him to join me.

David moved heavy-footed. He stood on one foot at times, balanced off his walking stick, took a deliberate step or two backward before pausing, then slightly changed his forward direction. If I hadn't known better, I would have thought he was performing in some sort of modern art installation.

"Are you okay, David?"

He didn't answer, and I understood to be patient as he went through his 'important' ritual.

While I waited, my eyes searched for that photo of the president that I so loved. There were two picture frames on the mantle, but the president's photo was gone. The Stephanie photo was still there but beside it was something new, the brightness of its colors contrasting with the faded image of Stephanie next to it.

"What happened to the president's photo?"

"Oh, yes." He stopped his idiosyncratic performance and

headed directly for the table. He pointed to the mantle. "Could you bring that photo to the table?"

The new photo was of a boy and a girl. The girl was maybe eight years old, the boy was older and much taller, in his later teens. My initial reaction was that the girl was Stephanie, as she had blond hair too, but comparing photos reassured me this was someone else.

What was more intriguing was how the children were dressed. The boy was in a bright blue regal military uniform complete with a white sash and wide black belt, epaulets in red with golden tassels dangling from his shoulders. He wore white gloves, one hand behind his back in a formal manner, and the other holding the girl's hand way over her head as she twirled dance-like under his arm. The girl wore a velvety blue dress with yellow puffy sleeves and a red flower tiara in her hair.

The boy looked at the girl with a mildly serious look. She wore a dreamy smile for the camera. All this in what appeared to be a beautiful, formal garden setting.

"What a gorgeous photo," I marveled. "Who are those two?"

"You don't recognize them?"

"Come on, David."

"Have a look at the back."

Neatly typed were the words 'Alice and David, 1981.'

"Grandma?" I squealed.

David's smile was now a wide grin.

"Grandma and you?"

He nodded, clearly enjoying my reaction.

"Oh my god, David!" I pored over the photo in detail, my heart pounding with excitement. Yes, I could recognize Grandma now, those round glistening eyes and the dipping hairline. It was harder to recognize David, as he was at an angle to the camera, but his chin gave him away.

"It was a day trip to a historical estate outside Concord City,"

David explained. "It was arranged by my older sister Heather—your great grandmother. A special festival where they had fancy dress costumes. Alice wanted to be a princess and, despite my protests, I was forced to be her Prince Charming. She bossed me around like a diva."

"That sounds familiar."

"I was so embarrassed that I wiped the whole event from my memory—until you came, keen to hear stories about your grandma. So, I asked Sarah to search my archives for anything related to Alice and she found this." He paused. "I want you to keep the photo."

"I'd love that. Oh, thank you, David. It's so beautiful."

I looked up from the photo to David, sitting in front of me, alive and grateful for my company. His presence in the photo bridged my connection with Grandma, taking me back to my simpler, happier times with her. My eyes returned to the photo. I focused on Grandma. My thoughts flashed with glimpses of the redemption that I had yearned for since she passed away.

"Do you think she'd forgive me?" I asked. "You know, for my decision about Mom?"

David leaned away as if caught by surprise. He looked into the distance. The wrinkles around his eyes contracted as his mind ticked over. "I have asked myself the same question … about Stephanie."

He turned to me. "Your grandmother loved you, even if she didn't like your decision. And your love for her was more powerful than any repentance you could have offered."

He studied my expression more closely as if confirming his thoughts. He nodded knowingly. "You would have forgiven your grandmother. It's time you forgave yourself."

My head lifted.

Thoughts like this had swirled in me for years, but never with enough gravitas to bury my doubts. Hearing the words out loud, from Grandma's uncle, made them a self-evident truth. He was giving me permission to forgive myself. No words were needed here. Just a fresh perspective unencumbered by remorse. The weight on my conscience was already melting away.

I reached for David's hand and squeezed it gratefully.

The sight of the ring on my thumb jolted me back to the purpose of my visit. "I have some news for you." News that seemed to carry even more meaning now.

His eyes turned apprehensive.

I readied myself and drew breath.

"There's no easy way to lead into this, so I'll get straight to the point." I paused. "I'm having a baby!"

He didn't react.

"Congratulations, Lily," Sarah offered. "That's wonderful news."

David stumbled. "Who's the f-father?"

"Matteo, of course!" I snapped. "What did you think?"

He didn't answer.

"And there's more. Are you ready?"

It took forever to get a nod.

"It's a boy and we're going to call him David," I announced.

He remained silent. I couldn't make out his expression.

"Is that okay? We ... we should have asked your permission before deciding on the name. We thought 'David' would be perfect. After all, Matteo and I wouldn't have met if—"

He raised his hand, stopping me mid-sentence, and beckoned for mine. He clasped my hand and stared at me with glistening eyes.

"Lily," he said in his gravelly voice, "you have given me something to live for."

The gloss in David's eyes brought back thoughts of my mother, who would never meet her grandchild. Tears welled up in my eyes, matching those in David's. Strange how tears attracted tears. When you cried at moments like these it was hard to tell the difference between joy and pain.

As I drew my hand back from David's, I wondered how much longer we had together. Would he hear my child talk? See him walk?

I looked down at my belly, then back up, and smiled weakly. I wasn't sure how things were going to turn out, but my sense of purpose and family had been rekindled. I just needed to believe in myself and get on with it.

Still, David's words stirred a fear I had submerged below layers of hope and fulfillment. Was it right to bring a child into a world of upheaval? Right now, we were living in an oasis surrounded by a desert of chaos. That wasn't going to last. What then? What dreams will little David have to aspire to? What will family mean to him? Was there even a future for him?

The sweep of time took me away. I saw myself in a distant place. In a cavernous room. My face was wrinkled, my breath rapid, my muscles tense. I sat waiting ... waiting for the assembled to come to order ... waiting as the vaguely familiar faces prepared to speak ... waiting for the judgment from my own grandchildren.

ABOUT THE AUTHORS

Michael Muntisov

Mike's professional expertise was in making drinking water safe. He was the editor of a non-fiction book on water treatment, proceeds of which were donated to Water Aid. After a global consulting career spanning 35 years, Mike finally got around to writing his first work of fiction. Before he knew it, he was a playwright as well.

Greg Finlayson

Having played in a rock band during his University days, Greg has recently returned to the music scene, where with his teenage daughter he does improv Jazz sets at local clubs. During the day, Greg consults for water authorities around Australia and the USA in fields such as desalination, integrated water management and climate change planning.

courtofthegrandchildren.com

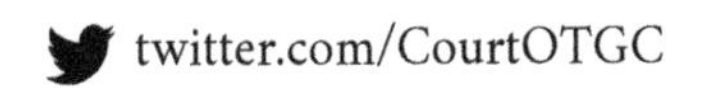
twitter.com/CourtOTGC

Printed in the USA
CPSIA information can be obtained
at www.ICGtesting.com
LVHW092034010923
756966LV00002B/200